S.B. ALEXANDER

COPYRIGHT

Cover designed by Hang Le
Cover copyright © 2022 by S.B. Alexander

The Union
Book three: Vampire Navy SEAL – Sam and Layla Series

First Edition: July 2022

E-book ISBN — 13: 978-1-954888-24-1
Paperback Print ISBN — 13: 978-1-954888-25-8
Large Print ISBN — 13: 978-1-954888-26-5
Audiobook ISBN — 13: 978-1-954888-28-9
Paperback Print ISBN — 13: 978-1-954888-27-2

1

LAYLA

My screams died in the wind as I plummeted to earth. If only my sweater hadn't ripped, or I hadn't chased after Sam, or I hadn't signed up for a job to capture the arrogant vampire in the first place. That night at the vampire club seemed like eons ago when in fact just over three weeks had passed. I had to stop kicking myself over meeting Sam Mason. I wasn't in a good place in my life, but Sam was the one good thing in the hell I was living. He might be an ass—arrogant, dominant, and possessive—but he was mine. He was the only one who loved me in a way no one had loved me before.

Still, so much had happened in a short time span that I couldn't process any of it quickly enough. But crying wouldn't save my life or that of my unborn child's. *Stupid, stupid me. I'm going to die. I'm going to splatter on the ground, and my body parts will be strewn over the open field.*

I would never see Sam again or see my baby at all. Hell, I would never have the chance to ask Dr. Vieira all the additional things I needed to know about having a supernatural kid. Above all, I would never have the chance to tell Sam I loved him.

Snow plastered my face as I continued to scream, thinking about all the what-ifs. But the number of what-if questions or regrets wouldn't save me. Tears poured out, and my pulse pounded in my ears. I had no clue how far up I'd been, and I was deathly afraid to look.

"Mom, Dad, I'm coming to see you in heaven. Jordyn, I love you. Rianne—" My other sister's name caught in my throat as anger overshadowed the panic gripping me.

I swore if I lived, I would kill my uncle Ray after I shook him for Sam's whereabouts. Then I would hunt everyone and anyone who had a hand in Sam's kidnapping, including my sister, Rianne. Trying to reason with her was a waste of energy.

But I was out of time. I squeezed my eyes shut, sucked in air, prayed harder than I ever had before, and braced for impact, preparing for the pain. But it didn't come. It took me a second to realize someone had caught me. He smelled like a mixture of pine and earth. Maybe I'd made it to heaven—or hell. My head spun like an F5 tornado as blackness crept in from my peripheral vision.

"I've got you, Layla," the man said, cradling me in his arms. The heat emanating off my savior competed with the chill coursing through my body.

"Sam?" I cried. Maybe this was all a dream, and the vampire I was hopelessly in love with hadn't been kidnapped. "You're okay."

"No, darling. I'm afraid I'm not Sam." He sounded sad with an undercurrent of anger. "We need to get you on the plane and warmed up. You're shivering."

"Plane?" I whispered as the face of the man who resembled Sam spun before me. "Steven?"

Sam's dad grinned, his green eyes high beams in the growing storm.

My heart split wide open.

"You're not dying on my watch," he said as if he read the questions on my face.

Tears streamed down my windburned cheeks and stung my chapped lips as I locked my hands around his neck. "I'm sorry. I wanted to save Sam, and I almost killed our baby in the process." I'd recently learned I was carrying a fanged creature—or maybe not. Maybe the embryo inside me would be born human, without fangs.

Normally when a male vampire impregnated a woman with Vel-negative blood, the child was human until the teenage years. At that time, the kid would have the choice to activate the vampire gene. However, Dr. Vieira had previously speculated the child would come out of my womb with fangs, ready to drink blood. My stomach protested as acid shot to my throat. The idea of a fanged baby was mind-blowing. But the thought of losing Sam was even more overwhelming.

"We need to find Sam." *How am I supposed to have a baby without him?* We were in this together. We were supposed to be a team.

I bounced in Steven's arms as we headed toward the plane. "We'll get him back," he said as certain as the snow was falling.

I rested my head against his. "Do you know where they're taking him?"

"No, but we know where to start our search."

Adrenaline surged through me. "Intech?" Killing my cousin Noah came to mind. Hell, murdering someone was on my list, and Jack's son sat at the top like a neon sign shining in the night on the Las Vegas Strip.

"We still don't know everything about Intech or Camden Industries, but we'll begin there." Steven continued to cross the large field.

I glanced up at the cloudy sky, snowflakes falling and melting on my skin. "I still can't believe I'm not dead." Maybe I had an angel on my shoulder. Or maybe my parents were watching over me.

"You weren't that far up yet. A little higher, and…"

I swallowed an elephant of emotions, thanking whoever was listening that Steven was a vampire. I doubted a human could've caught me with such ease. Again, I shook off images of my body being scattered over the open field.

When Jo's voice carried on the wind, I oriented my vision to find Sam's twin sister jogging toward us. Her black hair billowed behind her, capturing snow along the way. "Layla, thank the heavens you're okay." She walked alongside Steven and me.

"Why do you look like someone died?" I asked. *What am I thinking? I almost did.* Plus, the events of the day weren't exactly something to smile about.

Steven came to an abrupt halt not far from the plane. "What happened?" He hardened his jaw, his hold on me tightening.

Scanning the abandoned airport just outside of Chicago, I spotted Uncle Jack kneeling to my right on the tarmac a good distance from the plane. Flashes of Ray grabbing me flew back faster than the speed of light.

I squirmed in Steven's arms as my nerves teetered on the edge of destruction. "Put me down, please."

"I'm not sure that's a good idea. Your pulse is erratic, and your equilibrium is probably off."

My heart *was* trying to climb out of my chest, and I would probably collapse once I was on my feet. But it was crucial I speak to my uncles. Ray was the only one who could help, though I wasn't holding out hope he would. That didn't mean I wouldn't try like hell to glean information out of him.

"Please," I said. "I need to talk to Ray."

My uncle's words blared in my head. "You'll never see your vampire lover again." What had happened before Sam had been taken flooded my mind.

I rushed up to Sam just as the helicopter basket swung behind him. It was like the jaws of life were about to capture him.

"Run, Sam!" I screamed at the top of my lungs.

But he didn't. He stopped, turned, and raised his arms high above his head. Then he lowered one arm and closed his hand into a fist.

He was about to unleash his elemental powers. It was the same move he'd done to Roman that night on the naval base. But when Sam opened his fist, nothing happened. He quickly tried again. No fire. No wild weather. Nothing.

He looked at his hand a little too long.

I was about to bolt over to him when someone grabbed me from behind.

Ray laughed in my ear. "You'll never see your vampire lover again."

I screamed like a banshee, and Ray collapsed. I was ready to kick him in the throat when I noticed blood coming out of his ears, and that he wasn't moving.

I sprinted toward Sam, only it was too late. A guy, dressed in full SWAT gear, was shooting at Sam from the helicopter while another propelled down and shot Sam several more times, hitting him in the neck, legs, arms, and vest.

"Nooooooooo!" *I was about to run into the fray until another set of hands came around me.*

"*It's too dangerous,*" *Steven said in my ear.*

Jo came to a halt beside me and raised her arms, ready to use her elemental powers, but when she whipped her arms around, nothing happened. "My powers aren't working." She tried again. But failed. "They must have something stopping us," Jo said.

Steven tried to use his powers, but he failed too.

Sam stumbled to his feet and roared. The men just kept shooting and shooting and shooting until he became a rag doll. Then one of the men in the helicopter aimed his gun at us while his partner loaded Sam in the basket.

I shrugged out of Steven's hold. Screw this. I pulled out my gun and started shooting at the man on the ground. It took me three shots until he fell.

I rushed over to Sam, whose limp body was sprawled inside the basket. I reached in to drag him out when the helicopter lifted. If they were taking him, then they were taking me too.

I was about to hop in with Sam's lifeless body, but fate had other plans.

The feeling of icy fingers crawled up my spine as Jo's voice penetrated through the hell I was reliving. "I'm not sure Ray or the other one will make it."

I jerked in Steven's arms. "Ray? Is he dying? Why? How? I never touched him." Even though I'd wanted to kick him in the throat.

She gave me a sad smile. "I'm not sure what's going on with Ray. It could be a brain bleed or something else. But you did scream like a banshee."

I sucked in air along with snowflakes. "But a scream can't kill anyone. Can it?" Dr. Vieira's words sung in my head. *In our world, Layla, you'll learn that some things don't have an explanation, especially when magic is involved.*

Jo shrugged. "Not sure."

Whoa! Maybe I had banshees in my family.

Then she addressed her dad. "I tried to read Ray's mind, but my powers seemed to have short-circuited when the helicopter flew in. Can you try, Dad?"

Steven bobbed his head, easing me onto the snowy field. I

wobbled and stumbled like an alcoholic after a fifth of tequila. Jo had her arms out to steady me, but I took off and ran toward Jack.

"Layla," Steven shouted as he caught up to me. "You need to rest."

"There's no time for that. Sam's life is on the line, and if Ray is about to die, then we have to find out what he knows."

Jo jogged up on my other side. "I'll try to read the mind of the man that Layla shot. Maybe now that the helicopter is out of range, my powers will reengage." She stabbed a finger at her husband, Webb, and Tripp. Both of the Vampire Navy SEALs were searching the SWAT guy's pockets not far from Jack and Ray.

"Jo, a word, please," Steven said. "Layla, I'll be right there."

I ran toward my uncles before slowing to a walk, listing to one side on the slick, snowy tarmac. Steven was right. My balance was off.

Jack swiped his hand over his thinning red hair as he knelt beside Ray. "Don't you croak on me, brother."

"Where is Sam, Uncle Ray?" I asked through gritted teeth. "Huh? What did you do?" I clenched my freezing hands together, anger melting the chill and sending my adrenaline off the charts.

Lying flat on his back, Ray choked. His blue eyes were the color of gunmetal. His face was pale, and blood oozed out of his ears.

Jack glared at me, seething. "All you're worried about is your vampire? Can't you see Ray is in dire straits?"

I clenched my freezing hands together. The need to punch my uncle Jack made me itch. "Can't you see that Ray betrayed you?" The world was beginning to right itself as the dizziness waned and my mind sharpened. "Let me summarize the convo we had earlier today in the hangar. Ray knows where Noah is, and Ray brought you here as a ruse to help in the kidnapping of Sam."

"He didn't bring me here," Jack said. "I was the one who called the meeting with Steven."

I threw up my hands. My damn family would be the death of me before any outside enemy. Or I might be doing jail time for strangling one of them. "Fine. But Ray used that opportunity to set us up."

Ray pressed his bony fingers into his chest and choked. "Sorry, brother, but Layla is right."

I reared back as shock gripped me. Ray actually admitted I was right. My uncle had never once agreed with me on anything, and we'd argued on several occasions about different topics, particularly how to hunt vampires. Granted, he was my elder, but he was a hothead who had gotten us into bad situations, not only when it came to the family business, but his gambling debts had also taken a toll on the Aberdeen family.

Jack bared his teeth at me. "So what? That doesn't mean Ray should die for what he's done."

"I know that." I wanted to knock some sense into Ray, or even make him feel pain, but I didn't want him to die. "Ray, where are they taking Sam?" I toned down my ire just a bit and infused some kindness, or at least tried to, anyway.

"Fuck you," Ray bit out. "You'll die, Layla, if you continue to hang around vampires."

I was ready to scream at the top of my lungs again. "You're sprawled out on the ground, look like death, might be dying, and you are still being an ass. At least if I croak, I'll feel content, knowing I tried to save humanity. What you've done could just wipe out our existence. Handing Sam over to whoever won't only kill him but will turn humans into vampires. Is that what you want—more bloodsuckers in this world?" I shivered at the idea of Sam on some table in a lab or in a cage being treated like a test rat.

Jack tried to help Ray up. "I'm taking you to a hospital."

Ray winced as he climbed to his feet, holding onto Jack's shoulder. No sooner than he stood, he fell to the ground, taking Jack with him.

Jack scrambled to help his brother. "Ray, what's wrong?"

Ray clutched his chest. "I can't breathe."

"I'm calling an ambulance." Jack whipped out his phone.

Steven came out of nowhere and snagged Jack's cell before he had a chance to unlock it. "No. Get your car. I'll have Tripp go with you. The paramedics will alert the human authorities, and they'll have too many questions. We can't exactly give them answers, now can we?"

Ray swung out his hand to Jack. "If I don't make it, take care of my family."

Jack's forehead creased. "Don't say shit like that. You'll make it." Jack sounded like he was trying to convince himself more than Ray.

"If you want to save your brother, get the car," Steven barked at Jack. "He doesn't have much time." No doubt Steven could hear Ray's heart beating. "He might be bleeding internally."

Jack angled his head at Ray. "Or having a heart attack. They do run in our family."

My grandfather had died of one right in the middle of hunting vampires. My grandmother blamed his death on the fanged predator, but an autopsy proved the cause had been my grandfather's heart.

"Wait, Jack." Ray held out his hand. "I need you to do something for me. I need you to get the money they're paying me for Mason."

"Seriously?" I shouted. "You're probably about to take your last breath, and all you can think of is cold, hard cash?"

Ray snarled, inhaling a deep breath of crisp air. "My family needs it. I owe some people half a mil."

Steven regarded me with questions in his green eyes.

I shrugged. "My uncle has a terrible gambling addiction. Who are the people, Ray? The Mafia?"

Jack grabbed the back of his neck. "Please tell me it's not the Irvings."

I held my breath. That family owned several casinos, including the largest casino in Montana. The Irvings weren't the type of people to fuck with. The Mafia was a cakewalk compared to them.

Ray winced. "Talk to Noah."

Steven squatted beside Ray and held his hand. "Look, Ray. Do some good here. Tell us who you're working with. Is it Camden Industries? Intech? If so, we could be looking at a worldwide humanity crisis. Camden Industries builds weapons for the Department of Defense, which could mean they want to build super soldiers. It's been tried before by someone who wasn't working with the human government, and that turned into a war. We lost many humans to the genetic experiment. What we're facing now will be much larger and harder to control if the DOD gets involved. We can't risk human lives to turn them into someone like me." He mashed his lips together, seemingly holding back his anger. His patience was admirable given his son had just been kidnapped.

"Tell him, Ray," Jack pleaded.

"You'll never see your son again," Ray said to Steven while glaring at me.

Jack briefly closed his eyes.

Restraint was a monumental task on my part. My dad had always said never hit a man while he was down, unless the man was a vampire.

Steven's fangs shot out. "Careful, Ray. If you live, you might not like what you're heading into." Steven's caustic tone cracked through his placid veneer.

Jack sighed. "Please, brother." He sounded frightened. "Where are they taking Sam?"

I hated to think of what would happen if we couldn't find Sam. Steven would go on a rampage, and I would be right beside him with my heart shattering into a million pieces. More importantly, the little one growing inside me would suffer more. A child needed both parents. Even still, humanity? If we were right, and Sam's kidnappers wanted his DNA, then humans, including my family and me, were in trouble. Fuck, they could use me as a guinea pig, especially if they learned I was pregnant with a Mason baby.

Steven rose, his black shoulder-length hair blowing in the raging storm. "I can't read Ray's mind. My powers are nonexistent."

My eyebrows pinched together. "Sam's didn't work either." I couldn't even begin to speculate on a reason. Nevertheless, it was rather strange that the three most powerful vampires had lost their abilities in a blink of an eye. Maybe the helicopter emitted some kind of radio or sound waves that interfered with their abilities.

"Ray," Jack snapped in a harsh tone. "Tell us something. Where's Noah?"

"Jack, get your car," Steven said. "Ray isn't going to talk."

Jack hesitated for a second, frustration and despair washing over him.

Ray's eyes fluttered shut briefly. "I don't know where they're taking Sam. Noah is in Chicago. He's expecting me to call him."

"Go," I said to Jack. I was starting to fidget. I wanted to strangle Ray and save him at the same time. The selfish part of me thought Ray might be able to help us find Sam. My moral side had to spare his life. After all, he was my dad's brother, my uncle, and Ray had a wife and kids. I knew what it was like to lose a father, and I didn't wish that on my cousins, no matter how much Ray could get under my skin.

Jack finally dashed off to his car, which was about a football field away.

I stepped over Ray, knelt beside him, and grabbed his hand. "Uncle Ray, you're not that bad of a person. I understand you have a gambling addiction, but think about what it would be like if one of your kids was taken." I had to find some way to get through to him. He loved his kids and his wife, and despite the idiotic things he'd done, he was a good dad. "Who are you working with?" If he didn't have a clue where Sam was, he had to know who his bene-factor was.

Ray sucked in a large breath. "The guy from Carly's company." His breathing slowed.

"Lester Worthington?" I asked.

Tears leaked down his cheeks, and suddenly my heart was breaking for him.

"Talk to Noah," he whispered. Then his eyes widened as he stiffened.

The car engine blasted through the buzzing in my head. "Ray." I tapped his face.

Jack skidded to a stop, the car fishtailing on the snowy tarmac.

"His heart stopped beating," Steven said.

I checked Ray's pulse just the same. Nothing. I swallowed down my nerves and emotions, not ready to deal with his death.

Jack rushed over. "He's gone?"

I rose. "I'm sorry."

"This is all your fault, Layla," Jack shouted as he dove into action, administering CPR.

I ignored Jack's accusation, shoving them into a compartment for now. There would be plenty of time for us to exchange words and process what had happened. I would shoulder part of the burden, but I wasn't the only one with blood on my hands.

Jack gave Ray mouth-to-mouth, then I performed compressions. After my first round, Steven took over.

Several minutes later, when Ray didn't budge, Jack threw his head in his hands. "I don't know how this happened." Then he pushed his fingers through his thinning red hair with murder in his gray-blue eyes. "What did you do to him, Layla?"

I ground my back teeth together, trying not to yell at my uncle. "I didn't touch him. All I did was scream." Surely, I didn't possess that supernatural ability to wail right before an impending death, which if I wasn't mistaken, was the definition of a banshee.

Webb, Tripp, and Jo joined us, severing my crazy thought. I mean, if Mom had vampires in her family, maybe she had other supernatural beings.

Webb combed a hand through his brown hair, his blue eyes glowing in the waning daylight. "The SWAT guy didn't make it. Steven, we need to regroup. I'll get Sawyer and his tech team on the phone. Let's meet in the hangar." He glanced around. "With the snow coming down, we might be here for the night."

It was probably best we didn't fly in this weather. I wasn't afraid to fly like Sam, but I wouldn't chance it. Then something hit me. I only had a small amount of Sam's blood on hand, so time was of the essence for the baby and me.

2

LAYLA

After placing both bodies in the hangar, we had a moment of silence as we stared at Ray and the SWAT guy, who had a bullet hole in his throat. I'd never taken a human life before, and I'd been responsible for two deaths in less than a day. I took in a quiet breath, then released it. I repeated the sequence a couple more times in the hopes I could tamp down the nausea. I was sure that at some point later on, the weight of what I'd done would hit me even harder. My mind was too fuzzy to even think about how Ray's wife and kids would react when they learned one of their own might've murdered their patriarch.

As if Steven knew my struggle, he grabbed my hand and squeezed. I was sandwiched between him and Jack, who had his head down with his fingers locked together in front of him. He was probably silently swearing like a sailor or maybe plotting his revenge against me. I wouldn't blame him. Still, I wasn't that cold of a person not to sympathize with Jack. After all, Jack had lost his baby brother, my father, and now Ray.

A tear escaped. *Dad, if you're watching over me, can you please help me deal with the crap that is stacking up higher than a mountain? Give me a sign that will point me in the right direction.* Another tear trickled out as sadness comingled with anger. *I'm angry at you, Dad, for not telling me about Mom and her family. Who was Mom, really? Why didn't you tell me about her lineage? I might not be in this mess if you were still here.* If that were the case, I would've never met Sam, and that thought made my heart hurt.

You can't dwell on the past, girl, my inner voice supplied. *Stop brooding, stand up, and fight like the warrior you are. You're destined for this journey. Trust fate has your back.*

How could I put my faith in the unknown? It seemed like an impossible feat. But I could dig deep for that fierce strength I always had. Though, recently, with all the crap flying at me at warp speed, I was losing faith in myself.

Voices hummed around me, and one cracked through the war in my head, drawing me back to the present.

"I'll talk to the pilot," Tripp said as he stalked out of the hangar.

Then Jack left in a hurry.

I held my stomach. "I don't feel so well." Reality was setting in like a rotten apple. *Where do I go from here?* I had to find Sam. I was not raising a vampire child on my own. I wasn't one to wallow in self-pity, but I felt like I was heading in that direction. The poor-me syndrome was taking over my psyche like a vortex about to suck me in with no way out.

Jo skirted around the bodies. Her silver eyes held compassion and concern. "Come on, Layla. You're looking peaked. I'll warm some blood."

A giggle wriggled free, despite the feeling of hopelessness.

She curled black strands of her damp hair behind her ear. "You'll like it warm. I promise."

I quivered, suddenly realizing my clothes and hair were wet, my hands were still ice cold, and my nose was running. Warm blood sounded fantastic to counteract the chill. Still, whatever helped take away the nausea, I was all for it.

"Ray said he was working with a guy from Carly's company. Shouldn't we head to Chicago?" I asked. "That's where Noah is too." My tone dropped on the last line as images of my hands around Noah's neck played out in front of me like a silent movie.

Webb adjusted the sheath strapped around his leg, making sure his dagger was secured. "We need more intel. Then we can devise a strategy."

The hell with strategy. I was ready to march into Intech and demand answers. Carly was my cousin Junior's wife, and she would talk to me. If she was involved, she might not come clean, but reading a person's body language was gold. At the very least, I could snoop around.

Steven touched my shoulder, severing my idea. "You've had a rough day. Go with Jo."

His patronizing demeanor revved up my temper, but I had to choose my battles, and he was partially right. My day sucked the big one. Almost falling to my death, killing the SWAT guy and supposedly my uncle too, and discovering that, oh, I'm pregnant with a vampire baby was enough to set my mind ablaze. Besides, warm blood was calling my name.

I followed Jo out into the blizzard-like conditions and scurried across the tarmac, careful not to fall. Once inside the warmth of the plane, I sighed heavily, shuddering while Jo beelined straight for the galley in the back.

Voices filtered out of the cockpit as Tripp and the pilot talked about the weather. Then something dawned on me. "Where's Kendra?" She was the vampire who my uncles believed had a hand in my father's murder. Jack had brought her with him to allow me to talk to her about my father. But Steven had asked her to wait on the plane.

I ambled in Jo's direction.

"Not sure," she said as she poured blood into a glass.

If I were in Kendra's shoes, I would've bolted in a hot second, especially knowing that Ray and Jack wanted me dead. But given the raging storm, I was curious where she'd gone. But I couldn't worry about her. I didn't have the bandwidth, either, to talk about my dad. My head was brimming with enough problems.

I ducked into the bathroom near the galley. "I'll be right out."

Once I locked myself in, I leaned my head against the door and sighed. I took in several calming breaths, attempting to make sense of what had transpired in the last few hours. Or how in the world I was still alive. I said a quick prayer, thankful I was breathing, walking, talking, and that my body parts weren't scattered in pieces over the snowy field.

I rubbed my stomach. "I'm so sorry, little one. I promise I will do my best not to do something stupid like that again. I want to see you born. I want your daddy to witness your birth, so I'm going to find him and make sure he's with us from here until the day you're born."

I laughed quietly. I was talking to an embryo. It was hard to comprehend that I had conceived merely… I had to count back to the night Sam and I had intense, amazing, thrilling sex that would go down in history. Instead of trying to do the math in my head, I whipped out my phone and opened the calendar. Three weeks and one day from conception. I had so many more questions for Dr. Vieira about my pregnancy, but for now, I had to focus on Sam.

"Where are you, Sam Mason?" I would give anything to have a telepathic connection to him right now. I wasn't sure telepathy worked unless I was close to him. But… would dreaming work?

We had shared the same dream. I closed my eyes and recalled that lustful night in the women's barracks on the naval base. I'd been mortified when Sam had described every detail of my dream.

Water filled a bathtub tucked in an alcove, while a massive bed fit for six sat center stage.

I stepped into the room, my bare feet sinking into the plush brown carpet. "Hello." My voice was low and shaky.

The door snicked shut behind me, and that sudden euphoria was replaced with icy fear. My breathing became labored. My palms clammy. My legs weak and trembling. I ran for the door. Large, strong hands grabbed me out of nowhere. I shrieked, but nothing came out.

"No need to be afraid," the husky masculine voice said as he licked his way from my neck to my ear. "This is your fantasy." He lifted me and carried me to the bed.

I blinked several times, and when I did, I was completely naked. I oriented my vision, struggling to see who the voice belonged to, but he wasn't there. I fran-

tically searched around, and when my eyes landed on the virile man near the bathtub, I gasped.

A solid wall of muscle stood there, naked, built as if the gods themselves had carved him out of stone. Thick thighs, narrow waist, broad back, hair grazing his shoulders. He turned the water off, and when he pivoted on his heel, my eyes went wide.

I couldn't breathe. I couldn't form words. I couldn't even move.

Silver eyes glistened in the candlelight. Canines, sharp and deadly, seemed to drip with hunger.

My gaze traveled down his torso, tracking every breath he took, every dip and valley of his abs. I was prepared to go lower, but I couldn't look away. He stood like a Viking, every inch of him hard and ready to do battle.

My tongue darted out to moisten my lips.

He closed the distance between us, eyelids hooded, chest rising and falling, and his erection… I swallowed the dryness in my throat. He was huge, thick, long—and he was ready to show me a world I'd never set foot in.

He grinned, and his dimples emerged, giving him an even sexier look that had my pussy dying to feel him inside me.

"Layla." His voice was gravelly and caused goose bumps to blanket my body and my clit to throb.

I crawled to the edge of the bed, his voice pulling me, his body exciting me, and I wanted nothing more than for him to sink his fangs into me.

"Sam." I said his name like it was a prayer, pleading and desperate, and as though it was the most natural thing in the world, I closed my hand around his shaft.

His eyes rolled back in his head as he groaned. The sound was glorious and sent excited shivers to swirl in my belly. It felt powerful to have this man, this vampire, who could end me in a nanosecond, become putty in my hands.

He thrust his hips toward me, urging me to take control and to do as I pleased. I lowered my head, pumping him, and when I lightly licked the tip of his cock, he grunted so loud the walls shook.

A knock on the door startled me out of my lustful reverie.

"Layla," Jo said. "The blood is ready."

I briefly closed my eyes, practicing some yoga breathing as I cleared the cobwebs from my head and ignored the throbbing between my legs. "I'll be out in a minute." I would give anything to make that dream come true right about now. To have Sam standing in front of me, naked or not. His arms around me. His lips on mine. His woodsy scent seeping into me.

I had to find the man who owned my heart. The man I was hopelessly in love with.

I checked myself in the mirror. *Holy hell.* I was pale—whiter than the snow outside. My auburn hair looked as though it had been through a Category 5 hurricane. I pulled Sam's leather strap from my long, tangled locks. The one he'd given me right before he dashed off to patrol the airport. I dragged the strap under my nose and sniffed. A hint of his scent lingered, and a soft moan rushed out. Before I tortured myself, I tied the leather strap around my wrist. Then I splashed water on my face, hoping I could infuse a little more color into my cheeks and wash away my ghostly appearance. But the tepid water did nothing for my blue eyes, pale skin, or chapped lips that looked like shattered glass.

Despite that, I straightened and kicked my self-pity to the curb. I was strong, resilient, determined, and faced things head-on. I had to believe I could rise above adversity no matter how many curveballs were thrown at me. Otherwise, I would lose the fight before it began, and I didn't like losing anything.

3

LAYLA

J o handed me a glass of warm blood when I walked out of the bathroom. "How are you feeling?"

I shrugged, raising my glass. "I'm worried that we don't have enough of this."

She leaned against the counter. "I'll call Dr. Vieira in a minute. We should have some of Sam's reserves. But if we don't, you might be able to drink mine. In addition to our twin status, Sam and I have nearly identical DNA as vampires."

I rested my shoulder on the bulkhead across from the bathroom. "Whatever helps the baby." Which was the only reason I *was* drinking the sticky red stuff.

Tripp's voice drifted our way.

Jo glanced past me as I followed her line of sight.

Tripp closed the cockpit door, nodded at us with a concerned expression, then exited the plane.

I pouted. "I don't think we're taking off anytime soon." The snow was falling steadily. The wind was a factor, and with the cold temps, the plane probably had to be deiced before takeoff. A heaviness settled into my limbs, my heart, my entire being. The longer we stayed, the less of a chance we would find Sam. "That means our search for Sam has to wait." I took a swig of Sam's blood and couldn't help but pout. It was the first time I was drinking from a glass and not from his wrist. I briefly closed my eyes and imagined Sam smoothing a hand over my hair and whispering in my ear that he loved me, exactly as he had done at Jo's house in Maine. That day had changed everything. I'd known then I loved him but couldn't say the words. *Stupid me. What if I don't get the chance to tell him how I feel?*

"We might know exactly where he is," Jo announced.

I almost dropped my drink as hope sprouted like weeds after a hard rain. "Really? How? His cell phone?"

Her shoulders twitched in a light shrug. "Yes and no. Sam has a microchip implanted in him." She pointed to a spot on her lower right back. "I do too."

I bit my bottom lip. "Oookay. Is that a vampire thing or military?"

She flipped her hair over her shoulder. "It's some weird law we have within our government, although most, if not all of our kind, don't have chips. But those that work within our government do, like my father. But when Sam and I first turned, my dad gave Sam and me some story about how it was required. I think deep down, he was worried that we would be kidnapped, and he wanted a way to find us. But most of our adversaries know we have them, and they either deactivate them or scramble the signal."

I finished off the blood. "Let's hope either his phone or his chip comes through for us."

Jo held out her hand. "Do you want more?"

I gave her the empty glass. "I need to pace myself. We should check with Dr. Vieira on how much he has in reserve."

She whipped out her phone and put it on speaker.

Dr. Vieira answered on the second ring. "Jo, how did it go? Did you find out any intel on the cobalt oxide and where the Aberdeens purchased it from?"

One ingredient in the drug that I'd used at the vampire club the night I'd met Sam was cobalt. At the time, I had no clue what was in the drug that the man who hired me to capture Sam had supplied. Or that the drug had been given to my benefactor by my father before he'd died.

"Sorry, I didn't," she said. "Too many things happening. Sam has been taken by ex-special forces. Well, we think they're ex-military. But that's not why I'm calling."

Dr. Vieira expelled an exasperated breath. "Please tell me Layla is okay."

"I'm right here, and I'm fine. I'm a little concerned about Sam's blood supply, though."

"I have two weeks' worth," he said. "Sam was set to give us some yesterday, but then Tripp interrupted us. Layla, see how you react to Jo's. There's nothing in any of my training or medical books on what types of blood a pregnant woman needs for a vampire baby. I'm assuming Sam's since natural-born vampire babies who come out of the womb human will require their father's blood when they turn vampire at an older age."

Jo grabbed a dagger from her sheath, slit her palm, squeezed red droplets into my empty glass on the counter, and gave it to me. "Drink."

I brought the cup to my nose and shook my head. "I can't drink that."

She knitted her perfectly manicured eyebrows. "Why not?"

I placed the glass in the sink, then backed away as though it was poisonous. "It smells like broccoli, and I hate broccoli."

She busted out laughing. "What does Sam's smell like?"

I snorted. "I don't know. I've only drunk from his wrist, so normally it's his scent that I usually smell."

"You could drink from mine." She held out her arm.

I lifted my hands. "I'm good." I found the act of sucking on Sam's wrist erotic, so I wasn't eager to try it on Jo.

"Layla, you might not have a choice," Dr. Vieira said. "You could try Steven's. I just don't want you drinking the processed kind. And you might not like the taste, but remember, the blood is more for the baby."

"Not if I'm puking. But I'll try Steven's if I need to," I said. Maybe his wouldn't smell as bad as Jo's. "Dr. Vieira, when I return, can we chat about my pregnancy? Now that my shock is wearing off, I have so many more questions."

Dr. Vieira cleared his throat. "Of course. I would like to run more tests anyway. We'll need to calculate a delivery date, although considering you may not have a normal pregnancy, you might deliver early."

My forehead creased. "You mean, as in, the baby will grow faster?"

"Maybe," Doc responded. "Layla, I want to assure you I'm researching our historical records on pregnancies. A couple of questions before I go. What was your mother's maiden name? If she's truly descended from vampires, there's a good chance we might have records on her descendants. Also, I would like to get your medical records from your family doctor, if you had one growing up. Basically, I need to make sure we document your medical history and have it available in case of an emergency."

I understood the need for my medical data. "I am allergic to latex and penicillin. Just so you know. And my mom's maiden name was Drake. Also, our family physician was Asher Manning out of Bozeman. But I don't know if he's still in practice."

"If he isn't, I'm sure he's left instructions on how to secure a former patient's medical records," Dr. Vieira said.

I regarded Jo. "Any strange pregnancies in your mom's family? You know, vampire babies?"

Jo shook her head. "All my research on my mom so far hasn't shown any weird anomalies. The standard supernatural stuff—vampires and witches. No pregnancies where the woman delivered a baby with fangs and powers."

I sucked in a breath. "Witches?" I'd heard they existed, like shifters, but had never met a witch.

Jo's silver eyes glinted in the muted light. "I guess it's time to break the news to you. Right, Doc?"

"Go ahead," he said.

She crossed one ankle over the other, pressing her hands on the counter behind her. "We were waiting for the right time to tell you. Females with Vel-negative blood come from a line of witches."

I snorted, even though Jo was serious. Like I said, I knew witches existed, but no one had schooled me on them. My family had been focused on vampires and hardly paid attention to other supernaturals like witches and shifters. Still, I was curious if my mom had known or if she had Vel-negative blood as well. Par for the course, I guessed. My mom had been secretive her entire marriage, so I shouldn't be shocked. "So, I could have vampire cousins, uncles, aunts, or even witches in my family?"

Jo tugged the sleeve of her black sweater to cover half of her hand. "It's possible."

I tucked my hands into my coat pockets, hoping they would warm up soon. "It doesn't matter who I have in my family. What matters is my baby. So, Doc, do you think there's something in my mom's lineage that will tell us why you think I'm having a true vampire baby—you know, with fangs?"

"What in the world? You're pregnant?" Jack's voice sounded like a sonic boom behind me.

I froze as my jaw dropped open. Where the fuck had my uncle come from?

Jo's wide-eyed gaze darted past me. "Doc, we'll have to call you back." Jo ended the call at the speed of light.

I didn't know what to do. I wasn't sure I could speak. I'd been so adamant about Jordyn not spilling the beans, and fuck me, I was the one who announced it to Jack, of all people. The only thing louder than the mortified silence was my pulse pounding in my ears like a freaking war drum calling warriors into battle. "Help," I mouthed to Jo.

She rolled her shoulders back. "For fuck's sake. I was so absorbed in the conversation, I didn't hear him. I'm sorry." She skirted by me before I could tell her it wasn't her fault.

I should've been more aware.

"Jack, it isn't what you think," Jo said.

I held in a snort. It was precisely what Jack thought. I had no idea how she would convince him otherwise. Her supernatural mojo wasn't firing on all cylinders, which meant she wouldn't be able to compel him. But that wouldn't matter. Jack never went anywhere without taking a dose of the family's potion to block creatures like Jo from fucking with his mind.

"The hell it isn't," Jack yelled. "Layla Aberdeen, turn around and face me."

The hackles on my neck stood at attention. He sounded eerily like my dad had when I'd gotten into trouble. But this was far more than any trouble I'd been in as a kid. This was war, life, and death—at least to the Aberdeen family. It was bad enough my mother confessed on her deathbed she had vampire blood running through her veins. Equally, if not worse, my father supposedly had dated one —Kendra.

The exit door in the galley was calling my name, but I still couldn't move. The word *run* blared through my head, and that little voice in the back of my mind grew louder and louder with each breath I took. I wasn't one to bolt, but the bomb I'd just dropped wasn't one to stick around for. I didn't know what Jack would do with this shocking revelation, but I was confident I'd burned the hair in his ears.

Holy fuck and more fucks.

"Layla," Jack bit out as his teeth knocked together like a snapping turtle.

I inhaled as deeply as I could, and the area around me spun like I was on a merry-go-round. If I wasn't cast out of the family before, I was now. I could never step foot in Montana again.

But it's only Jack you have to worry about. Ray is dead. The Aberdeens are diminishing in number.

Not exactly true. Jack Jr. would slide into his father's seat at the helm. He was the oldest of my ten cousins. Ray's two boys and two girls weren't of legal driving age yet, although his oldest, Shelby, was probably close. Despite their ages, my cousins could carry on the family business for generations to come, which meant they would hunt me until I was fifty feet in the ground.

Jack growled through a sigh.

"Jack, please sit," Jo said. "Your pulse is severely high." Her concern for my uncle was jarring since Jack's brother and son were responsible for Sam's kidnapping.

"Get out of my way, vampire!" Jack shouted.

Jo didn't need to fight my battles. I could handle Jack, though my stomach protested, as did the *boom, boom, boom* of my heart punching my ribs. In addition, I didn't want him to croak like his brother.

I spun on my heel and shook the cobwebs from my brain. "I've got this, Jo." My voice didn't sound as confident as I intended it to come out.

Jo wavered as she regarded me. "Are you sure you'll be okay?"

I wasn't afraid of Jack, and I didn't think he would be as brainless as Ray and hurt me with Steven, Tripp, Jo, or Webb nearby.

"My niece will be fine with me," Jack said to Jo.

I nodded at her. I appreciated her concern, but Jack and I needed to talk.

"I'll be in the hangar with the others," Jo said as Jack gave her room to pass.

I fisted my trembling hands inside my jacket pockets and stayed rooted to the spot near the bathroom.

Jack gripped one of the leather seats halfway down the aisle, looking defeated, angry, and confused.

"Where did you go when you rushed out of the hangar earlier?" I asked, hoping to lessen the tension between us.

He stuck out his chin. "That's not important right now. Are you pregnant?"

My insides were a ball of tangled knots, but I had to own my shit. Whatever happened from this minute forward, I was ready for it, or I prayed that I was.

4

LAYLA

My gaze drifted out the window. "Does it matter whether I am or not? You've already cast me out and made your judgment."

Steven started to leave the hangar when Jo grabbed him by the arm. She shook her head, and Steven stabbed a thumb at the plane. I imagined she was trying to convince her dad to allow Jack and me a few moments to air out some things.

"Layla, you realize it's an abomination for you to be pregnant with a vampire baby." Jack's deep baritone voice punctured my eardrums.

I snorted at the word abomination but wasn't surprised at his reaction. I more than understood why he thought it was a disgrace, a monstrosity, a curse. We were vampire hunters—generation after generation of hunting the bloodsuckers who had killed several of our family members.

"Maybe it is a curse, Uncle Jack. Maybe it's also fate. Maybe I'm carrying Sam's baby for reasons beyond what you and I could ever imagine. But I can't do anything about it now."

His grayish-blue eyes darkened. "You most certainly can."

My blood instantly boiled. I'd had a hard time coming to

25

terms with my plight, but I wasn't about to end the life of my unborn child. "I'm not getting rid of it, if that's what you're saying."

It wouldn't be easy to raise a little Mason with fangs, but I'd chosen to sleep with Sam. Even if I'd known I had that rare blood type, I wasn't sure the outcome would've been any different. He and I were drawn together like magnets—polar opposites, but we fit together, completed each other. We might rankle each other's nerves, but that worked for us. I was meant to be with Sam. It became more apparent with each passing day. He was my yin, and I was his yang. The universe or fate wanted us together, and I was sure the reason or reasons would reveal itself in due time.

He sat on the arm of a seat. "You just keep throwing oil on the fire. When will you learn, Layla?" His tone softened as though he'd given up on me. "You'll be hunted. Is that what you want?"

I inched closer to him and settled four rows away. "By who? You? Noah? Rianne? Then so be it." I kept my tone even. I was tired of arguing with Jack. "I love Sam, Uncle Jack." Sam didn't know that yet. I'd been about to tell him when we walked off the plane. But he had to patrol the airport, and we'd been minutes away from meeting with my uncles.

Jack threw his hands in the air in a huff. "You were raised to kill those creatures"—he pointed out the window toward the hangar —"not give birth to one or fall for one."

I itched to stomp my foot like I had when I didn't get my way as a three-year-old. "When will you hear me? Those people out there want the same thing as us—to protect humanity."

He gaped at my stomach. "That has nothing to do with your situation."

"Maybe not," I said. "But let's focus on what we're up against. Uncle Ray set us up. He sold Sam for his DNA." I was 99.9 percent sure on that. "Which means we have bigger problems. I know you agree with me on that point."

He rubbed his fingers along his nape. "We do see eye to eye on that. I will not stand by and watch humans become supernatural predators."

I sat on an arm of a seat, relief flooding my veins that we agreed. "Uncle Jack, I'm tired of fighting with you."

He lowered his shoulders, defeat washing over him.

I had a perfect opportunity to say my piece one last time, although I'd thought I'd done just that when he and I had a tense conversation at his Montana ranch not that long ago. But the topic then was about sleeping with a vampire, not about being pregnant with a vampire baby. Still, if he chose to shun me, kick me to the curb, so be it. "I understand where you're coming from on my pregnancy. Well, on all of it. I'm having a difficult time too. I mean, my father dating a vampire, my mom's admission on her deathbed that her bloodline is part vampire, and now my situation." I twined my fingers in my lap. "I struggle to make sense of Sam and me. But he and I fit together. I believe I'm in his life, and he's in mine, for a greater cause… and that's humanity." I swallowed the dryness in my throat, fidgeting under his scrutiny. "I'm so, so sorry about Ray. As much as I wanted to strangle him, I didn't want him dead."

He gave me a sad smile. "I know. I'm trying to figure out how I missed Ray's setup," Jack mumbled. "I'd been so blinded by Noah going missing and his scheme to kill Sam."

I tilted my head. "Didn't you want Sam dead?" Uncle Jack wanted all vampires dead, though he'd never hunted the Masons. My gut told me it was because he knew he didn't stand a chance. The Masons were the most powerful vampires among their kind.

"Killing him would only start a war that we would never win," Jack said on a sigh. "My parents wanted to, but my father had decided a long time ago that it would be suicide."

My intuition was right. "You know, Noah, Rianne, Ray, you, me —we want the same thing. We're just going about it differently. Granted, Ray's actions were driven by money, but he wanted the human race to thrive. Noah and Rianne do as well. I know Rianne is trying to protect me." I loved my sister for that. "In your gruff sort of way, you're trying to do the same as her. I appreciate that, Uncle Jack. But what we're facing isn't about me or you. It's about humankind."

Originally, Jack's son, Noah, and my sister, Rianne, had teamed up to kill Sam, but were unsuccessful. Then Noah had conspired with our uncle Ray to kidnap Sam. As far as Rianne's whereabouts, that was still a mystery. She'd disappeared shortly after she helped Noah string Sam over a firepit at our old hunting grounds in Montana.

"We need to push our differences aside and fight with Steven and the others," I said. "I'm not suggesting it because I love Sam. The Masons and the Vampire Navy SEALs know how to handle a situation like this. They've done it before."

His tired gaze never wavered from mine. I prayed he truly absorbed every word. "I'm exhausted, Layla. I don't want to fight with you anymore. You're headstrong and stubborn like your father. I guess that's why I've been an asshole to you. You remind me of him. And…" He looked at his boots or the floor, rubbing his lips together before shoving his hand through his hair. "I blame myself for his death."

I remembered Aunt Tab sharing that last sentiment with me. Still, to hear his confession had my eyes bulging.

"Your dad was only trying to find proof of what your mother told him. He'd been searching to find if she had any relatives." He scrubbed a hand across his jaw. "I should've listened to him. I should've helped him. He'd been so distraught over not knowing who your mom really was, and he wanted answers."

I'd wished my dad would've confided in me. Maybe I could've helped him. But I couldn't change the past. "Is that where Kendra comes in? Or is she the one who murdered him? I'm a little confused about her."

He looked around. "By the way, where is Kendra?"

I rolled a shoulder forward. "I guess she took off."

His Adam's apple bobbed. "I don't blame her. Ray was eager to stake her. Anyway, your dad had been spending a copious amount of time with Kendra. I'm not sure who she really is or if she is responsible for your dad's death."

I scratched my neck. "You said he slept with Kendra. Is that a lie?"

He massaged his bicep. "I assumed he did."

Oftentimes, Jack assumed things. A flaw that got him into trouble. Regardless, I wasn't about to scold him. We were breaking through some stone barriers in our relationship.

"I have many things to atone for, Layla." Remorse coated his tone. "I do care about you." He swallowed audibly before a long-suffering sigh escaped him. "I know my actions have shown otherwise. Your aunt Tab sees the good in you, and despite your predicament… I'm starting to see that too. I'm extremely relieved nothing happened to you after you fell out of the helicopter basket. I'd promised your dad long ago that if anything ever happened to him, I would take care of you. So, it might shock you to hear me say this, but I owe Steven Mason for saving you."

Tears burned the backs of my eyelids as a host of emotions surged to the surface. "I *am* surprised. Thank you for telling me, Jack."

"I don't know where we go from here," he said. "My head is one big mess, but I need answers from Noah."

I spotted Steven walking with a sense of purpose across the tarmac toward the plane. A brush of excitement stirred. Maybe he'd found Sam's location through one of his tracking devices.

Steven dusted snowflakes off his head as he entered the cabin. "Everything okay?" He scrutinized Jack, then me.

It was uncanny, the resemblance between Steven and Sam—forest-green eyes, black shoulder-length hair, and he was as tall as his son. But Sam was more muscular and didn't have the fine lines around the eyes that Steven had.

Warmth spread through my chest at Steven's concern. "We're fine. Did you find Sam?"

Steven tucked his hands in the pockets of his black cargo pants. "No. His phone and his microchip are a bust."

I frowned. It figured that we couldn't catch a break.

"Steven, we should talk," Jack said as he stood.

Hopefully, my uncle would side with us. He might be the only one to knock some sense into Noah.

"Give me a minute. I need to check on something with the pilot." He banked left, knocked on the cockpit door, then entered.

"Dan, can you pull up the radar?" Steven asked, closing himself and the pilot in.

I rose and stretched my achy body. My butt was numb from sitting on the arm of the seat.

Jack ambled to the front. I thought he was about to leave until he folded his bulky body into one of the front-row seats.

I joined him and sighed when my ass met the comfortable leather cushion. I briefly closed my eyes, relishing the quiet moment —the lull before the storm. I knew we were in for a wild ride ahead. I just prayed no one else died.

Voices filtered in from outside before Webb, Jo, and Tripp came in. The three of them studied Jack and me.

I adjusted the leather strap on my wrist. "We're good." I wouldn't say Jack and I were best buds, but we'd made some strides in our relationship.

As if those were the magic words, Tripp and Webb strutted toward the galley.

Jo closed the plane door, then eased into the seat across the aisle from me.

"Are we leaving?" Hopefully, our next destination was Chicago and not the naval base in Massachusetts. It was vital that we find and question Noah. Considering the potential for a blizzard, it seemed safer to make the two-hour drive to Chicago than what I imagined would be a thirty-minute flight.

Jo brushed snow off her black leggings, her silver eyes probing Jack and me as though she was trying to read our minds. "Not sure yet."

I crossed one leg over the other. "Have your powers returned?"

Her silver eyes glistened. "They have. My dad thinks that the sound waves from the helicopter coupled with your scream blocked our powers. Apparently, sound waves displace air particles, causing a disruption in the equilibrium of the particles, which might've created an invisible shield around us."

That made sense to me. I'd even thought along those lines earlier. I was relieved she had her mojo back. Whatever we were about to face, we needed all the magic we could muster.

Steven emerged from the cockpit and stood against the wall across from Jo. "Dan will move the plane into the hangar for the night. We'll load the bodies into the cargo hold for now."

The word bodies gave me a chill, and at the same time, I slumped in my seat, relieved to know we weren't flying in this weather.

"We found a hotel nearby," Jo said. "We'll work out the logistics in a few minutes."

Once the six of us were gathered together, Steven crossed his arms over his chest. "Jack, what are you planning? When you left the hangar earlier, where did you go?"

Webb swiped a hand over his brown hair as he rested a shoulder against the bulkhead. Tripp was in the chair next to Jo but sitting on the edge so he had a view of Jack and me.

For a beat, the tension in the cabin escalated. I didn't need to be an empath to feel it either. The vampires stared at Jack, and no doubt Jo was reading Jack's mind like an open book. Regardless, I got the vibe that they had already initiated a plan of their own, which was the reason for Steven's question.

"He called his wife," Jo said.

I'd assumed he contacted Noah.

"He tried to call Noah," Jo added, responding to my thought. "But Noah didn't answer."

Steven gave Jo a fatherly scowl. "Please, let Jack speak for himself." Steven could read minds, but only when he was touching someone.

Jack leaned forward and dug his elbows into his thighs. "Why? She can read everything I'm thinking. Besides, what do you want me to say? I don't know what the fuck is going on. As far as my intentions are concerned, I want to take Noah back to his mother and knock some sense into him. I don't want humans turning into supernatural predators. But I'm not sure I can do anything here. Remember, I came to you for help, not only to find my son but to help in your search for Roman Brown. Ray was excited to hunt Roman for cutting off his finger. I didn't know he'd been scheming behind my back."

I would've joined Uncle Ray to find Roman. The bastard who ran a successful blood syndicate was a thorn in my side. Actually, Roman had escaped a vampire prison. So the SEALs were chomping at the bit to capture him.

"Here's what I suggest," Steven said to Jack. "It's best if you return to Montana. We'll handle things from here."

Jack straightened. "I'm not going anywhere without my son."

Webb cast a vacant look at Jack, but behind those blue eyes was a calculating soldier ready to fight. "Until we get answers, Noah will be our guest."

"*If* you find him, but you're not holding my son prisoner." Jack's voice was deep and scary. "The Aberdeens handle their own."

The vampire SEALs would blow up buildings and chase down anyone who knew Noah until they found my squirrelly cousin.

Steven's green eyes flashed to silver, his fangs lowering. "The fuck we won't. Jack, I want to make something crystal clear. If you stand in our way, I'll have no choice but to lock you in a cell along-side your son."

Jack flew off the chair, fists clenched. "I'll handle my kid, bloodsucker."

My uncle had some balls. He was the minority among these powerful creatures who could squash him in a nanosecond.

Tripp, who had been quiet, was on his feet, fangs front and center, bronze eyes shifting to inky black. All vampires, except for the Masons, had black eyes when their emotions changed.

Webb straightened, primed to intervene if he had to.

Steven got in Jack's face, his green eyes now gunmetal silver. "I am so fucking tired of my family being hunted, used, abused, and nothing but a commodity for some psychotic asshole who only wants to profit off us." Steven bared his fangs before running his tongue over one canine. I swore he was testing if his teeth were sharp and ready to rip Uncle Jack's throat out. "So know this. If anyone, and I mean anyone, thwarts my efforts to save my son, I will take no prisoners. Are we clear?"

A stabbing pain seized my chest as I held my breath.

Jack inched back a step. "I swear if you hurt Noah, you'll be the one hanging over my firepit."

Steven chuckled. "I've got to hand it to you, Jack. You've got some huge fucking balls." Then his features tightened. "But let's be real. What would you do in my shoes?"

Jack snarled. "The same fucking thing."

A phone rang, slicing through the tension.

Jack snagged his cell from his coat pocket. "It's Noah." He pursed his lips as he answered. "Where the fuck are you?" he shouted, the color of his face deepening to red. "Your mother has been worried sick."

Jack didn't need to put the call on speaker. I could hear Noah as though he was in the cabin with us.

"Dad, chill." Noah's voice was loud, clear, and condescending.

"I'll ask again. Where are you?" A muscle jumped along Jack's jaw.

"I need to talk to Uncle Ray," Noah said. "He's not answering his phone. Where is he?"

"Son, I suggest you talk to me. What you and Ray have done has put our family in jeopardy."

Noah growled like an animal. "What did those bloodsuckers do to Ray?"

Noah might be a dickwad, but he was perceptive. Then again, he had to have known that once Sam was taken, the shit would hit the fan.

"That's not your concern right now," Jack said as calmly as he could. "I understand you're in Chicago. Are you with your brother? Is Junior involved too?"

Dead silence.

Jack checked his phone. "Either we lost the signal, or he hung up."

I would bet the latter, which wouldn't surprise me. For Noah's sake, he should run. It wasn't the vampire military he needed to worry about, and it wasn't his father… it was *me*.

5

SAM

I jolted upright, sucking in a breath. My head felt like someone had smashed it with a hammer several times.

A gloved hand landed on my chest. "Easy," an unfamiliar female voice said.

I stiffened as I tried to move my arms, but they wouldn't budge. I blinked, and the room slowly came into focus, revealing the one-inch cobalt cuffs around my wrists. I pulled on the chains locked to the table and the fucking cobalt burned my skin.

I rounded my gaze on a dark-haired woman. "Who the fuck are you?"

She gave me a blinding smile, her brown eyes glinting as though she'd caught the largest bear in the forest.

I gritted my teeth, quickly taking inventory of my surroundings.

Medical equipment—operating tables, IV equipment, and heart monitors set up one by one and in perfect alignment with one another across from me. Then my memory rushed back like a fucking flash flood. The helicopter, Ray Aberdeen running for his life, guns pointed at me, a basket dangling from the helicopter, and Layla. I gulped in air. She'd screamed like a seasoned actress in a horror movie.

Where the fuck is she?

Slowly, I released a breath, scanning the ample space for my gorgeous huntress. No sign of Layla or anyone other than the petite woman and me. That didn't mean Layla wasn't in the hands of whoever the fuck these people were.

"Again, who the fuck are you? Where am I?" I jerked on the restraints, and the cobalt singed my skin even more.

She pressed her small hand into my chest. "Lie back, Mr. Mason, or you'll hurt yourself."

I bared my fangs at the woman who didn't have a name tag on her hazmat suit. A wild laugh broke free. "Why are you dressed like I'm contagious?"

She inched back as fear dripped off her in buckets.

I grinned like a starving animal. Fuck, I was hungry and extremely thirsty. My enemy's fear excited me. It boosted my adrenaline and fueled my powers.

She raked her gaze over my lower body as she wrinkled her button nose.

I sniffed the air. My skin burned like a slab of meat on a charcoal grill. "Smells great, doesn't it?"

She pressed her coral-colored lips into a thin line. "Mr. Mason, please relax. My work will go a lot easier if you do, and you should be thanking me, by the way."

I roared with laughter. "I should be feasting on you until your heart stops beating." I flicked my tongue over one of my fangs as my bloodlust grew stronger.

She shuffled back another step, her rapid pulse music to my ears. The taste of fear smelled so fucking sweet, and I hungered to cool that burn scorching my throat.

She plucked a horse needle off the tray beside her. "I don't want to use this." She aimed the syringe at me.

I snapped my jaw shut, and my fangs punctured the skin below my lower lip. I'd been in this position several times when my uncle Patrick used me as his personal lab rat. The first time, I'd been human with no abilities to fight back. Several times after that, I hadn't honed my elemental powers, so my efforts to escape had been weak. Fast forward five years, and I was a much stronger and fiercer vampire. This woman had no idea who she was dealing with. I briefly closed my eyes, inhaled, and concentrated on each body part, allowing the energy in the room to seep in. A prickly sensation coursed through me, growing stronger with each intake of breath. Once my nerve endings sharpened to pinpoints and rage filled my veins, I pulled on the chains so hard I bent the hook attached to the table.

She blanched as she leaned away.

I flashed my fangs at her, my eyes changing from green to silver, my vision preternaturally clear. "It's only a matter of time before you become my next meal."

She stuck out her chin, the color draining from her rosy cheeks. "You're not the first vampire to bite me."

Brave woman, even though her terror was drenching me, giving me the edge to keep my focus despite any drugs she'd pumped into me. "Maybe not, but I will be the first one to drain you." I loved a challenge. I loved when people were so sure of themselves that they were caught off guard by their overconfident attitudes.

She tore her gaze away from me.

I tracked her line of sight to a windowed room above us and scorching anger had me jerking on the chains like a crazy fuck when I recognized the woman staring down at us.

"I'm going to have so much fucking fun ripping your head off, Rianne Aberdeen." I didn't know if she could hear me. My bet was she could because her smug grin grew wider as though she was untouchable.

Rianne stood stoic, chin out, shoulders rolled back, and her brown hair was tightly wound on top of her head. Layla's sister wagged her finger at me with a look that said she'd won. In whose fucking universe did she win? This was only the beginning. She leaned to her left and said something to Lester Worthington. Another brazen-faced fuckwad decked out in black, whose brown hair was slicked back. The two chatted as if they were discussing the plot of a movie they'd recently seen while the dude beside Lester watched me with a keen eye. He was about a head taller than his counterparts, with a broad chest that filled out his expensive black tailored suit. I was quickly reminded of Roman Brown, who'd come to a fight dressed in a suit. But this dude had brown hair, not blond, and brown eyes, not blue. And if I had to guess, he was the head honcho, the one who spit out orders and was fucking with the wrong vampire.

Rianne threw her head back and laughed.

I thrashed around, tugging hard on the chains, and the hook bent even more.

Then Rianne's voice blared through the speakers from somewhere in the room. "Carly, give him another dose. Now!"

I whipped my head at Carly. "So, you're Carly Aberdeen. I was told you were in charge of the tech department, not the lab."

She kept the needle pointed my way but didn't move a muscle. "I wear many hats for Intech."

"What are you waiting for?" Rianne asked.

I snarled at the bitch. "Why don't you come down here and do it yourself?" My mouth watered to slice and dice her. I turned to Carly. "Who's in the driver's seat? You? Rianne? Lester? Or that sharp-looking man in the suit?"

She lowered the needle. "I don't want to use it, Mr. Mason. The tests I'm about to run require you to be awake and lucid. So cooperate with me, and I'll make it worth your while."

I gave her a condescending grin. Still, my empath side told me she wasn't exactly pulling my leg. "You have nothing to give me in return unless you'll let me leave here."

She sighed. "I'll give you an update on Layla."

I glared daggers at Carly. "Where is she? Is Layla here?" I restrained myself from spewing idle threats. I would rather show her how much damage I could do. If anyone laid a finger on Layla, they wouldn't have a heart left.

"Carly," Rianne warned.

Images of me dragging Rianne through an inferno danced before me as heat hurtled along my arms. My fire element was ready to set alight anyone and anything in my wake.

Carly set the syringe on the table as though she knew she was a gnat's ass away from smelling her own skin charring. "Rianne, I'm running this show, not you." Her demeanor changed from half-scared to full-on bold as fuck. "Or did I miss a memo, Mr. Emery?"

Even though Carly wanted to use me as a lab specimen, I was digging her fearlessness with Rianne. "Fred Emery?" I mumbled. He was the dude who had given Jordyn Aberdeen the creeps when she'd met him. He was also the head of security for Intech. Plus, he could be the same Fred guy who had been talking to Roman Brown on the phone when my best bud, Ben, had been in Roman's clutches.

Carly shook her head. "Adam Emery," she said to me while keeping her attention glued to the threesome, waiting for an answer.

Must be a family business.

Emery nodded as his deep baritone voice filled the hospital room or lab or whatever the fuck they called this place. "Do what you need to but make it quick. We have a lot of work to get him ready."

I cocked an eyebrow. "Ready for what?" My gut told me Carly wasn't in the market to extract my DNA, but something far worse.

Rianne, Lester, and Emery left as two guards dressed in full SWAT gear entered the room above and positioned themselves at the corners. They each opened a small window and aimed their sniper rifles at me.

"What are you about to do to me?" I again asked Carly, knowing she wouldn't tell me. Considering Intech and Camden Industries built computer programs and weapons for the Department of Defense, that bad feeling only multiplied.

She scurried over to what looked to be an MRI machine near a glass room that resembled the one my uncle Patrick held me in when he'd been poking and prodding me.

No fucking way was she about to mess with my brain or strap me to the table in that glass room.

Think, man. If I tried anything, the two SWAT dudes would pump drug-filled bullets into me. I knew they didn't have cobalt bullets, but only because Carly needed me alive.

I lay back, visualizing snapping off Rianne's head, slitting

Lester's throat, and burning Noah over a firepit. As I did, rage consumed me, a prickly heat blazing down to the tips of my fingers. I inhaled, the searing feeling growing hotter and stronger, as though I was touching a plug with a wet hand, only fifty times more powerful.

Heat filled my palms, but it wasn't enough to melt the cobalt. I had to set myself on fire, scorch my skin so I could slip my hands and ankles through the cuffs, or allow the cobalt to burn me to the bone. Gritting my teeth, I kept feeding my fire element with my intense fury. I tuned out all the sounds as the table beneath me quaked like a ten on the Richter scale.

Carly rushed over just as I had one hand free. "Impossible. Your powers shouldn't be working."

I lurched forward and howled like the animal I was. When I did, my other hand slipped through the cobalt.

Carly shouted, "Shoot him!"

Come and get me, motherfuckers. In a flash, I vaulted off the table and dodged medical equipment, throwing fireballs at one guard and then the other. My aim was off, and I set a cabinet below them on fire. The water sprinklers engaged, and alarms blared.

I had maybe five minutes at most before the cavalry came in. I hauled ass toward Carly, who was running in the direction of the elevator.

I loved a good chase, but I was faster than her. I caught her before she had a chance to either hit a big red emergency button or dart onto the elevator.

She stumbled backward under the low ceiling beneath the room above. "Mr. Mason. You don't want to do this. Think about Layla."

I *was* thinking about Layla, which was fueling my powers like gasoline.

My fangs dripped with saliva as my skin sizzled. "Where is she?" I desperately needed blood if I wanted to heal quickly.

"She's going to be okay." Her voice cracked. "She got caught in the helicopter basket when we captured you."

My heart stopped for a beat as I grabbed her by the throat, not sure if I believed her. But if she was telling the truth—fuck me.

What did that mean? I couldn't remember much past her scream. "Is she hurt?" Knowing Layla, she would do everything in her power to save my ass. She had once before when Noah and Rianne strung me over an open fire. But with our child growing in her, she wouldn't put the baby in jeopardy. Then again, if I were in her shoes, I wouldn't think twice about risking my life for hers. "Answer me!"

Carly choked, her face turning scarlet red.

I loosened my grip. "Speak."

"She's fine." Her voice was squeaky. "She's in a room on level four."

I cocked an eyebrow. "You're lying." Her heart was racing too fucking fast.

She swallowed, her brown eyes staring right through me. "I'm not."

I didn't believe her, but I had an idea. "Take me to her, then once I see Layla isn't hurt, I'll be your pincushion or whatever the fuck you want to do to me." I was the one lying now, but I doubted she could tell.

A deep crease dented the smooth spot between her eyebrows. "You're serious?"

"Whether or not you believe me, you have no choice. Live or die."

She frowned as though she was losing her best friend. "Fine. But you need to do one thing for me. There are guards on every floor, and Adam Emery will have an army waiting for you, so I need you to be a good vampire and not attack anyone. I'll handle the rest."

In part, I believed she would ensure I wasn't harmed, since she needed me awake. But I also needed her. Other than her boss, she was the key to driving whatever fucked-up plans they had for me, so she was about to become my human shield, my ticket out.

"Adam Emery was the man standing beside Lester, and he runs the show? Is he related to Fred Emery?"

She grabbed my hands, trying to pull them away from her throat. "Yes. Adam owns Intech and Camden Industries. Fred is Adam's brother and is head of security for both companies."

I set her on two feet, and she was whirling around toward the elevator when I caught her arm. "One more thing." I sunk my fangs into her neck.

She yelped like a dying animal. But I didn't care. The only way to take on guards was to have my powers at 100 percent. I drank, pulling in her sweet fear.

She cried again. "This wasn't part of the deal."

I held her steady as I sucked harder, the blood sliding down my throat like an expensive bottle of smooth whiskey. Every fiber in me came alive as the burn eased and my skin healed.

Once I was sated, I released her. "Now we have a deal."

She covered her neck with her hand as she hurried, stumbling to the keypad and pressing her thumb on the screen. I made a mental note of her action in the event I was trapped in here with her again.

The elevator doors whooshed open. Once we were inside and moving, I hit the stop button.

She flattened her back against the wall across from me. "What are you doing?"

I folded my arms over my chest as images of Layla and me in the elevator came to mind. I grinned, replaying our steamy scene when I'd first had her alone in the elevator on the naval base, but I quickly shook them off.

"Well?" Carly swiped a hand over her short black hair before ripping off her bloodstained disposable white suit. Then she dumped it on the floor and brushed a hand down her lab coat.

"I want to have a quiet conversation before we jump into battle. Tell me the truth. What am I doing here? What did it mean when that Emery dude said, 'We have a lot of work to get him ready'?"

Her pulse was steady, her fear not as strong as earlier. "Before I answer you, I'm confused about something." She swept her gaze over my sweaty body.

My chest was bare, but I still had on my black cargo pants and boots, although both were charred at the ankles, and my weapons were gone.

"I see why Layla is drawn to you. You're handsome, muscled, and your green eyes suck a person in. But you could drain her dry, and she's okay with that? I mean, I'm not disgusted with your kind like my husband and his family are. I'm utterly fascinated with the supernatural."

I rolled my eyes. "What's your point?" We didn't have long before guards either tried to pry the doors open or came through the ceiling, and frankly, I didn't give a fuck about her obsession with my world.

She sighed. "We've injected you with good amount of—"

"Ketamine, gelsemium, wolfsbane, and maybe even cobalt oxide." As soon as we'd touched down at the abandoned airport, Doc had informed us what had been in the drug Layla and her sisters had used that night at the vampire club.

Her mouth dropped open. "You've done your homework. But I only used ketamine and gelsemium on you. The latter should counteract your powers and even paralyze you. I need to increase the dosage."

Maybe the antidote I'd taken before I'd left base worked on the gelsemium. It sure as fuck didn't work on the ketamine. Five years ago, Dr. Vieira and Jo had developed the antidote to work against a drug Edmund Rain and my uncle Patrick had used on us to knock us out. I would guess the ketamine wasn't the same one. Still, I made a mental note to tell Doc and Jo about the newfound info on gelsemium. My other thought was that maybe gelsemium didn't work on certain vampires. My DNA was unique, after all. Not only that, but Jo, my dad, and I were the only three vampires in my world who could wield all four elements—earth, air, wind, and fire.

"You can try any concoction, but you can't keep a Mason down." Ketamine had had the intended effect, but my powers were a different story. "How long have I been here?"

She tucked her hands into the pockets of her lab coat. "Not long. A few hours. Your turn to answer a question. Tell me how you compelled Rianne. I heard she was in a vegetative state." Her fascination with me screamed she didn't want to be human, which didn't shock me.

"Do you want me to show you? Or I have a better idea." I closed the distance between us. "How about I erase your knowledge of me and all vampires?" If I did, then she couldn't use me as her test subject. One problem out of the way, and a thousand more to go.

She slinked away from me as terror jumped off her and rammed me in the gut. "I swear, I will tell you the truth. But please don't erase my memories. If you do, Adam Emery will only find another person to do the job, and I can promise you, you want me performing the tests."

I sneered. "I don't want anyone using me for their science project or whatever else the plan is. How would you feel if I stuck needles in you? Would you be happy? I am sick of anyone thinking they can use my DNA or sell me on the open market. Frankly, the last two people who tried are dead."

She jutted out her chin as she rested against the back wall, not fazed by my last statement. "I know. I'm well aware of Edmund Rain and Patrick Mason."

I flinched. I had to have marbles in my ears, or maybe my vamp hearing wasn't up to par. "Come again?"

She stood straighter, as if proud of dropping that bomb. "I've been studying your uncle Patrick's formulas and notes."

What the fuck? My eyebrows disappeared into my hairline. "That's impossible. We burned all that data."

She shrugged. "You may have, but Patrick had been sending his research to Adam Emery on a regular basis as a backup if something ever happened to him."

I laughed, albeit crazily. "So, what? You want to follow in his footsteps? For money? Power? My uncle failed in engineering vampires out of humans." Not entirely. Ben was a hybrid—half human and half vampire. Then there was Alia Costner's son, Matthew. He was also a product of my uncle's experiment, and the only human out of hundreds to turn into a true vampire. "What makes you or Adam think you will be successful?"

"We're close. But we're lacking in certain areas."

Figures. The exact reason my uncle and Edmund Rain had kidnapped Jo and me a few times had been to further my uncle's research and find the Holy Grail. "And that's why I'm here," I said through gritted teeth. "You'll never find the right ingredient to make the perfect clone of me. I was born with vampire DNA." My theory about why Matthew Costner drew the lucky card was because he had vampire blood running through his veins. His mother was born with the vampire gene, but she'd decided not to turn so she could have children. And even though Matthew probably had the right DNA makeup to give up his humanity, he lacked one important component—a vampire father, since Alia had married a human.

Nevertheless, I was beginning to understand what my grandfather had relayed to my dad about a war coming when he'd been in a coma. If Intech was close to a genetic serum of sorts to alter human DNA, then humanity was at stake—big time.

I had to get out of here more than ever. I couldn't allow Carly to perform any tests on me, although maybe she already had when I'd been out.

Suddenly, my eyes burned.

Carly squinted as she glanced up at the vents, choking.

I gagged too. *Motherfucker.*

Carly slid down the wall as her body went limp.

My limbs became weak as the small space spun on its axis. Then everything went black.

6

LAYLA

I ran under a canopy of trees as the rain pelted down. Sticks, rocks, and dead leaves embedded in my feet, the adrenaline keeping me from feeling any pain.

I tossed a look over my shoulder, but I still couldn't see who was chasing me. The area was as black as the inside of a closed coffin.

Keep running, *my inner voice supplied.* Whatever you do, don't stop.

I gulped in the cold, crisp night air as I struggled to regulate my breathing. A wolf howled in the distance, heightening my senses and frying my nerves. I swallowed the sandpapery feeling in my throat as I ducked under a branch, but not low enough. My forehead took the brunt of the impact, and I fell backward, my hands disappearing beneath the packed, wet vegetation covering the ground.

I scrambled to my feet, but the panic coursing through me made me stumble, only to fall on my ass again. Fuck! I sat in the sea of leaves, the rain soaking my hair and running down my face, competing with the tears leaking out of my eyes.

A ray of light shone up ahead, causing my heart to sputter and relief to stir. I pushed to my feet, and this time I managed to skirt under the branch without any problems.

I wiped my dirty hands on my wet clothes as the light pulled me forward. The minute I walked into a clearing, my jaw came unhinged. I blinked several times.

A man stood in the distance—tall, muscled, with shoulder-length black hair and green eyes lighting up the darkened sky. Butterflies took flight in my stomach.

"Sam?" I whispered, running through the squishy earth, ready to jump in his arms.

Suddenly, the terrain changed, and I was in a room with bright lights and windows all around me. The rain outside pinged off a metal railing rimming the perimeter. I inched over to one side and scanned the area. Lush green treetops spanned the landscape for miles. For a beat, I struggled to figure out where I was. When I spun on my heel, my surroundings changed once again.

The expansive room was sterile, the air cold, and I hugged myself, shivering. The lights were bright, almost blinding, but something in the distance caught my eye. I slowly walked in that direction, squinting to read the three letters within the red circle stamped on the wall. The first letter was a capital E *followed by a capital* M, *but the third one vanished when a shiny object to my right caught my eye. My pulse went haywire when my gaze landed on a stainless-steel table. But it wasn't the table that had me sprinting over to it.*

No. No. No. My bare feet slapped against the tile floor that felt like a slab of ice. I pumped my legs hard, my arms in sync like I was running the 100-meter dash in the Olympics.

Hurry, Layla. You need to save Sam, *that small voice in my head whispered.*

I pushed myself harder, but it was futile. I wasn't gaining any ground. The table seemed to be moving farther and farther away.

"Go back, Layla," a familiar husky voice said overhead. "It's not safe for you here."

I came to an abrupt halt. "Sam?" My eyebrows pinched together as I glanced at the ceiling. "Where are you?" I swore it was him on that table.

"Baby doll, please, run. Run now!"

Confusion snaked through me, and when I returned my attention to the table, the body was gone.

A wave of heat whooshed over me, and I was standing in the middle of a road. Fire danced along the edges, the flames licking their way up the trunks of trees. The snap of a branch made me whip my head forward.

His black hair fell around his strong jaw. His green eyes were luminescent. His bare, brawny chest was slick with sweat. Sam held out his hand, beckoning me to him.

But my gut kept me rooted to the warm pavement. I tossed a look behind me. Fire encircled us.

"Come to me, Layla." Sam's husky tone made my belly flutter despite the evil grin etched on his handsome face.

I shook my head. "You're not Sam." I wasn't sure how I knew that, but the man who stood about ten feet from me wasn't the sexy vampire I was in love with. I stiffened. "Who are you?"

The Sam look-alike threw his head back and laughed. "I'm your worst nightmare, Layla Aberdeen." The man's face morphed into Ray's. "You're going to hell for killing me."

I screamed at the top of my lungs, and when I did, the fire died. Before I could take a step, I was spiraling down a long metal tube, my screech sounding hollow, echoing and blasting in my ears. I landed in a bin of towels with an oof. I was hurrying to climb out when a hand gripped my arm. I toppled into a hard chest, my back to his front. He spun me around, and I came face-to-face with Sam.

My breath rushed out of me like a fast-moving train. His manly scent, his cocky grin, those forest-green eyes that caused my heart to skip a beat indicated he was Sam. I touched his unshaven jaw. "Is that really you, Sam?"

He grinned, his fangs lowering slow and steady before he pounced. His strong arms banded around me, and quick as a whip, he sank his fangs into my neck.

I became a rag doll in his arms as he fed on me like a hungry animal who hadn't eaten in months. I scraped my nails up his bare back, and he moaned, drawing my life into him. Minutes went by, and the more he feasted, the weaker I became.

I pushed him away, but he wouldn't budge. "Sam, stop. You're taking too much blood." My mind became fuzzy and my eyes heavy. "Sam, please," I begged, wiggling and pushing as a faint ringing sound cut through my soupy consciousness.

The sound grew louder and louder as Sam vanished, and slowly I became alert until I was gulping in air and sitting upright in bed. My tank top clung to me like a wet rag as I brushed hair off my forehead.

The ringing stopped as I rubbed my neck. "What the hell was that?" I said, feeling like I'd just been through hell and back.

I flopped back onto the pillow, cleared the sleep from my eyes, and stared at the popcorn ceiling of the hotel room. We'd found a place to crash about fifteen minutes from that abandoned airport. A lot of good that did if I couldn't get any rest.

I sighed, rifling through my nightmare—a table in an empty room and the letters *E* and *M*. Sam and I had been connected through one of my dreams before, so I believed he had to be giving me a sign. I puffed out my cheeks. I didn't have much to go on.

A ray of light wormed through the crack where two curtain panels met in the middle. The *drip, drip, drip* of the bathroom faucet played a soft tune.

I checked the clock on the nightstand. One damn thirty in the morning. I'd only fallen asleep two hours ago. After a rough day at the airport, I had a feeling I wouldn't be able to sleep until we found Sam. I laughed, my voice echoing in the room. *Rough day. Ha.* I would bet hell had to be a cakewalk compared to the day I had.

I quivered at the remembrance of plummeting to earth. A shaky laugh erupted. I was a complete idiot but grateful fate was on my side. Now I just needed a sign, a clue of Sam's whereabouts.

I swung my legs over the edge of the bed, dragging a hand over my carotid artery, checking again. I could almost feel Sam's fangs in me.

My phone rang, and I flinched before a dose of excitement stirred. Maybe Jo or Steven had news on Sam. I fumbled to snag my cell from the nightstand. Jordyn's name brightened the screen.

My voice was raw and rough as I answered. "Hey, sis."

"Sorry to wake you," she said. "This is the first chance I've had to do anything, and I wanted to catch you before things got busy again."

"I was awake. Steven tells me you're helping Sawyer and his tech team." On the way to the hotel when I tried to call Jordyn and she hadn't answered, Steven informed me that she was on the naval base, working alongside Sawyer.

"Yeah, so talk to me. I'm so sorry about Sam. We're busting our butts to find something that will lead us to him." She yawned. "Sorry, I haven't slept."

"Did anyone fill you in on any of the details?" I'd asked Steven not to share the part about me falling out of the sky or Ray's death with Jordyn. I wanted to be the one to tell her. I wanted her to hear my voice and know I was okay.

"Just that it was chaos and Uncle Ray betrayed Jack, which I can't say I'm surprised about. Why? Did something else happen? Is the baby okay?"

I didn't even know where to begin or how to tell her I was responsible for our uncle's death. I cleared the emotions lodged in my throat. "The baby is fine, as far as I know." I was still craving blood, so to me that seemed like a good sign. "Uncle Ray is dead." I held my breath.

The sound of her shriek blared through the phone. "What the fuck! How?"

I bit my bottom lip. "I think I'm partly responsible. But everything happened so fast. The more I think through things, the fuzzier they get, but Uncle Ray grabbed me when I ran toward Sam, and I screamed at the top of my lungs. Uncle Ray collapsed, and blood oozed out of his ears. Not long after that, he was dead. I'm so going to hell." Guilt encased my heart as Ray's dead body flashed before me.

A viscous silence stretched over the line.

I dug my fingers into my chest, hoping my heart would stop jackhammering against my ribs.

"Sis." The softness of her tone helped to slow my pulse slightly. "Can a scream cause someone to die? I understand we're dealing with the supernatural here, but you're far from acquiring powerful abilities. Sure, you probably have some since you drink Sam's blood, but nothing that would kill a person."

"I've been trying to rationalize the correlation between my scream and Ray's death, but nothing is jiving. You're right, though. I have minor abilities from Sam. But we also can't discount Mom's family. Jo told me that females with the Vel-negative blood type come from a line of witches."

She snorted. "For real?" Her giggle sounded a little wild. "What else will we learn about our mysterious mother?"

"I shudder to think." I then filled her in on Kendra.

"Do you think Kendra knows something about Mom?" she asked.

I stretched my neck. "Not sure. But she's gone, and she's not our concern right now. But I think you should have Dr. Vieira test your blood."

"No," she said emphatically. "I'm not ready to go down that road."

"Fair enough, but don't sleep with a vampire." I snickered. "You might end up like me."

We both laughed.

I rubbed a hand over my carotid artery. I swore it still felt like Sam had sunk his fangs into me. "Anyway, back to Uncle Ray. He was complaining he couldn't breathe."

"Heart attack, you think? They do run in our family."

"Maybe so. But I can't help but think if I hadn't screamed, he would still be alive." I couldn't face his wife or kids. Aunt Deb was a decent woman, and we'd gotten along okay.

"Listen to me." Jordyn's voice was motherly, reminding me of when Mom scolded us. "I'm sad about Uncle Ray. I am. But we can't control fate, and whatever happened to cause his death, it wasn't intentional. So shrug off the self-pity. You're tough and resilient. Dig deep for that strength. Sam needs you. Your baby needs you. I do too. Fight with all you have, of course, but be careful. You're carrying my niece or nephew. But for fuck's sake, none of us have time to mourn or allow guilt to take over. Do you hear me?"

A gloom-ridden laugh escaped. "Yes, ma'am."

She sighed heavily. "Good. I need to go. I've been surfing the dark web for any chatter on Sam, and I want to continue my efforts."

"You mean the supernatural dark web?"

"That, and the human one too," she said. "I found a chat room that might give us some leads."

I straightened. "Tell me more."

"Not much to say yet. Get some rest. Tomorrow will be a long day."

She might be right, especially if we were snowed in. "Love you, sis."

"Ditto," she said, then hung up.

Blowing out a breath, I combed my fingers through my tangled hair and climbed off the bed. On my way to the bathroom, hunger pangs struck. What the hell? I'd eaten a juicy hamburger about three hours ago. I placed my hand on my stomach. "Hey, little one," I said. "I'll find us something to snack on." I had a craving for something sweet and not blood… yet.

I didn't have any money with me, so the vending machine was out. But there was a store adjacent to the check-in desk. If I remembered correctly, the store was open all night.

With that in mind, my mouth watered for a Reese's or a Mounds bar.

7

____

LAYLA

Fifteen minutes later, I stood in the hotel's all-night store with a Reese's, a Mounds bar, a package of white powdered donuts, a Kit Kat, and a chocolate protein bar in my hands. I set everything on a wood counter connecting the store to the check-in desk. It was time I started to keep snacks with me so when the hunger struck, I would be prepared.

The brunette night clerk sat on a stool, reading on her phone. "Are you ready?" she asked, not looking at me.

"I am," I replied as the elevator dinged. "Can you add these to my room? I'm in 432."

She smiled at whoever had just stepped into the lobby. "Evening, sir."

I couldn't see anyone from where I stood. But maybe the guest had the same idea as me.

Then she typed a few strokes on her keyboard before she hopped off her stool and ambled over to me. "Can't sleep?"

"Nightmare," I said. One I didn't care to discuss.

She tipped her head toward the lobby. "That handsome guy over there must have the same problem." She proceeded to add my snacks to a plastic bag.

52

Hotels were hard for me to sleep in. After my sisters and I had buried our dad, we'd traveled around the country and spent many nights in motels. I should be used to the uncomfortable beds, musty odors, rough sheets, and disgusting bathrooms. But the high-end hotel I was in that night was not a cheap one. The memory-foam mattress was by far more comfortable than any I'd slept on in a long time, if only I could sleep.

Damn nightmares. Damn screwed-up life. The way things are headed, I'm on a trajectory to hell.

She handed me my items, then we exchanged pleasantries. I pulled out the Mounds bar, my mouth watering in anticipation. Even my stomach growled. With my luck, I would be as big as a cow in another month or two.

Walking out of the store, I was concentrating on ripping off the wrapper when I bumped into a hard chest.

Hands grabbed the sides of my arms. "Miss."

I glanced at the blue-eyed valet dude who had helped us when we'd arrived. Webb's assistant had booked the hotel and a rental car. Then Steven and Tripp borrowed Jack's car to pick up the SUV while the rest of us waited. Shortly after Jack and Steven's tense conversation, I would've bet a ton of money Jack would take off to Chicago. But he surprised me and stayed, although he'd attempted to reach Noah several times. Jack assumed he'd lost the signal, and that might be true. My guess was Noah was running scared.

I smiled at the burly valet. "Sorry." I held up the candy bar. "Important stuff right here."

"That's one of my favorites," he said as he skirted by. "Enjoy." He went right toward an office.

I went left, biting into the chocolate-coconut sweetness. My taste buds did a happy dance, and I moaned, rounding the corner into the lobby.

Webb sat stiffly on a couch, absorbed in something on his iPad. A crease formed between his brows. He was seemingly irritated with whatever he was reading. I debated whether to disturb him or not. Frankly, as good-looking as he was, he scared me. He had that vibe that if I fucked with him, he would embed his canines in me and not let go, and that gave me the freaking chills. Webb's fangs were longer than most vampires'. At least they appeared that way to me.

Chewing and savoring the taste of the Mounds, I stopped behind a wingback chair in a lounge area outside the hotel bar. "Hey. You can't sleep either?"

Without looking up from his iPad, he said, "You should be more aware of your surroundings, Layla." His tone was rigid, as if he was talking to one of his soldiers.

I flinched, silently berating myself that I hadn't kept walking. "Come again?"

Still not looking at me, he asked, "What if that valet snagged you?"

The candy bar was melting in my hand. "He didn't. He's not working with the people who have Sam," I fired back as anger twisted my gut into a tight knot.

Ever so slowly, his chin lifted, then his eyes, angry and calculating. "Do you know that for sure? He could be working here incognito, watching us."

Frustration crept along my arms. I was mad at myself because what if he was right? But I was also annoyed with how easily he put me on the spot. He and I had had a shitty day, to say the least. We were both on edge. But that didn't mean he could take out his frustration on me. Unless he blamed me for what had happened. After all, he probably considered me the enemy since I was an Aberdeen.

Instead of lashing out, I finished off the Mounds. The darn thing was melting fast, and I didn't want to waste it. We stared at each other while I wiped my chocolate-coated fingers on my jeans.

He opened his palm toward the couch on the other side of the coffee table. "Have a seat." The man was a rock—impenetrable, emotionless, and cold.

I guessed he wasn't done scolding me. Frankly, I wasn't in the mood to argue. The crappy day, an emotional convo with Jack, a weird dream that made no sense—or maybe it did—were overwhelming, to say the least. Still, I had a ton of respect for Webb, and I wouldn't mind hearing what he had to say. He, Tripp, Steven, and

Jo had probably already planned their next moves. One of them was to snag Noah.

Once I was seated, I tossed the empty wrapper into the bag.

Webb's hard glare made me edgy. Placing my hands in my lap, I dug my nails into my palms. "So, here we are."

A long stretch of silence followed.

At any second, I would draw blood from my nails piercing my skin. "Are you going to talk?"

He tilted his head, his blue eyes hollow, empty. "If you're not trained to know your surroundings right down to the speck of dirt on the ground, you'll get yourself killed." His tone was firm and unyielding. "While you're with us, you will abide by our rules."

"You don't own me or command me. I'm not one of your soldiers." I struggled to keep my tone even.

His features hardened even more. "I won't argue with you. Are we clear?"

Whoa! I raised my hands. "I'm not the problem."

The way he examined me critically from where he sat told me otherwise. "I beg to differ, Layla. You don't think before you act. Today was a perfect example of that."

Lowering my hands, I grunted out a laugh. "Are you saying you wouldn't do the same if it were Jo? I highly, highly doubt you would sit idle while assholes took Jo." I didn't care if I pissed him off, if he cut out my lungs, or banned me from ever stepping foot on the naval base again. He was madly in love with his wife, and he would never convince me he wouldn't react to save the woman he loved.

"I'm not in the spotlight, here," he said. "And I'm not pregnant. You put your life and your unborn child's in jeopardy. Steven told you it was too dangerous to run after Sam."

Guilt rode me hard, and he succeeded in making me feel like crap. I couldn't argue with him on that point, and if I was reading between the lines, he was more concerned for the Mason child growing in me than for Layla Aberdeen. I couldn't fault him for that. We hardly knew each other, and again, I was related to one of his enemies.

"You're right. I panicked when they captured Sam. I'm in love with him, and I don't want to lose him."

He scratched his scruffy jaw. "I understand, Layla. But you need to listen to me, Steven, Tripp, and Jo. It's admirable you want to save Sam. We do as well. But until we know what and who we're dealing with, I can't have you going off half-cocked or pulling a stunt like you did today. You're lucky Steven reacted as fast as he did."

An avalanche of regret tumbled into the pit of my stomach. In part, Webb was right. But love had a way of driving people to act without thought, to do stupid things, and I wasn't immune to that. Still, I wasn't sitting around and twiddling my thumbs. My family was in the fray, and I knew them better than Webb did.

He pushed to his feet with his iPad in his hand. "We're returning to base tomorrow. We'll meet in the lobby at six a.m. sharp." He gave me a long blank look. "Before you ask, we are not going to Chicago. We don't have any firm leads."

"I thought you wanted Noah. He's in Chicago."

"Maybe he is, but I have people who can snatch him," Webb said.

I rose. "We should talk to Carly then." We couldn't just jet off without at least trying something. Besides, even if Carly knew nothing about Sam, she might have answers on Noah's whereabouts or even Rianne's. I wanted to find my sister. She and I had some unfinished business. Whether Webb agreed or not, I was tracking down Rianne. Maybe in the process I would find answers to where the SWAT men had taken Sam.

I couldn't help but think of my dream. I might be crazy, but Sam was giving me a sign. I could feel it.

A muscle ticked in his jaw. "And what do you think she'll tell you? That Intech is responsible? That they have Sam? Layla, we're not about to rush into a situation when we don't have all the facts." His tone was even.

Defiance bubbled to the surface, and I angled my chin up. "Who says we're rushing? Carly's family anyway. I have every right to talk to my cousin-in-law."

He gave me a long look. "Lobby. Six a.m." Then he strutted over to the elevator.

Despite his orders, I wasn't sitting on the sidelines.

8
───────

LAYLA

I'd left the hotel about an hour after Webb scolded me. I admit I was as stubborn as my dad or any Aberdeen. But I couldn't leave the state without talking to Carly or her husband, Jack Jr. If they didn't know where Noah or Rianne was or about the game the Aberdeens were playing, then no harm, no foul. At least I would walk away knowing I tried. Besides, they would talk to me before they opened up to a complete stranger, like Webb.

I kept my chin tucked in my coat as I walked out of the parking garage not far from Intech in downtown Chicago. The Windy City was holding true to its name. The crisp, cold air blew my hair in all directions. A pedestrian breezed by at a brisk pace, scarf wrapped up to her mouth and hands tucked in the pockets of her wool coat as she beelined it for the Starbucks on the corner. Coffee sounded mouthwatering, and I might need to grab a cup to settle my nerves.

The weather was far better in the city than it had been at the hotel. A two-hour drive had taken me almost three. The highways had been fairly clear, with snowplows working overtime. I wasn't an amateur driver in winter weather since I'd grown up in Montana.

My phone rang just as I approached Intech. The building stood tall and spanned a city block next to its sister company, Camden

58

Industries. I peeked into the lobby as I strolled by. Other than a security guard, who sat behind a half-moon-shaped desk, all was quiet, which at six thirty in the morning wasn't a surprise.

My phone stopped ringing, only to start again. I suspected Webb was blowing up my phone, or it was Steven, Tripp, or Jo. Or the caller could be Jack. After all, I had borrowed his car. Never mind that I hadn't asked for permission. Flirting with the valet I'd bumped into in the lobby had made him putty in my hands. I'd set a Mounds bar on his desk, then explained I needed to get something out of the car. He didn't ask questions. He'd taken the candy bar and handed me the keys.

I pictured Webb fuming, his fangs down and steam coming out of his nose. So be it. I wasn't in Chicago to piss him off. I also wasn't one of his soldiers, so I had free rein to do as I pleased. Besides, I would like to think I would make a good detective, which was something that had always appealed to me.

Suddenly, nausea churned in my stomach. *Damn it.* The last thing I needed was morning sickness. I had two of the candy bars tucked in the inside pocket of my coat. I also had the remaining two vials of blood with me if my throat became scratchy—a sign I needed it. But a pastry sounded better than a candy bar, especially paired with coffee, and like the perfect remedy for morning sickness. I couldn't meet with Carly while puking my brains out, and I didn't want to give her any indication I was pregnant. Women have a sixth sense about that. The less she knew, the better, particularly if Junior hadn't told her about vampires.

I crossed the street and went into the Starbucks. The minute I entered, a wave of heat washed over me, and the aroma of caffeine seeped into my nostrils. I ambled to the counter that was full of sweets and treats.

Aside from two baristas, a man dressed in a suit minus the jacket sat at a corner table near the entrance to the restrooms, typing on his laptop.

The cute blonde waiting to take my order smiled. "Morning. What can I get you?"

I gave her my order of a soy latte and an apple turnover, then found a seat in one of those comfy chairs near the window. My phone trilled again the second my butt hit the chair. I plucked the annoying piece of technology out of my coat pocket and was ready to turn it off but stopped. Jordyn's name flashed on the screen.

Ten to one, Steven had asked her to call me. "I'm fine," I said to her as I answered. "I just want to talk to Carly." *Nothing reckless.*

"Then call her," Jordyn said in a harsh tone. "Where are you anyway?"

The hiss of the latte machine as the barista frothed the milk rattled my nerves. "I don't have her number, and she probably wouldn't answer my call anyway. Besides, I want to gauge her body language. Do you have her home address?" It didn't matter where I talked to her or Jack Jr. Or Junior, as we called him.

"No," Jordyn bit out. "I'll text you her number. Again, where are you?"

Glancing past the car stopped at the red light, I bent my head slightly and scanned the windows of Intech as far up as I could from where I sat. Lights were on in several offices.

"I'm sitting at a Starbucks for a quick bite before I go into Intech."

"You won't get past security."

"Then what are you worried about?" I asked.

"I don't know. That place gave me the creeps when I interviewed with them. Well, their head of security is scary."

"What's his name again?" I remembered her telling me about him.

"Fred Emery," she said in abrasive tone. "He's maybe five foot ten. He has military-cut brown hair and brown eyes. The eerie part of him is he has a scar that starts from his left ear and ends near his mouth. If you see him, get out of there."

A chill gripped me just from her description.

"Layla, you need to listen to Webb and Steven. They *will* find Sam."

The blonde barista came over and set the apple turnover and my soy latte on the table. "Enjoy." Then she checked on the businessman.

I pressed my lips into a thin line. "I understand you're worried. But this isn't just about Sam. We're dealing with our family. Carly might have answers on where Rianne is. Junior might too. Or Noah could. It's not like I won't come out alive." A shiver racked my body.

"You are so like Dad, and dare I say, Uncle Jack too," she said. "But I would do the same," Jordyn added, finally acquiescing. "It would be nice to know what our sister is up to. I wish I could be there with you."

A yellow cab pulled up to the curb in front of Intech, and an older lady climbed out. When the taxi sped off, the lady tossed a look over her shoulder in my direction.

I squinted. It couldn't be. The short reddish-gray hairstyle and gold-rimmed glasses on the woman reminded me of someone closely related to me.

"Um… Jordyn. Where is Grandma Aberdeen? Is she still in Fiji?" My pulse pounded in my ears.

The older woman stood on the sidewalk, her gaze lingering in my direction.

I gulped in the caffeine-laden air.

"What?" Jordyn asked. "Why are you asking about Granny?"

That nauseous feeling multiplied. "I think she's standing outside Intech." I couldn't exactly see that well. The light inside Starbucks was bright, and the streets were still somewhat dark, which made it difficult to see from this distance. Plus, I remembered my grandmother with black-rimmed glasses, not gold.

"No way," Jordyn rushed out.

A nervous laugh hurtled out, my head on a collision course with a brick wall. "I'm fairly sure Harriet Aberdeen is about to walk into Intech."

"She's probably there to see Junior or Carly." Jordyn sounded as though she was trying to convince herself. "Maybe Carly and Junior are working."

My grandmother, if that was her, scanned the area one last time before heading into Intech.

"Maybe you're right." Junior worked as a security guard for the company, and I was at Carly's place of employment to see her too.

Suddenly, something dark and twisted squeezed my insides. "What if Granny is working with Noah and Ray?"

Jordyn choked. "Where did that come from?"

Silence stretched over the line as I noodled on my own idea, and I knew Jordyn was too.

"You know, with what's been happening, that might not be off the mark," Jordyn finally said.

I gnawed on my bottom lip. "Plus, Granny wouldn't jet back to the States unless something was amiss." Things had just taken a weird turn. "More than ever, I have to go in, sis." My curiosity would probably bite me in the ass, but knowledge was power, and the old saying "keep your friends close and enemies closer" was singing in my head. Or rather, keep my family closer.

Regardless, Harriet Aberdeen wasn't a woman to mess around with. She was the matriarch of the Aberdeen family and a ball-buster, much like her son Jack. I wasn't afraid of much, but the woman frightened me. She had one of those sweet demeanors, but underneath she was a viper waiting to strike.

"Holy hell." I sucked in air. "When she finds out about Ray, watch out." I was a dead granddaughter walking. Maybe I should run for my fucking life. I'd thought to ask my uncle Jack to accompany me, but I'd decided not to in case he stopped me. But I was kicking myself now. Then again, part of me didn't trust Jack, so maybe I'd made a good choice.

"You're not responsible," Jordyn bit out. "Stop thinking that."

"Easier said than done," I mumbled. "Remember what happened when she learned Dad died?" My grandmother tore up Montana to find the person who'd murdered my father. In the process, she'd tortured several vamps before she'd strung them over the firepit and burned them alive. Not that she would do the same to me, but she might have other ways to make me sweat. What those were? I wasn't sure and didn't want to find out.

I brought the latte to my lips, my hands trembling. "Maybe I'm seeing things." I took a sip, swished the delectable drink around, then closed my eyes, sighing as I swallowed, hoping that it would ease my jitters.

"Maybe Rianne called her," Jordyn said. "You know Rianne and Granny have a special connection. Our sister seeks Granny's advice when she feels the need."

I stole another swig before setting my cup on the table. "Possible." Rianne and Harriet had always been close since Rianne was a little girl. Granny felt sorry for Rianne because she was the middle child like my grandmother had been. Granny had never gotten the attention from her parents the way her younger sister or older brother had, and she always made a point of telling us that as she doted on Rianne.

Jordyn sighed. "Did Uncle Ray say anything about Rianne before he died?"

"No. He only mentioned Noah."

"Maybe our sister wants Granny's help to knock some sense into you about falling for a vampire."

That sounded plausible and scary. Rianne knew that Harriet Aberdeen had the power, at minimum, to intimidate me. Plus, if my grandmother knew I was sleeping with a vampire, she would teleport here from Fiji if she could, maybe slap me around, or finish what Rianne and Noah had started—kill Sam. My heart sputtered.

"If Rianne did call Granny, does that mean our sister is at Intech?" she asked.

"Only one way to find out. Jordyn, call Uncle Jack. Find out if he knows his mother is here." I would like to think he didn't. He'd clearly been dumbfounded when he learned Ray had set us up as a ploy to kidnap Sam. Or maybe he was putting on a good show to throw us off. Still, the thread of trust between him and me was weak at best. "Call Steven and let him know what's happening as well. I'll check in with you later."

"Watch your back, sis," Jordyn said.

"Always." Though the way the crap kept flying at me, it might be difficult to protect myself.

After we ended the call, I dug deep for courage. I didn't want to go in with guns blazing. I had to be calm, a little devious, and act as innocent as I could, even though I was far from the latter.

9

SAM

I startled awake. "Layla." I gasped for air as my mind kick-started and panic gripped me by the balls. If the dream I'd just had was real, Layla was in trouble. How? I wasn't sure. But she was running through a forest, clearly panicked.

I sat up or tried. A fucking cobalt collar was strapped around my neck and burning the fuck out of me. I moved my arms. Same response. Ankles too.

Rage coiled in my muscles, and the bed beneath me shook. *I will tear out intestines, throats, livers, and rip limb after limb until these fuckers are nothing but a heap of human bones. Think, man.*

But I lost all thought when the stench of something very familiar penetrated my nostrils.

Then a moan of laughter echoed, followed by, "Still an arrogant fuck."

I slowly turned my neck to the left and did a double take. "What's a mutt like you doing here?"

Dane Gray, alpha to the Gray Pack and an asshole shifter, was secured to a bed like me—collar around his neck, arms and ankles chained, and a metal contraption over his white hair.

His dark eyes met my green ones. "Do you think you're the only

64

one on the most-wanted-supernatural list?"

Confusion wormed its way into my head. "Dude, don't sound so fucking proud of that." I was wanted by every fucker, human or vampire, hungry for money and power. Or if they were anything like my uncle Patrick, who'd been human when he was killed, then their goal might be to become the very creature who could drain them dry. Which had been one of the reasons my uncle tried to develop a serum to engineer humans into vampires. He'd never had the opportunity to turn before his father had died, since the only way for a human born with the recessive gene to become a full-fledged predator like me was by drinking his vampire father's blood.

Yet, if the goal was to build an army of super soldiers, then it made perfect sense to have a variety. I wasn't one to panic, but humanity was in serious trouble.

"Doesn't a shifter's bite change a human?"

"Only an alpha's," he said. "Which I suspect is the reason I'm here. They want to study how and why."

"Welcome to my world, but we can't let these fuckers use us." I pulled on the restraints. I'd gotten out of them once before, so I could do it again.

"You can't free yourself," he said. "I tried to shift while you were snoring, but I can't. I think she injected me with something to block my ability."

Ignoring his barb, I said, "I did it once before." How long ago? I had no clue. For all I knew, I'd been here for weeks or even months. The last thing I remembered was the elevator and some type of gas knocking out Carly and me. "We need to blow this place."

"You're the one with elemental powers, right?" he asked, evenly this time. "I'm dead in the water unless I can shift."

I inhaled deeply. "Who set you up?" The Aberdeens played a role in my capture, but I didn't think they had with Dane.

"Roman Brown, and I will enjoy sinking my canines into that bastard when I get out of here."

"I'll join you." At least Dane and I agreed on something. "If you'll help me take down a few Aberdeens."

His low growl shook the table he was on. "Fucking a vampire

hunter was your downfall. I blame you for this. If it weren't for your sorry ass at that nightclub, we wouldn't be in this shithole."

That night my team and I had been at the club to gain intel on Roman Brown, head of one of the largest blood cartels. We'd left with intel but not much on Roman. Instead we'd met three humans, Jordyn, Rianne, and Layla Aberdeen—vampire hunters who fucked up their job to capture me alive. They'd been hired by a former CIA agent who'd wanted revenge on me for erasing some of his memories and screwing up his life. His end goal had been to turn me over to the CIA.

Nevertheless, meeting Layla had been the highlight of that night and each one since then. I wouldn't say it was love at first sight. But man, it came fucking close.

I bared my fangs. "You should be blaming that fuckwad, Roman. He's the reason why you're here, not me."

His table shook again as he muttered swear words.

"Seems like we have a battle on the horizon," I mumbled, spotting a camera above me.

"A fucking war is more like it," he added.

I grinned like the cocky bastard I was at whoever was watching me. I would bet my vamp ass Rianne had a front-row seat. My blood boiled to torture the fuck out of her. Or better yet, compel her into oblivion like I'd done that night at the club. Her brash attitude and idle threat to blow up my sister Jo's house had gotten Rianne a room at the crazy house with the way I'd compelled her.

"We're being watched," I said, grinning like I was happy to be there.

"You two look so sweet together." Rianne's voice grated on me as it filled the glass room Dane and I were in. "Matching headgear and all."

"I swear you're a dead bitch," I snarled.

When will the fuckers learn that they can't keep me down? If they want to play Whac-A-Mole with me, bring it the fuck on.

"Tsk, tsk, tsk, Sam," Rianne said. "Don't you know I hold the upper hand?"

"The only thing you'll be holding is your neck when I squeeze the air out of you," I spat.

She let out a condescending laugh. "Aw, sticks and stones may break my bones, but you'll never see Layla again."

"Wanna bet?" I fired back, even though the bitch might be right. I could burn myself out of the wrist and ankle cuffs, but my head was a different story. "Rianne, I can't wait to skewer you over an open flame."

"I'll gladly help you," Dane said, sounding more furious than me.

Rianne's laughter slashed through me like a dagger cutting into me over and over again. "You're such a cocky motherfucker, Sam. You know that attitude of yours is why it was so easy to capture you. Besides, Layla will never let you kill me." Her confidence was larger than her ego.

My feisty huntress Layla might have a take-no-prisoners attitude. But even Layla had a breaking point. The scary realization, though, was that Rianne could be spot-on. Layla had a huge fucking heart when it came to her sisters. I didn't fault her for that in the least. I would die to protect Jo. But she had her husband, Webb, to take the lead ahead of me. Still, I wouldn't allow anyone to hurt my sister.

"Where's Layla?" I might as well try to find out as much as I could, not that the bitch would tell me unless I goaded her. With her egotistical attitude, she was chomping at the bit to tell me. I only knew that because I had the same fucking arrogance.

"Somewhere you'll never find her," she said in a pompous tone.

Fury as hot as a forest fire blistered, scorched, and charred me. My bed rattled as I strained my neck against the cobalt collar. The stench of my own flesh permeated my nostrils, and that tingle that always came before my elemental powers kicked in raced down my arms. If I could at least free my hands, then I could pull off the neck brace.

"I swear, I'll kill her for you," Dane said as though he was reading my thoughts.

"I might pay you for it," I muttered between clenched teeth.

Two beeps resounded while that prickly sensation grew stronger.

I fought against the restraints, salivating with anticipation in the hopes that Rianne was entering the room. A panel of glass cracked —a hairline fracture, but it was still progress.

Then Carly rushed over, her brown eyes filled with outrage. "Rianne, shut up." She glanced at the camera. "How many times do I have to tell you, you're not running this show."

"Maybe you could kill her for me," I said.

Facing me, Carly smiled, showing perfect white teeth, as though she'd been thinking that very thing. She placed gentle hands on my head. "Lie back, Mr. Mason." Then she adjusted whatever was on my head before she checked the metal device covering Dane's white hair.

"Where's Layla, Carly?" My nostrils flared. "Tell me now!" She'd touted that Layla was in the building. Fourth floor, if I remembered correctly. "I want to see her."

"Carly," Rianne warned. "Keep your mouth shut."

She flipped Rianne off as she went over to a computer on wheels that sat near the door. "Layla is fine, Sam." She spun the computer around so the back of the screen was angled toward Dane and me. The *rat-a-tat* of her nails banging the keys helped to somehow dull my rage until I read the sticker on the computer.

"What in the fucknation?" I asked.

Carly peeked around the computer, her eyebrows pinched.

Dane muttered, "What is it?"

"Emery Mason Laboratories?" I asked.

My uncle Patrick was probably laughing from his grave. My old man wouldn't be when he learned of the shit Carly had freely admitted to me so far.

She shrugged. "Adam Emery wanted to honor your uncle."

"Your uncle is involved?" Dane asked. "So you're as much to blame here as Roman."

I snarled at the alpha. "Fuck you. Do you want to get out of here or die here?"

War was definitely coming. All that effort five years ago to stop Patrick Mason and Edmund Rain from experimenting on humans was for nothing.

"Carly, hurry up," Rianne said.

Carly huffed. "She needs to go."

"You don't like her, do you?" I asked for nothing more than to drive a stake further between Carly and Rianne. Maybe then Carly would ditch her fucking job and loyalty to Adam Emery and work for us. Not that we would practice genetic engineering, but Dr. Vieira would welcome another scientist who would be eager to learn from him. My sister was studying genetics and hematology, and so far Dr. Vieira had taught Jo quite a bit. I had no doubt my sister would be in charge of our medical team one day.

Carly focused on the screen. "Rianne and I have different agendas."

I'd gotten that vibe the first time I woke up and found myself in this place. "What's yours? More vampires and mutts in this world? Doesn't that go against what the Aberdeen family stands for?" After all, Carly was married to an Aberdeen.

"In part, yes." She continued to pound the keys.

Suddenly, a high-pitched sound blared in my head before blinding pain throbbed like a motherfucker. It felt as though someone was crushing my skull.

Dane let out a howl that sounded as though he was dying. Hell, we both might be.

I saw fire and flames and images of a person I couldn't make out. Then the pain stopped, and another flash of darkness hit me before the light overhead brightened. Where was I? I tried to sit up when a burning sensation gripped my neck.

A cold hand touched my chest. "Easy, Mr. Mason."

"Carly?" Her voice sounded like Carly's, but I was having difficulty distinguishing her and my surroundings.

Laughter blared from somewhere above, a familiar voice etching its way into my psyche.

A click sounded, followed by another, then my thoughts short-circuited, and a feeling of consciousness took over. I blinked several times.

"Mr. Mason." Carly said my name as though she wasn't sure it was me.

Fuck, I wasn't sure I was me. *Did she just fry my brain cells?*

She stood over me and shone a penlight in one eye, then the other. "Do you know who I am?"

That grating laughter overhead snaked its way into every fiber in me.

I growled. "Seriously? You're the next person on my kill list after Rianne." Hatred clung to every word.

"Say my name, Mr. Mason," Carly ordered in a caustic tone.

"Why? I don't need to do shit."

"That's him," Rianne said.

Carly bared her teeth as she glanced at the camera. "I might strangle her."

I laughed. "Wanna team up, Carly?"

She lost that mean look that had her cute face all creased and scrunched. "I just might take you up on that."

Then she examined Dane, whose bare chest glistened with sweat. When she was done, she pocketed her penlight. "You two are coming along just fine."

Dane thrashed around on the table. "I hope you have life insurance, human, because when I'm finally free, you're my next meal."

She giggled, masking the fear coursing through her. "No, you won't." She stuck out her chin. Then her phone rang. She plucked it out of her lab coat and answered. "What is it?"

"Your guest has arrived," the lady on the other end said.

"I'll be right there." Carly pocketed her phone and said to Dane and me, "I'll be back later. For now, rest. I need both of you on point for my meeting." Her heels clicked against the tiled floor.

When the door snicked shut, I closed my eyes, taking inventory of my body, moving my feet, hands, and fingers. Whatever had just happened to me, I didn't want to hang around to find out what else Carly had in store.

"It's time to blow this joint," I said to Dane.

I gathered my fury simmering on the surface and dug deep for my elemental powers. They'd served me well earlier, and they were about to help me again.

10

LAYLA

An astringent odor coupled with the chill in the air made me shudder when I entered Intech ten minutes later. Before I'd left Starbucks, I'd eaten a sliver of the apple turnover and almost puked, thanks to nerves.

Swallowing a ball of emotions, I inched up to the security guard, my pulse sprinting, and my breathing shallow. Jordyn's description of Fred Emery didn't match the man behind the desk. The guard had a short crop of wavy blond hair, and I didn't see a scar. That should ease the tightness in my stomach, but it didn't.

A voice in my subconscious was shouting for me to turn around and leave. Run, and run fast and far, but my legs kept moving forward.

You're here to talk to Carly, nothing more. Yet, if my grandmother *were* here, then the stakes of the battle I was about to fight just escalated. How? I wasn't sure. But when Harriet Aberdeen was involved, nothing good came out of it.

I let out a soft, agitated laugh. I wasn't afraid of vampires, but I was frightened of my own kin. Another laugh escaped. I could go head-to-head with Jack, but not his mother. The sweet lady had a deadly bite.

Johnson, as his name read on his uniformed shirt, glanced up from the glass-topped desk, his brown eyes lasering in on me. "Are you lost?"

I feigned a smile as that knot in my stomach wound tighter and tighter. "Good morning, Mr. Johnson." Kill him with kindness. I was taking a play from my grandmother. "I'm Layla Aberdeen, and I'm here to see my cousin, Carly Aberdeen. I know it's early, and she may not be in yet. But I'm worried." I stabbed a thumb at the Starbucks. "She was supposed to meet me for coffee before she came into work." *Liar.*

He flipped his mechanic magazine over. "I'll check to see if she's in. Mrs. Aberdeen tends to work around the clock sometimes." He typed on a keyboard.

After I thanked the nice man, I ambled around the empty lobby to keep the blood flowing and the jitters at bay. A bank of elevators was carved into an alcove to the right of the lobby desk. Three tall fig trees covered with mini white lights were scattered around. Two benches were positioned in front of the wall of windows that overlooked the city street, and an antibacterial station stood at the entrance to the elevator area.

"Take that, Webb," I mumbled to myself. "I am aware of my surroundings." My dad had taught us girls that very thing when hunting.

"Search high, low, and everywhere around you," he'd said many times. "Never let your guard down." As hunters, we couldn't. We always had to be on high alert. And when faced with a life-and-death situation, we didn't have time to think. If we did, we died.

Maybe Webb was right. Maybe I'd been reckless when I tried to save Sam. Maybe I should've been more aware of the valet. Maybe I was too hasty in my decision to come here. I could second-guess myself all day long. But the only way to move forward was to get answers. I knew the SEALs had their rules and regulations. They did things by the book—or rather, by the vampire book. I was more than certain human Navy SEALs didn't follow some of the regulations that the Vampire Navy SEALs did. Where the supernatural was involved, rules tended to be different. But I wasn't military and didn't work for Webb. Above that, I wanted answers from my family. Whether they owed me any was a different story. But I would try like a hellion to force them to talk.

The security guard had the phone to his ear. "Yes, sir. I will." Once he lowered the phone, he said, "Ma'am, you're in luck. Carly is in the building. Head to elevator three. Someone will be down in a moment to escort you."

Again, I thanked Mr. Johnson for his help, my pulse beating like a racehorse galloping around a track. That eerie feeling in the pit of my stomach grew by leaps and bounds as I strolled over to elevator three. Suddenly, I had a craving followed by that burn stinging my throat. I slipped my hand into my coat pocket and had my fingers wrapped around the small vial of blood when the elevator dinged. *Damn it. No time to fuel my thirst.*

The rotund security guard with Treadway engraved on his gray uniformed shirt held the door open until I entered.

Smiling, I brushed past him, squeezing the vial as though it would give me a shot of courage.

Silence ticked by one floor at a time until we were exiting onto the third level. Treadway strutted out. The *swish, swish, swish* of his black pants rubbing against his legs scraped along my already frayed nerves. For the next several minutes, we traveled one hallway after another without encountering any doors, offices, or even sounds. I swore he was escorting me into the belly of the beast—or maybe he was taking me to hell.

As I trailed behind him, I hurriedly downed the blood. The initial jolt of power warmed my insides, and I sighed heavily.

Treadway looked over his shoulder. "Are you okay?"

I nodded quickly, licking my lips when he stopped at an ominous solid wood door.

I glanced over my shoulder, debating whether to run or confront my demons.

You got this girl. Go forth and conquer. A wild laugh broke free in my head. *You're not facing a gang of vampires in the dark woods on a foggy night.* Maybe not, but whoever is on the other side of that door isn't a vampire, which in my mind meant I couldn't kill them.

"You know, I think I need to use the bathroom." I held my stomach. Coupled with the shot of Sam's blood and my pulse dancing to a fast tune, I was dizzy.

"There isn't a bathroom nearby, and they're waiting for you." He grabbed the handle.

"They?" I asked.

He ignored me and opened the door.

Instantly, a whoosh of perfumed air floated out, and I stiffened. If I had any doubts that the woman I'd seen climbing out of the taxi was my grandmother, I didn't anymore. Her rosewater scent gave her away. The pungent fragrance that had embedded in my nostrils since I was five years old was a smell that always made me wrinkle my nose.

"Go," Treadway said.

It took me a second for my eyes to adjust to the muted light since the room wasn't as bright as the hallway. On my last blink, the eight theater-style chairs facing closed curtains that traveled the length of the rectangular room came into view. Whatever was behind the ugly paisley drapes jabbed a sharp blade of fear into my chest.

That fear morphed into terror when I laid eyes on three men seated and waiting for the show to begin. My attention rounded on Lester Worthington. Next to him was a man with thick wavy brown hair who I didn't recognize, and Jack Jr. I had no time to process Junior's involvement when Rianne stepped out from the shadows. She looked like a Viking ready to fight—black sweater, black leggings, and military boots with daggers secured to the belt around her waist. She glared at me, hatred swimming in her brown eyes.

My heart fell to my feet. I couldn't understand how in an instant, our sisterly relationship went to shit. *Stop trying to figure that out,* my inner voice supplied. *You have bigger problems.* The understatement of the century.

Rianne got in my face, breathing fire. "Where's Noah? What did your bloodsuckers do with him?"

Noah? I was surprised she didn't ask about Uncle Ray. Nonetheless, I cocked an eyebrow, snarling at the woman who had been everything to me. "How would I know?" I pushed her, and she flew back as though I had the strength of the Hulk. "I didn't do anything to asshole Noah."

She landed against the wall of curtains. As quickly as she fell, she was on her feet and lunging for me.

"Bring it, Rianne. I'm in no mood for your childish rage." She had a temper, but so did I. When we'd fought as kids, fists flew.

"Now, girls," a sugary voice warned.

The hairs on my neck sprang to attention. That syrupy tone had a way of scoring my skin like a serrated blade. She was the type who could destroy a person with her kindness.

I swung my head to my left, and my grandmother glided out of a dark corner. Leave it to my family to hide and only show themselves at just the right moment.

Adjusting her black silk scarf that brought out her blue eyes, Harriet Aberdeen scrutinized me. She hadn't aged a day since I'd last seen her at my father's funeral over two years ago. A foolish thought breached through my confusion. *Had she found a way to turn into a vampire? Or maybe she was a guinea pig for Intech, which was why she was here.*

She flattened her small, cold hands on my cheeks. She might be a short woman, but her attitude made her ten feet tall. "So good to see you, Layla. I thought that was you in the Starbucks. I would've gone over, but I was pressed for time." Her sugary tone scraped my nerves. "You look pale. Are you eating?"

Yeah, my favorite food these days is blood. "When I can." I inched back. I needed air, clean air, not the suffocating kind laden with roses. "What's going on?" My pulse was pounding in my ears like a stampede at the Running of the Bulls. "I came to see Carly. Is she here?" Although now that I knew where Rianne was and had confirmed my grandmother was in on the scheme, a discussion with Carly was a moot point.

Junior's features were pinched, his shoulders hunched up to his ears as he studied me like I had five heads. He dragged a hand through his red crop that was shaven on the sides. Frowning, he prodded me with his blue eyes as if he was trying to tell me to keep my mouth shut.

Shit. Something happened to Carly. That's the reason Junior is here.

He knew I wasn't one to shy away from much—except Harriet. Though I would like to think I'd grown thick enough skin that she couldn't intimidate me with a look or her narcissistic attitude.

"Harriet, it wasn't a good idea to bring Layla here," the man next to Junior said.

She lowered her hand and scrutinized me. "Adam, if you want my money, then she stays."

The man she'd addressed as Adam must be the one in charge. I held back the need to fidget under her stare.

"You're not the only one funding this project," he sniped back.

She squared her shoulders. "I don't care about your other investors. You need my money, and Layla needs to understand how good our efforts will be for mankind."

"We're not saving humanity," Junior mumbled loudly. "We're killing them."

A host of emotions caused my heart to thrash around inside my chest despite knowing my grandmother and sister were knee-deep in this demented scheme.

I swallowed thickly. "You're engineering humans into vampires."

Lester Worthington gave me a patronizing glare. "You're very astute, Layla. Please, sit. Enjoy the show."

Spine-chilling terror coiled through me like a rattlesnake was about to sink its fangs into its prey. I didn't want to see any show. I would flip the fuck out if Sam was on the other side of those curtains, and somehow, I knew he was.

Rianne rubbed her hands together. "Ooh, I can't wait to see your face." Excitement filled her brown eyes.

If I was previously unsure if Intech had kidnapped Sam, I wasn't anymore. Glaring at Harriet, my legs wobbled. "Why would you agree to add more vampires to the population? What happened to our family's mission?"

A noise vomited out of Rianne, sounding more like a high-pitched squeal than a snarl. "You're not part of the clan anymore, sis. Remember, you traded sides by sleeping with a vampire."

I gritted my teeth so hard, I think a tooth cracked.

My grandmother overlooked Rianne's comment and tried to force me to open my fingers. "Just think, dear, we can have a team of supernaturals do what we've been striving to do for centuries. We're failing, Layla. There aren't many humans out there who want to hunt, and with more predators roaming the planet, we need help. Our family has grown tired of beating a dead horse. Ray is right, and I'm glad my son called me. He doesn't want his kids hunting, and I don't want my grandkids to have to take the reins."

Ray had been far from right. All he'd wanted was money to pay off his gambling debt to the Irvings. I wondered if she knew about that. I recalled the fights my grandmother had gotten into with the patriarch of the Irving family. But I wasn't standing before her to throw that stone in her face. In fact, I needed to run out of there as fast as I could and not look back. But I couldn't if Sam was there.

"Does Jack know you're here?" I asked my grandmother.

"He doesn't," Junior answered. "My dad has no clue what's going on, and neither do I."

I found the last part of his statement suspect. After all, he was married to Carly. How didn't he know what was going on? He lived with the woman. But it wasn't my business.

"I'm not sure I do either," I mumbled. My mind was scrambling to figure out how Ray, Rianne, and Noah had gotten involved with Intech. Noah had been seen talking to Lester outside of Intech from the images Tripp's team had gotten hold of. Did that mean Lester cornered them in Montana? He must have.

"It's easy," Rianne said. "Carly started all this. She was the one who sent Lester to talk to Jack that day Sam was at the ranch. You see, when she found out we knew Sam, she jumped into action. But Noah and I got to Sam first, not knowing who Lester was or his intentions until after our plot to kill Sam failed. I'm glad it did. Now we can make the arrogant fuck suffer."

Junior was as red as a tomato. "Until recently, I had no idea about my wife's involvement. I never told her about the Aberdeen business. Color me surprised when I learned she knew about vampires all along."

Sleeping with the enemy. I refrained from laughing. In a way, I'd slept with my enemy. But at least we knew where each other stood. *Shut up, brain. Focus.*

"And how does Ray fit in?" I asked.

"Since I didn't have a chance to meet Jack, I struck a deal with Ray when he showed up at the Deer and Elk waiting for Noah and Rianne," Lester said. "Well, not until after I heard Sam wasn't dead."

"You offered Ray a ton of money," I said.

"Money always talks," Adam added. "If we're done, I would like to continue."

Adam could wait. I grabbed the side of my neck and rubbed at a kink in my muscle. "And where do you come in, Granny?"

"Ray called me immediately after he talked to Lester. He filled me in on you, what you've done, the mess at the military base, and how my son, Jack, has lost his way. So I'm here to bring my family back together and take control. Something I should've done a long time ago. Where are my sons? I understand they were with you."

"And Noah?" Rianne added.

To drop the bomb or not about Ray's death. That was the question.

Adam's nostrils flared. "I'm not going to say this again. If I have to, Harriet, I'll cut you out of the deal. Your family problems can wait."

My grandmother sneered at Adam as though she was running things around here and not him. "Layla, where's Ray and Jack?"

I shrugged. "I don't know. I stole a car and came here." Part lie. Part truth. "I wanted to talk to Carly and ask if she knew where you were." I eyed my sister. "I see that you're fine."

The temptation to run ignited my adrenaline, but again, I couldn't do that if Sam was behind curtain number one.

"I'm glad you're here to see your vamp boyfriend in action," Rianne said with too much vigor.

"You won't succeed." Though a corporation with money, resources, and a large team behind it had the means to win the war, what it didn't have was supernatural powers. At least not yet. Or maybe its team had already altered humans into vampires, and I was about to witness the progress.

"Oh, we will," Rianne said, as sure as I was trembling where I stood. "Your bloodsucker will be our shining star."

I dove for Rianne and tackled her to the floor. Before I could throw a punch, strong arms banded around me.

"Layla," Junior said in my ear. "Not now." He lifted me off her but not without one last-ditch effort from me.

My fist connected with her jaw. "What happened to you? You changed overnight."

She grinned, massaging the spot I'd hit. "I didn't. You did." She climbed to her feet.

Junior ushered me to the end seat away from my grandmother and Rianne.

"Finally," Adam said. "And Harriet, if you bring your family problems into our next meeting, I'll cut our deal in half."

Harriet's smile was lethal as she nodded at Adam.

A drumbeat thumped in my ears as I processed what I'd just learned. Carly was the mastermind? I couldn't articulate how I felt about that, but I sure as heck hadn't seen that coming.

11

LAYLA

I bounced my knee, waiting for the curtains to open. I had no idea how my heart would fare when I laid eyes on Sam. Based on Rianne's statement that Sam would be their shining star, I had a feeling, whatever Intech had planned, there was more than just Sam's DNA at stake.

Rianne was messing with a switch near the microphone. Adam was restless, Lester had a satisfied smirk on his face, Junior was biting a nail, and my grandmother was texting on her phone. I suspected she was trying to contact Ray and Jack.

"Rianne, what's wrong with the mic?" Adam asked.

"It's the switch for the curtain," Rianne replied. "It isn't working."

Adam went over to inspect things.

The waiting ate at my stomach lining, and the need to scream clawed at my throat.

Harriet leaned over Lester. "Layla, you'll come to see that what we're doing is the right thing."

I doubted that.

"You will," Lester said as if I'd spoken my comment out loud.

I threw him the finger. "Fuck off."

Junior placed a hand on my leg and mouthed, "Chill."

I narrowed my eyes at him despite knowing he was right. I had no control over whatever was about to happen. But I was in charge of my actions, and I was ready to wipe the condescending smirk off Lester's face.

"Layla, language, please," Harriet said in a brusque tone.

Funny she didn't scold Rianne earlier when she swore.

Rianne snorted. "See, sis. There's a new sheriff in town. Uncle Jack and Ray are puppets now."

If Ray weren't dead, he would fall in line and kiss my grandmother's ass. Jack, on the other hand, wasn't the type to allow anyone to jerk his chains, not even his mother. He'd always stood up to Harriet.

Adam banged on the switch, swearing. Then he found the drawstring, fiddled with it, and the curtains slowly opened. "Rianne, hit the lights."

My pulse was knocking hard against my skin. Gripping the left arm of the chair, I braced myself. When the room below came into view, I squinted at the bright lights and shiny, empty stainless-steel operating tables. A whoosh of air flew out of my mouth. I was relieved that Sam wasn't lying on one of them, and even more so that humans, or anyone, for that matter, weren't either.

But my relief screeched to a halt when I spied the emblem on the wall adjacent to the door in the distance. The same letters I'd seen in my dream, or at least the first two, *E* and *M*, were encased in a red circle. I had no idea what EML stood for, but I was pretty sure either Sam had been reaching out to me in my dream or I had a magical ability to see into the future. I'd had visions here and there since meeting Sam, which was a result from drinking his blood. At least that was the theory.

If there was a show planned, nothing was happening. "Is this a joke?" I asked. "What are we supposed to be looking at?"

Adam searched below.

All of us were on our feet and looking too.

"If Carly is the leader, where is she?" I asked Junior.

A deep, cavernous crease dented the space between his thick reddish-brown eyebrows. "I don't know."

Rianne curled her fingers around the microphone and lifted it slightly, as though she was about to conduct Beethoven's Fifth Symphony to a packed theater. "Carly, where are you? We're waiting."

Adam dragged his hand through his brown hair. "Something is wrong. Lester, find out what's going on."

Lester hurriedly obeyed the command, running out.

Junior pulled on the collar of his golf shirt. "This is so wrong."

My grandmother wagged her finger toward Junior and me. "You two need to straighten up and get on board."

Her matriarchal tone shredded the last of my nerves. "I will not listen to you. I think Fiji fried your morals and smashed your brain cells. In whose universe do you think the world would be a better place with manufactured clones of vampires?"

"Super soldiers," Adam said proudly.

An acidic taste coated my mouth. "I thought Carly ran the tech department."

"In a way, she does," Junior was saying when a loud crash resounded.

The five of us were riveted to the window.

Then Lester soared through the air. His limp body crashed into a cabinet before falling to the floor.

Adam and my grandmother were frozen as they waited for Lester to stand, but the man wasn't moving.

"I swear that bloodsucker is getting on my nerves," Rianne bit out. "Why the fuck can't Carly keep him down?"

I shouldn't be laughing, but it was comical. Rianne, of all humans, knew what Sam was capable of. She'd been a victim of his anger when she'd made a false threat to blow up his sister's house. Though maybe someone else had thrown Lester.

Junior leaned close to my ear and whispered, "I know a way out." He wrapped his fingers around my wrist and tugged when Sam marched into view from somewhere directly beneath us.

I jerked my arm from Junior and squealed, slapping a hand over my mouth as my heart stopped cold. Then it cracked in two when he glanced at us with his silver laser beam eyes, his fangs dripping with blood. But what had my stomach churning with horror was the metal device on his head. Frankenstein's monster came to mind until Sam zeroed in on me. Confusion replaced the savageness on his handsome face.

A sharp pang punctured my heart. *He must think I'm with them.* That I conspired with Rianne and betrayed him.

I pressed a fist to my heart to urge the darn thing to beat or race or do anything but cut off my blood supply. "I'm not with them." My head moved back and forth in quick successions like I had a nervous tic. "I'm not." With his sharp hearing, he had to have heard me. *Please hear me.*

A large wolf trotted out, severing my attention away from Sam. The white-haired beast sidled up to Sam and shot his gaze upward, his red eyes glinting.

"They're using shifters too," Junior said.

Suddenly, the memory of that snowy morning when we'd fought Roman, Vera—a shifter—and her alpha in the form of a white-haired wolf reared its ugly head like a predator caught off guard.

But the flashback vanished when two military-looking men entered in stealth mode, guns trained on Sam and the wolf whose name escaped me.

I banged on the window. "Sam, behind you!" I screamed holy hell. The high-pitched sound rattled my eardrums and cracked the window.

I pivoted on my heel, ready to save the man I loved, when horror careened through me. Once again, my body went rigid. *No, no, no. Not again.*

Harriet, Adam, Rianne, and Junior had keeled over.

The sound of glass breaking jolted me out of my stupor. I was about to check Junior's pulse when he moaned, holding his left ear, which was oozing blood.

While the sounds of fighting echoed toward me, I checked the others. Adam, my grandmother, and Rianne had blood trickling out of their ears too. Just like my uncle Ray had before he died.

Junior held his head. "Carly. I need to help her." He tried to stand but couldn't. "What happened?"

I helped him up. "I'll tell you later." I would—if I could make sense of why my scream caused them to conk out.

Once he was on his feet, he wobbled as he wiped the blood from his ear. "What the fuck?" Then he glanced at the other three on the floor. "Did your scream do this?"

I shrugged. "I think so. Don't ask. I don't even understand it."

"I feel like I have vertigo." He swayed on the way to the door.

I rushed over to Harriet and Rianne when an animalistic roar rented the air. I peeked below. The lab was bathed in chaos as Sam sunk his fangs into a guard before throwing him across the room. The wolf leapt at the other guard, his growl sending shivers through me.

Then Sam launched fireballs.

I didn't have time to watch the show. "Help me," I said to Junior, who was holding onto the doorjamb.

"No. Carly is in trouble."

"It's Granny," I said. "And my sister. You wouldn't leave your siblings or your parents for dead." No matter how much I disagreed with their decisions and their involvement, I didn't want them dead.

He cocked an eyebrow. "Noah, I might leave. But that's beside the point."

My grandmother whined, her eyelids opening. "Layla, what's happening?"

"See," Junior said. "She's fine. Let's move our asses. Otherwise, you'll be her prisoner. Harriet's plan is to take you back to Montana and lock you up until she can persuade you away from the Masons. If I don't conform to her plan, she'll do the same to me."

She'd said she wanted to bring the family together and take control. What better way than to lock us up? *No, thank you.* Ice flowed through my veins. If she found out I was pregnant, she would... If she didn't have a stake in Intech's plan, she would kill my baby. But the game had changed. My unborn baby was a Mason who would be powerful like Sam. Therefore, she might salivate at the notion she could gain power from my child. *Screw that.*

My grandmother reached out. "Help me, Layla."

"Move, cousin," Junior shouted on his dash out of the room.

Without a word, I bolted out, kicked my legs into gear, and pounded my feet into the carpeted floor.

Junior was running, appearing as though the vertigo he complained of moments ago wasn't bothering him. Then he made a sharp left and shoulder checked a door. "This way. Hurry!"

Once in the stairwell, he stopped for a second, shook his head, then took the stairs two at a time.

"Where are we going?" I asked.

"The lab," he said.

"It's on fire." I wanted to believe I'd learned my lesson when I tried to save Sam from the helicopter, and from what I'd seen, Sam was handling himself just fine.

"I need to save Carly," he said.

It was admirable he wanted to help the woman he was in love with. I would do the same. But did he truly know who she was?

"I can't go with you. We need to get out of this building." I had to show Sam and Webb and the others I wouldn't throw myself into danger. Coming here to talk was one thing. Running into a fire with no way out was suicide. Sam had lived through an explosion when the house I'd been renting in Massachusetts blew sky-high from C-4, so he would make it out of here alive. I had to believe that.

Junior stopped short and glared up at me with fear and desperation in his blue eyes. "Please, Layla. Carly's life is in danger. Mason or the shifter will kill her. You can distract Mason while I tackle the shifter."

A laugh bubbled free. "No offense, cousin, but you don't stand a chance with that beast." The wolf was by far no animal a human wanted to mess with.

"Then help me. Please!" His voice cracked.

My hands were tied. I had no clue how to get out of there, but Junior did. I needed him as much as he needed me.

I grunted in frustration, and when I did, a vision of Rianne driving a dagger into my stomach came out of nowhere, and my chest tightened.

"What is it?" Junior asked.

I held my throat and swallowed. "Nothing." He wouldn't understand, and we were pressed for time anyway. I climbed down the steps toward him, trying to clear my head.

At that moment, I believed without question that Abbey's premonition of Rianne killing me would come true. Webb and Jo's adoptive daughter had the ability to see into the future, and she didn't know how or when I would suffer at the hands of my sister, but I was beginning to.

I shook off the weirdness of why I had the vision and waggled my finger at Junior. "When we get down there, you have two minutes. Then I'll find my own way out."

"Thank you," he said.

Once we reached the bottom floor, and he threw open the door to the lab, I stopped short.

Sam was walking through a plume of smoke, carrying Carly. Her arms dangled and her head flopped backward, but I didn't see any blood on her. But déjà vu whacked me hard. Sam had strutted out of the fire and wreckage, carrying Rianne's body from the rubble of my rental house.

Was this the way my future was heading? Explosions, fire, running, fighting, war? I didn't want any of that for my child.

"If you've hurt my wife," Junior said, "I'll slit your throat."

Sam snarled, showing bloody fangs. "I wouldn't hurt her. I need her."

"Then why is she out cold?" Junior asked.

"Talk to Lester Worthington." Sam glared daggers at Junior. "Let me guess. You're Jack Jr."

"I'm also your savior," Junior said, sounding like his father with that deep, patronizing tone.

"You're an asshole like your old man," Sam muttered as he deposited Carly in Junior's arms. Then he set his sights on me.

Holy hell. Millions of butterflies flapped their wings inside my stomach. My heart was ready to leap into Sam's large hands. I was on the brink of bursting into tears—happy ones. It didn't matter that a fire burned behind Sam. It didn't matter that my own family wanted to lock me up and throw away the key. It didn't matter that my life was in a never-ending cyclone of death and war. All that mattered was Sam Mason.

My mouth went dry, my heart hammering as he stalked toward me with a sense of purpose, his silver eyes probing me, bringing a welcomed fresh wave of fluttering inside my stomach. He grinned, showing dimples that only made those butterflies swarm into a frenzy. He whisked a large hand through his unbound black shoulder-length hair—or tried to, but his fingers caught on that contraption he wore. He ripped it off and flung it to the side.

I wanted to run to him but was afraid if I did, I would fall flat on my face since my legs were trembling.

The closer he got, the more my pulse soared. Breathing seemed like a monumental task as I clutched my chest, ready to jump into his arms, kiss him until I couldn't breathe, feel him inside me, and so much more.

He gave me that snarky grin I so loved, desire and intent rippling over his handsome face. When we were toe to toe, I pressed my hands on his soot-covered bare chest and moaned.

We stared at each other for a minute or maybe ten before he nuzzled his nose into my neck, his fangs grazing my skin.

Goose bumps popped to attention as I grasped the waist of his cargo pants.

"Fuck, if you're not a sight for sore eyes," he whispered in my ear. "I want to be inside you so fucking badly."

I giggled as my lady parts awakened after a long winter's nap. "We're in the middle of battle."

He eased away. "How's my baby mama?" He placed his hand on my stomach, showing his dimples that softened his hard exterior.

"I told you never to call me that, vampire," I teased.

"I don't want to know what he means by that. But follow me." Junior shook his head as he carried Carly out.

Whether or not Junior connected the dots, I didn't give a fuck. All that mattered was Sam and our child.

12

SAM

I couldn't wait to get Layla alone, naked, and screaming my name over and over again. She was the reason I'd managed to break out of the restraints. It had been comical that each time Carly knocked me out, I woke up stronger, and I credited that strength to the woman running beside me. The woman who glowed like the sun on a hot summer day. The beautiful goddess carrying our baby. The more I'd thought of my unborn child, Layla, and what my future would be like with them in it, the less anything could keep me down.

After I'd torn off my restraints, I'd freed Dane, and he instantly shifted.

I grasped Layla's hand and wasn't letting go until we were breathing outside air and fifty miles away from wherever the fuck we were.

Ahead, Junior struggled to hold on to his wife as he bounded along a hallway that was a mile fucking long.

Layla was breathing heavily as her pulse beat rapidly.

"Baby doll, are you okay?" She appeared to be in great shape— no cuts or bruises or blood anywhere on her that I could tell.

She snorted. "I should ask you the same. What was that thing on your head? Were they doing brain surgery?" She took a breath.

"And was that Vera's alpha? Where is he?" Her pulse was extremely high.

"Dane should've gone out the other door, and I'll explain later." If I could. I didn't know what Carly had been doing to my head or Dane's. Fuck if I wanted to know. My uncle Patrick had extracted tons of blood and DNA from Jo and me, but he'd never messed with our brains. I felt normal. I had my powers, and my mind was working fine.

"How did you get out of that glass room?" Junior tossed over his shoulder.

"How do you think, moron?" I fired back. "I *am* one of the strongest vampires." Although it hadn't been as easy as the first time. The drugs had hindered my abilities, and it had taken several misfires before my elemental powers finally ignited. "The question for you is why didn't anyone see Dane and me on camera?" Rianne certainly had before I'd busted out. I'd been prepared for the onslaught of guards or someone gassing me like they had in the elevator.

"Carly turned off the camera after she left you and the shifter in that glass room," Junior said. "She and Rianne were butting heads."

Layla sneered at the mention of her sister's name.

Interesting reaction.

I grinned. Perhaps there was hope for Carly, or I could sway her to join my team. Or just maybe she intentionally wanted Dane and me to escape. Come to think of it, my wrist restraints hadn't been all that secure—or at least I didn't think so.

"Baby doll, I'm stoked you're here, but where are the others?"

My old man, Webb, Tripp, and Jo should've busted in by now. Not that I wasn't excited to see my feisty huntress. At first, when I'd laid eyes on her, I'd thought she betrayed me. For a whisk of a half a second, I'd died a thousand deaths until I heard her siren voice filter into my ears, pleading and assuring me she wasn't a traitor.

Junior slowed to a walk, then his knees buckled. Carly tumbled out of his arms and hit her head on the floor. Junior collapsed alongside her with blood trickling out of his ear.

"What in the hell?" I whipped my perplexed gaze at Layla.

She shrugged as she dropped to her knees beside her cousin. "Junior." She lightly slapped his face, then felt his pulse. "He's alive." She released a long-suffering sigh.

Carly stirred before sitting up and mashing the heel of her palm against her temple. Her head had to be pounding after Lester threw her into a wall. Then there was the fall just a second later. I wasn't a doctor, but she probably had a concussion.

Disoriented, she glanced around. "What happened? Where am I?" When she pinned me with a hard look, she stumbled to her feet. "You?" She closed the distance between us on wobbly legs. "You need to return to the lab." She attempted to push me.

I laughed like a maniac. "Fuck if I will." My fangs clicked into place. I kind of liked Carly. I believed she was a lost soul, trying to understand a world she didn't belong in. I also felt sorry for her. It seemed like research was her first love, and she was struggling with taking orders from Adam Emery. Regardless of how I felt about her, she was not about to use me for whatever she had planned. "I am not your puppet or lab specimen. The next time you try to stick a needle in me, or one of your idiot guards shoots at me, Aberdeen or not, I'll fry your heart with my bare hands." That was a promise I would etch in blood.

She gave me a casual shrug. "No matter. I'm pretty certain I have what I need to start testing."

"You won't be testing squat. You're coming with me. It's your turn to find out what we do to humans who fuck with us." Steam practically blew out of my nose.

She squared her small shoulders, giving off a bravado she couldn't handle. Underneath her fake façade was a frightened girl. She seemed like she was ready to say something to me when Junior stirred.

Layla helped him to his feet.

Carly blinked. "Jack." With shaky fingers, she wiped the blood from his ear. "Why is he bleeding? What did you do to him?" she asked me.

"I didn't do shit. We're wasting time." Before long, police and firemen would be descending on the place. "Which way is out?" I asked harshly. I was growing tired, and frankly, I was in dire need of sating my bloodlust. Grabbing Layla's hand, I stuck Junior with a glare. "Lead the way."

Carly fastened her hands on her hips. "I'm not leaving."

I had to applaud her for standing her ground. She had to be five feet, if that, but man, she acted like she was six feet tall and could take me on. "Oh, the fuck you are, even if I have to carry you out."

Junior slid between Carly and me, though he wasn't very stable. "Touch my wife, and I'll gut you."

I shoved him out of the way, snagged Carly, and threw her over my shoulder. I had no idea where the exit was, but I stalked ahead. I didn't need Junior. "Come on, Layla."

The sooner we got out of there, the better for everyone, because I was a second away from unleashing my wrath on the fucking place.

Carly screeched. "Put me down." She punched my back with her small fists and kicked her legs. "I have to finish my work."

"Not on my watch," I said, checking over my shoulder that Layla was on my heels.

Layla took hold of her cousin's hand. "You'll be better off with us."

Junior grunted through a sigh and acquiesced. "There's a loading dock around the corner." He skirted past me with Layla at his side while Carly continued to beat me.

The second we turned the corner, an explosion blew the loading dock door in. The impact threw the four of us backward. Luckily, the blast wasn't fatal. Still, Carly fell from me. The second she was out of my hold, she climbed to her feet and took off.

Junior groaned, seemingly in one piece, hopped over Layla, and chased his wife.

I crawled over to where Layla was holding her head, appearing dazed and confused. I checked her body to be sure she wasn't bleeding. "Talk to me. Are you hurt? Anything broken?"

She blinked several times as she sat up.

"Baby doll, say something." Terror wedged between my shoulder blades as I wiped the drywall dust from her pretty face.

She winced. "I love you, Sam Mason. I'm hopelessly in love with your vampire ass."

Those three little words packed a punch that made me dizzy and high. "I'm not sure I heard you correctly." Of course I had. I had to hear her say it again despite the fact we didn't have time to get all warm and cozy.

Her smile was blinding, and my soul did a happy dance. She stuck her finger in her chest. "I love"—she pushed her finger into my dimple—"you. You make me crazy, mad at times, happy, horny, and sometimes I don't even know what, but I would die without your stubborn, arrogant, bossy, sexy ass in my life. We fit perfectly together."

I grinned like a kid on Christmas morning. "Have I told you lately I love your huntress ass?"

She giggled and blanched at the same time. "Can we get out of here? I want a shower, a bed, you naked, and a night of blissful sex."

I was ready to kiss the fuck out of her when my father's voice peppered the air.

Layla and I jerked our attention at the gaping hole just as my father climbed through, gun at the ready.

I rose, then helped Layla to her feet. "Can you walk?"

She rolled those ball-squeezing electric-blue eyes. "Does a cow moo?"

Whether she could or not, I lifted her into my arms just the same.

"I said I could walk, vampire." Her protest was weak at best.

"Too bad. I need to feel you against me." She was the only one who could temper my rage and the urge to blow this building all to hell.

Once we were through the cavernous hole, Webb stood on the other side and jerked his head at the SUV idling in the loading dock. "We need to move."

Daylight flowed down the incline of the driveway, and a hint of the car's exhaust hung in the air.

I was curious as to how my father had known where we were in the building until I remembered the tracking device in my lower right back. I'd hated when my old man had the microchips embedded into Jo and me after we turned into vampires. He'd been worried about finding us if we'd ever gotten kidnapped. A lot of good that had done. Whenever Edmund had kidnapped Jo or me, he'd known to scramble the signal since Edmund had been a vampire and had a chip in him as well. But Intech didn't know about my chip, or at least I didn't think so.

My father kept his gun aimed at the blown door as he backed toward us slowly. "Your chip didn't have a signal until about thirty minutes ago," he said, reading my mind. "I suspect wherever they were keeping you was blocking the signal."

Layla squirmed in my arms. "What about Carly and Junior?"

I held her tighter to me. "Too risky." I desperately wanted to snatch Carly to pump her for information, particularly about what she'd been doing to my head. I also wanted to gather every last fucker involved and put them in a dark cell with a hoard of rats, never to see the light of day again. Rianne came to mind first.

Layla shuddered. "I guess you're right." She sounded highly dejected. "Junior doesn't want any part of this fight."

"Too bad. He's an Aberdeen. The shit comes with the territory." I set her on her feet outside the SUV. "It's odd you're worried about Carly and Junior. Not Rianne?"

Her bottom lip jutted out. "I'm done with my sister. There's no saving her, Sam."

I think my love for Layla grew twenty times stronger. It had to be difficult for her to say that. Yet, deep down I knew that if she had the opportunity again, she would try to knock some sense into Rianne.

Webb had gone go through many emotions when he learned his sister, Kate, had been a traitor who'd sided with our enemy. It had been harrowing to watch but equally as agonizing to feel as an empath. It had taken Webb a long time to come to terms that he couldn't save Kate, and he tried many times. And when she took her last breath at Jo's hand, Webb tried to revive her. He'd wanted nothing to do with Kate, but he didn't want her to die either.

Sadly, my gut told me Rianne and I would face off eventually, especially if Abbey's vision about Rianne ending Layla came true.

Layla scraped a soft hand along my scruffy jaw, jarring me out of my reverie. "Did you hear me?"

I blinked, then opened the back door. "Sorry."

"I believe Junior can be swayed if we can convince Carly to join us," she said.

I kissed her on the forehead. "I agree, but now is not the time." I swung out my arm, gesturing for her to get into the SUV.

Leaning forward, she eyed the blown door as if she was ready to run.

I stepped into her line of sight. "We'll discuss Carly and your cousin later. I promise."

She flashed her big blue eyes at me and climbed into the car.

Once I was seated beside her, I asked, "Are you sure you're not hurt?" I didn't see any cuts or blood, but she could have broken bones. Even worse, our unborn baby could be hurt. My pulse was machine-gun fast, praying her pregnancy hadn't been compromised.

She wrapped the seat belt over her before it clicked into place. "I'm fine, Sam."

I loved her badass attitude, but she was talking to me, an empath. "Liar."

"Just bruised." She propped her head against the seat, her chest heaving with a sigh.

Webb jumped behind the wheel, and my dad climbed into the passenger seat.

"It happened again," Layla said. "More than ever, I'm sure I killed Ray."

Webb and my father exchanged a worried look. As for me, while I was dumbstruck, I threw mental high fives in the air. Ray Aberdeen had been a schmuck of epic proportions.

My dad peered around the seat with an unsettling look in his green eyes. "Explain."

Layla shivered. "When I saw the guards about to shoot Sam, I screamed. Then I turned around, and Junior and the others had collapsed with blood coming out of their ears, just like Ray. I'm responsible for my uncle's death. I can feel something changing inside me, and I'm not talking about the baby. It's a weird feeling I can't articulate." She gulped in a large amount of air as her color turned pasty.

13

———————

SAM

A dense silence filled the inside of the car for a beat as I processed Layla's statement. "Are you saying your scream kills people?" I'd never heard of a human doing such a thing. "You did sound like a banshee in there." I'd also remembered her doing the same on the tarmac when the helicopter flew in.

She had some abilities from drinking my blood, but those were weak at best. As far as I knew, I didn't have any shrieks that caused a person to die. However, that would be pretty fucking cool.

"We don't know that Ray's death was a direct result of your scream," Dad said. "It seemed to me his heart gave out."

Layla righted her head. "Maybe so. But my scream affects people. Don't they say something like more than three occurrences is a pattern?"

"Does it work on vamps?" I asked, curious now that my little huntress had a unique ability to protect herself. Then I realized what I'd asked. I hadn't passed out from her scream.

Webb threw the SUV in gear.

"Do you want to see if it does?" she teased.

"No!" Webb and Dad said at the same time.

She snickered.

"We aren't affected," Dad was quick to add. "But your eardrums might be damaged for a bit."

She closed her eyes briefly and blew out a breath, turning whiter.

Maybe she needed blood. I bit into my wrist. "Drink."

Without hesitation, she sucked, but then quickly drew back, scrunching her nose. "That tastes nasty."

Oh, fuck! "Spit it out. Now!" I was an idiot. Carly had pumped so much shit into me that it would likely have a severe effect on her.

Dad tossed a water bottle to Layla, and she downed half of it.

I slapped a hand on my chest. "I'm sorry. I wasn't thinking." My heart cartwheeled like a gymnast in a floor routine.

She wiped her mouth with the back of her hand. "I didn't take that much."

Thank fuck! I couldn't live with myself if I was responsible for hurting Layla or our kid. I snaked my hand over to hers, then interlocked our fingers. A bolt of electricity crackled along my arm, rivaling the supernatural charge Jo and I experienced when we joined hands. Odd. Layla shouldn't have that much elemental energy. Unless the baby was giving her powers. Doc believed we were having a baby who would be born with fangs—a true vampire who wouldn't have to wait until his teenage years to turn. Or maybe we were having a human child who would possess magical powers like Abbey.

Webb pressed on the gas, and the car moved an inch before he slammed on the brakes.

Layla and I leaned into each other and peered through the windshield.

The short, plump woman who had been in the room over the lab strolled alongside Adam Emery.

I let go of my beautiful goddess and grabbed the door handle, ready to end them once and for all.

"Don't, son. I'll take care of this," Dad said.

"Is that Harriet Aberdeen?" Webb asked.

Layla was frozen, fear leaking from her pores. "You know my grandmother?"

I cocked an eyebrow. "Is your whole family scheming to…?" I didn't know what the fuck the Aberdeens were up to. In one instant, Noah and Rianne had me strung by my ankles over a firepit, intent on seeing my ashes blow in the wind. In another, they were selling me off to yahoos who wanted my DNA, which had me scratching my head since the Aberdeens staked, burned, and murdered my kind. "I don't understand the Aberdeen motive anymore."

"Join the club," Webb said.

Layla shuddered. "My grandmother is one of Intech's investors funding Adam's project." She gnawed her bottom lip as her nerves clogged the air. "Her plan is to have a team of supernaturals she can control."

My dad laughed. "When will people learn they can't genetically restructure a human into one of us? My brother tried it and failed, except for Ben and one other."

I believed Alia Costner's son had come through Patrick's experiment as a full-fledged vamp because he was born with the vampire gene, thanks in part to his mother. He hadn't been able to turn because his father was human. Ben, on the other hand, was an exception or an anomaly. He had no supernatural DNA running in his family. Doc was constantly trying to figure out why Ben became half human and half vampire.

"It's not just us, Pops. They had Dane Gray."

Webb's knuckles blanched around the steering wheel. "Dane, alpha to the Gray Pack?"

"Yep," I replied. "Hopefully, he got out in time before the lab burned to the ground."

"Motherfucker," Dad muttered as he got out of the car and met Harriet and Emery at the bay door not far in front of the SUV.

Layla rolled down the window about an inch to hear the convo.

With his backside to us, my father asked, "Harriet, what brings you back to the States? I thought you were living on some island in the South Pacific." Dad's voice echoed.

"Family issues," she said with a fake smile.

Layla was behind Webb's seat, but in order to see Harriet, she had to lean in toward me. "She wants to lock me up and force me to see that what she's doing benefits humanity."

My gut twisted into a knot the size of the planet. "And she'll kill our kid."

Layla choked. "I'm not sure she would." She kept her voice low. But as loud as my dad and Harriet were talking, they wouldn't be able to hear what we were saying.

Layla bit her thumbnail as she watched her grandmother exchange words with my dad. "If or when she finds out I'm pregnant with a Mason, she might want to control our child. Her other goal is to run the Aberdeen family. She's home to take the reins."

I shoved my hand through my hair. "She isn't coming near our kid." A conversation between Doc and me blared like a sign on Hollywood Boulevard. He'd warned me about Layla's grandmother. He hadn't gone into detail, except he was confident that the Aberdeens would never let our child enter the world. "She doesn't know you're pregnant?" Not much scared me, but that boulder in the pit of my stomach was ready to explode.

Layla flashed her big blue eyes as terror sprung off her and strangled me. "No, but Jack does. He overheard Jo and me talking." She swallowed. "And don't forget you kind of dropped the news in front of Junior."

"Motherfucker," I mumbled.

She flinched. "It doesn't matter, Sam. They'll know soon enough when my belly starts growing."

"Not if they don't see you." I ground my back teeth together.

Her nostrils flared. "You are not hiding me away. If you even try to, I'll cut off your balls."

I snorted. "I would like to see you try."

Webb sighed through a grunt. "Children, this isn't the time."

Layla pursed her plump lips together, looking sexy as anger soaked her to her core.

To cool my temper, I had to change the subject. Otherwise, my elemental powers would destroy the vehicle and everyone in and around it. "By the way, where is my sister?"

"Jo and Tripp are on a quick assignment," Webb responded.

"Does that assignment have anything to do with capturing Noah?" Layla asked.

Webb eyed her through the rearview mirror. "Never let anyone tell you you're not perceptive."

"Webb. I want to apologize for taking off against your wishes. I know I put you and Steven in a bad spot, but if I hadn't come, then I wouldn't have known about my grandmother. I also needed to confront my family. Please understand that." She raked her teeth over her bottom lip.

"Thank you," he said. "Did you find out anything else?"

"Carly is the mastermind in all this." She leaned her elbow on the armrest between us.

My old man was still exchanging words with Harriet while Emery listened to them. Harriet and my father seemed to be old friends catching up. But I knew better. My dad was probably waiting for the right moment to touch Harriet so he could read her mind.

"Not only Carly, but the fucker standing beside Harriet," I said. "According to Carly, Adam Emery is an old college buddy of my uncle Patrick."

Webb swiveled his neck toward me, his blue eyes morphing to black. "And you're about to tell me Emery has Patrick's research?"

I nodded once. "Yep. Patrick sent his data to Adam as a backup."

Webb emitted a low growl. "But we picked apart his computer, emails, and passwords. There was nothing to indicate he sent his files to anyone."

I couldn't answer him on that. "I don't know what's true, but if Carly is right, then she has what she needs from his research and whatever the fuck she did to Dane and me to start testing, which means humans will begin to disappear."

"Get out of my way, Steven," Harriet practically shouted. "I want my granddaughter."

Dad blocked her. "Which one?"

She waved her hand in the air like some magician in a magic act. "Don't play coy with me, Steven. I will have both Jordyn and Layla in my custody if I have to rain hellfire down on you."

My father chuckled, but it was more deadly than funny. Bending his head so he was level with Harriet's short stature, he leaned in. "May I remind you who you're dealing with?"

"Pfft," Harriet returned. "You don't harm humans."

My father straightened. "Who said you were human?" Acid burned each word. "The way I see it, you're the monster, and I'm defending myself and my family."

She glued her hands to her wide hips. "Layla isn't *your* family."

"She's under my protection," my father replied in a poisonous tone. "Until you and your clan understand the importance of that word and what it means to protect your own instead of attempting to murder them, you'll have no access to Layla."

Harriet laughed for a second before a bloodthirsty expression washed over her. "Steven, we both know your son and my granddaughter are shacking up." She wagged a gnarly finger at my old man. "That is a sacrilege. No kin of mine will live with a bloodsucker, or bed with one, for that matter."

"I'm so screwed," Layla muttered. "Maybe she *will* end my pregnancy if she finds out."

I rolled my eyes at my beautiful goddess. "The fuck she will."

"Sam." Horror stole any remaining color from Layla's face. "Maybe we do need to go off the grid for the next nine months. My belly will be big soon, and it will be hard to hide."

My gaze fell to her flat stomach. I couldn't wait to feel him kick, to listen to his heartbeat, or see him on an ultrasound. Or maybe it was a *her*, but I was sticking with him. I wanted a boy. Of course, I didn't have control over the sex, and I would be over the moon with a little girl. However, I would be overprotective of her, and she might hate me for that. Well, there was only one solution —I would have to train her to fight the moment she entered this world.

I lost all thought when my old man said, "If Layla agrees to go with you, I won't stop her."

Fuck me sideways. No way in hell was Layla leaving with that evil old lady. Not that Layla would. At least I hoped the fuck not.

"That isn't happening." Layla jumped out of the car.

I practically tore off the door as I flew out and rushed to stand behind Layla. "I'm right here to protect you."

Harriet closed the distance between her and my baby mama as she focused on me.

I smirked, showing Harriet my fangs.

I didn't feel any fear from Harriet as she clutched the sides of Layla's arms. "These creatures are not your friends." She smiled at her granddaughter warmly, yet cold and calculating.

"How do you know? You haven't been around since my dad died. You don't know anything about me anymore, Granny," Layla said through a sneer, pressing her back to my front.

I grasped her hips, guiding her away from the old lady.

Harriet's jaw hardened. "Think really hard about your next move, Layla. This is your only warning."

Layla laughed, albeit a crazed one, inching into her grandmother's personal space. "Or what, Granny? Do you intend to hurt me too? Or keep me prisoner until you can knock some sense into me? Well, news flash. I'm not yours to control. And in case no one has told you, I have supernatural blood running through my veins. My mom made that shocking announcement on her deathbed."

Harriet's thin lips parted. "You're lying. My sons would've told me."

Layla straightened. "Maybe if you were around more, they might have. But that's beside the point. Before you start down a path that will only lead to your demise, think really hard, Granny. You won't win."

Harriet narrowed her blue eyes. "Are you threatening me, young lady?"

"If the shoe fits," Layla volleyed back.

A cunning smile washed over Harriet's weathered face as she flicked her chin at me. "By the time we're done with him, you'll be running for your life."

I had enough. I stepped in front of Layla, shielding her with my big body. "Old lady, you'll never control me. If you so much as come near Layla again, I'll snap your neck in two."

"Son," Dad warned.

I swung my gaze to Emery. "Don't think for a second that you have the upper hand because you have my uncle's research."

A deep rumble belted out of my father. "You knew my brother?"

Sawyer had been researching Camden Industries and Intech, and he probably was still compiling data on Adam Emery. I was certain when he had a full workup on Emery, it would reveal that he'd known my uncle.

Emery nodded, confident and brave as he regarded me, then my father. The fuckwad should be pissing his pants unless he had backup hiding in the shadows.

I sniffed, and the only aroma floating around was… I wrinkled my nose. Dane's wet-dog scent flooded my nostrils before he leapt on all fours from the grassy incline on the right of the driveway, bloody saliva dripping from his canines.

Harriet and Emery stiffened.

"Layla, in the car, please." My voice was teetering on the edge of destruction.

She started for the vehicle when heavy breathing and footsteps filtered into my ears, growing louder by the second.

I glanced at my father, who tossed a look over his shoulder.

I didn't want to take my eyes off Harriet or Emery.

The car door opened before Webb said, "Layla, get behind the wheel." Like me, he had to have heard someone running hard toward us.

My father could handle Harriet and Emery, and with Dane behind them, they weren't going anywhere.

I spun on my heel to make sure Layla obeyed Webb as my heart jackhammered against my sternum. I might not leave here, but she would if it was the last thing I did before I went down. Not that I was planning on becoming a lab specimen again.

She was about to climb into the driver's seat when Rianne launched herself through the gaping hole of the loading dock door with a semiautomatic aimed at me.

"The party has begun." My heart flipped out of control as happiness ballooned inside me. Now I could murder the bitch.

14

LAYLA

I glanced in the side mirror to see what had Sam ecstatic. Rianne was sporting a grin like she'd won an Olympic gold medal. She aimed the gun at Sam, and the blood in my veins gelled. But this wasn't his fight. She was mine to do with as I pleased. I was ninety percent sure she wouldn't shoot based on everything my grandmother had said in that viewing room. If she did, though, Sam's reflexes were too fast. She wouldn't have time to pull the trigger.

Sam stiffened—his muscles were corded, his jaw tight, and his arms open and primed to unleash his elemental powers. There was no mistaking the hatred stringing him and Rianne together.

I jumped in front of him. "She's mine, vampire."

Without breaking his connection to Rianne, he shoved me behind him. "Fuck no."

I pushed him to the side. "Sam Mason, move. She won't hurt me. I promise." Part of me was confident my grandmother didn't want me dead. Not yet anyway.

"You have two minutes," Sam bit out before eyeing Webb, who had his gun trained on Rianne.

I remained as steady as I could, ambling toward my sister with my hands in the air, though I was nauseous and my adrenaline was spiking higher than a druggy snorting too much coke.

Rianne's shoulders were tight. Her brown eyes were narrowed and her lips tightly mashed together.

I fought hard to understand how two people who grew up together, loved each other, and protected one another could turn on a dime. She hadn't even attempted to reason with me or talk to me about my feelings for Sam.

I kept my hands in the air. "I'm sorry for the way things are turning out." I was more than sorry. I was heartbroken. Fighting and arguing with her wasn't accomplishing anything, and neither was reasoning. But I was a glutton for punishment. When Rianne made up her mind, she never changed it. Yet I had to believe my sister was in there somewhere—that I could get through to her.

But hatred was a hard nut to crack, and Rianne's revulsion for Sam Mason had begun that night at the vampire club when Sam bested her. Rianne lived for revenge. Poor Kim Lauder, Rianne's nemesis in high school. The pretty blonde cheerleader had slept with Rianne's boyfriend. Because of that one incident, my sister spent her last two years of high school bullying Kim any chance she had. The circumstances were now vastly different, and yet they weren't.

I studied my sister, searching for some emotion or a sign she cared. But her brown eyes were hollow and empty. "Stop this charade," I pleaded. "You're mad that I like Sam. He saved you from that bomb. If it weren't for him, you would be dead."

My grandmother said something I couldn't comprehend. I hoped I cracked through a chink in her armor, and she appreciated that a bloodsucker cared to save her granddaughter. Granny needed to know precisely who Sam, Webb, and Steven were as people— living, breathing members of society who wanted to live in peace among humans and not as creatures of the night.

Rianne shrugged as she held her arm steady, pointing her weapon at me. "He compelled me into a vegetable-like state, and have you forgotten he's a monster? It's wrong to live with him. He probably used compulsion on you to fall in love with him."

My forehead creased. While that was possible, it wasn't true. "You're upset that he bested you. Let's not forget you threatened his sister that night."

Rage popped the air around her as daggers shot from her hardened gaze. "Let's not forget you slept with him."

That revenge Rianne took out on Kim Lauder in high school had come down to betrayal and jealousy. But Rianne's animosity with Sam wasn't about either one of those things. Or was it? As teenagers, Jordyn, Rianne, and I had wondered what it would be like to date a vampire, but that was as far as our fantasies went. Every time we returned from a hunt, that fantasy became a nightmare. As handsome as some of them were, they'd been evil, pure and simple. Sam, on the other hand, had a nefarious side when going up against his foes, but he had a heart.

"Why do you care so much? Jealousy? You had fantasies of dating a vampire. But you hate yourself for that. Don't you?"

She blinked. "You don't know what you're talking about."

It wasn't the time to psychoanalyze my sister, but part of me was right. "Where's the woman who wanted to enlist in the air force to fly jets?"

"I guess I took a play out of your book. You wanted to join the police academy. Instead, you're living with bloodsuckers. So, I'm on a mission to end them, especially that asshole." She briefly glanced past me.

I couldn't see Sam, but I didn't have to. I could almost feel his need to kill wrapping around me like a heavy coat of armor.

"You're angry because you think he took me away from you. He didn't, Rianne. I'm still your sister. I love you." Sure, she wanted revenge on him for defeating her, but if I peeled back her layers, I was certain her malicious intent was steeped in jealousy. "But none of this means you need to point a gun at me."

"If I hurt you, I hurt him," she said as Sam's growl echoed in the cavernous space.

Getting through to her was pointless. I was wasting my time —*again*.

"Rianne, you'll have your opportunity," my grandmother said. "Lower the gun."

A maniacal laugh zipped around in my head. If they hadn't succeeded in keeping Sam barricaded in a lab, they sure as shit wouldn't be able to stop him from tearing off heads.

I finally lowered my arms. "Listen to Granny. Look, sis, you realize that Carly, Granny, Emery, and whoever else is part of this experiment are murderers. I'm not okay with killing innocent humans for someone's sick plan to build super soldiers. Are you?" Given that she aligned herself with Intech and Granny, the answer was clear, but I needed to hear her say it.

Revulsion and disgust flared in her gaze that once again drifted past me. "Granny was right. We need help as well as a new plan to rid the earth of the monsters that these fuckers are, and Sam is the biggest one of them all."

A low, venomous growl rumbled from Sam. "Careful, Rianne."

Rianne lifted her chin with a diabolical smirk. "Or what, bloodsucker? You won't touch me. But I promise you the next time we meet, I will be able to best you."

Sam's chuckle sounded like a Hemi engine firing to life. "How? By becoming one of Carly's test subjects?"

A gasp raked from my lungs as I tossed the question around in my head. If that was her goal, it was suicide. Clear fucking self-destruction, all because she wanted revenge. Rianne Aberdeen was not stupid. She acted without thinking many times, but those were incidents that had never involved altering her DNA or physically hurting herself. "Please tell me you're not thinking of that, Rianne. That's suicide."

She snorted. "Living with a vampire is too. The only way I can end Sam once and for all is to be like him." Desperation and animosity drenched her words. "It's a brilliant plan."

My throat closed. Madness—sheer and utter madness. My sister had a screw loose. She was the one who had to have been compelled recently. I swished saliva around to unglue my tongue from the roof of my mouth. "Who compelled you?" It was the only reason I could grasp onto that could explain her idiotic decision. "Don't answer that. I'm done. Completely over this shit with you."

Tucking her gun into the back of her black jeans, Rianne grinned as though she'd won. "Don't you want to turn, Layla? That way, you can live for eternity with your vampire lover. Don't tell me you haven't thought about that."

A scoff broke free. I was sad I wouldn't have forever with Sam and our child, but I wouldn't become a lab experiment. "Live your life the way you want and leave me alone. Also, if I were you, I would join the military like you intended. Experimenting on humans will only end in anarchy." I spun around, brushed by Sam, and marched toward my grandmother. She had her arms crossed over her jacket and was wearing a proud smile. "You would allow this asswipe"—I stuck my finger at Emery's hooked-nose face—"to experiment on your granddaughter? Did you persuade Noah too?" My uncle Jack would never allow his son to do something this imbecilic. My father wouldn't either, if he were alive.

My grandmother gave me a nonchalant look. "They're adults who can make their own choices."

I dug my nails into my palms, causing myself pain to prevent me from slapping the Aberdeen matriarch across the face. I was better than her. Than Rianne. I stormed over to the SUV, seething as my heart broke in two. Before I got in, I flipped off my grandmother and Emery.

Everyone seemed to be statues, not moving a muscle or saying anything. It looked as though the vamps and Dane were preparing to attack the humans.

Rianne bumped Sam's shoulder as she strutted past him, muttering swear words.

Sam held steady, a severe and dark expression crossing his chiseled face.

With his gun targeted at our enemies, Webb stalked to the driver's door.

Steven stood in front of the car. "Harriet, I'm glad we had this talk." His superior attitude shone through his words.

Sam finally snapped into gear and came over to my side.

"Emery, if I were you, I would watch your six. Because the next time you fuck with me, you'll find yourself hanging from a fifty-story building by your toes."

Emery gave Sam an inferior nod. "Highly unlikely."

"Gentlemen, can we get the fuck out of here?" I asked.

The only one not whipping his ego around was Webb. If I were on the opposing side, I would be more frightened of the quiet one.

Once the men were inside the car and the engine rumbled to life, I released a weak sigh. We weren't out of the woods yet and wouldn't be until Intech was in our rearview mirror. The fight of my life was only beginning.

"What about Dane?" I asked. "We can't leave him."

Webb gunned the gas, forcing our enemies to shuffle out of the way.

I rolled down the window. "Dane, come with us."

The white wolf ignored me, keeping his red eyes and sharp attention on Rianne, my grandmother, and Emery.

Sam grasped my hand. "He'll find his way home."

I twisted my upper torso to glance out the back window. "What if they drug him again?" No sooner than I asked the question, Dane darted up the driveway and took off in the opposite direction.

Webb sped like a demon heading to hell.

My head hurt with everything that had just happened.

Sam's husky timbre broke the soupy silence that had followed us for ten minutes. "Well, that was eye-opening."

"Mind-blowing is more like it," I added.

Steven's phone dinged. He read something on the screen, lowered the cell to his lap, and said, "Jo and Tripp couldn't find Noah."

"Where's my uncle Jack?" I asked.

"Not sure," Webb offered. "We left him at the hotel. Since you took his car, I would guess he rented another one and went to find Noah too."

I thought for a split second about Jack's rental that I'd stolen but then discarded any need to return it. We didn't have time, and I didn't have the energy to care what happened to it.

Surprisingly, Sam didn't say a derogatory word or threat about either Jack or Noah. Frankly, I wanted nothing to do with either of them or anyone else in the Aberdeen clan, except Jordyn. She was going to have a stroke when she learned what Rianne was about to do.

Mounds of snow blipped by along the highway as the hum of tires on the salt-laden road lulled me into a trance. I tuned out Steven's voice as he talked about their next move. The next nine months—or sooner, if I delivered early—were more important. I wasn't one to run and hide. But Sam was right. Going off the grid would keep me safe until our child was born.

15

SAM

I sat up in a bed that wasn't mine. For the last forty-eight hours, I'd been Doc's hostage in the infirmary at the naval base until he gave me the all clear that Carly hadn't fucked me up. I'd been worried about my head. Doc speculated that she might've been comparing my brain function to a human's to check for any similarities or differences. Since I wasn't exhibiting any signs of memory loss or anything to indicate my mind was fried, Doc didn't think we had anything to worry about.

The bad news—I wasn't sleeping beside Layla. She'd spent one day in the infirmary. Then Dr. Vieira discharged her. She'd hung out in my room for a bit and told me about her exam with Dr. Vieira, complained about Rianne, and poured out her emotions over her family.

Every bone and fiber in me thirsted to take away the emotional pain Rianne inflicted on her sister. The only way I knew how was to murder the bitch. But in doing so, I would only hurt Layla. But I couldn't promise her or myself that I wouldn't do something drastic when it came to Rianne. If she had any notion of taking out Layla like she had on that loading dock, I would kill Rianne without even blinking.

III

On top of that, I'd almost lost my mind after Layla explained what had happened at the airport when I'd been taken. I'd never been more grateful to my old man than I was for saving Layla and my unborn child. Carly had mentioned something about Layla getting caught in the helicopter basket. But as Carly fucked with my head, I hadn't registered the true terror of Layla dangling by a thread.

Regardless, the woman I was hopelessly in love with continued to put her own life on the line for me, which was why I didn't go apeshit on her. How could I? I would've done the same fucking thing.

It tore my heart out to see her emotionally distraught and tired as fuck. I recommended she go to my apartment where it was quiet, which would give her the freedom to kick back and relax. Plus, I wanted her close. The infirmary and my apartment were in the same building but on opposite ends, so if she needed me, I would be there in a flash, and if our enemies got any ideas about storming in, I could get to Layla quickly.

Doc strolled in with a stethoscope around his neck, pens poking out of the chest pocket on his lab coat, and a bright smile on his face.

I clutched the blanket over my lap. "I hope your smile says you're discharging me." It was approaching midnight, and Doc had been working around the clock to ensure I had no more drugs in my system. Carly had pumped enough drugs into me to feed an army of addicts who craved their next fix, which was the main reason I hadn't left the infirmary and not only because of Doc's orders. I couldn't risk Layla drinking from me, not until I knew I didn't have crap in me that would jeopardize her or our kid. Otherwise, I would be snuggled up to a naked Layla, taking away her pain, and fucking her into next week.

"You're good," Doc said, removing the IV from the back of my hand.

Hall-e-fucking-lujah. Layla, here I come. My dick jerked at the thought of pounding into my beautiful huntress.

"But before I let you leave, I need to draw blood. I have minimal reserves here, and if something happens again, I want to be prepared. Not only if you're injured, but for Layla and the baby."

I couldn't argue with him despite my desperation to be with Layla. She and the baby came before my dick or my blue fucking balls. "Is it imperative that Layla has my blood?" We needed a backup plan if I was missing in action for an extended period of time.

He switched out the IV bag for an empty one. "It's hard to say. I'm still researching our historical records. But so far, I haven't found anything to help me with Layla's pregnancy. However, if she doesn't have access to your blood, I suggest Jo's or your father's. The processed ones we drink have too many additives, and it wouldn't be good for the fetus."

I rubbed the back of my neck. "So it's not for sure our kid will come out with fangs?"

He stuck a needle in my vein. "No. Her Vel-negative blood indicates she comes from a line of witches. Therefore, that's a possibility, or it could end up being a combo."

"Like Abbey?" My niece had never been dubbed a witch. But she'd been born with magical powers. She was a special little girl, and if the prophecy was correct, she didn't need her father's blood to turn into a vampire. According to our late grandfather, Abbey would slowly lose her humanity as she aged and at sixteen would be a full-fledged vampire.

We were seeing her change right before us. At ten years old, her powers were getting stronger. Her ability to read the future was becoming sharper. She could open a door with a wave of her hand.

"Possibly. As you know, Jo is still looking into Abbey's mother's family."

Jo and Doc suspected that Rachel, Abbey's birth mom, came from a powerful coven of witches.

Dark red liquid flowed from my arm into the bag as Doc continued. "I understand Layla's scream has an effect on humans," he said. "If that's the case, I don't know any vampires with that ability."

"When I held Layla's hand the other day, a bolt of electricity connected us," I said. "It was stronger than the supernatural charge when Jo and I combined our powers. Layla shouldn't have that much elemental energy. Is it coming from the baby?"

Doc scraped a hand along the side of his face. "From my calculations and her exam yesterday, she's just about a month along. So until the fetus develops more, it's too early to tell." He released a breath. "On another note, she will probably require more and more blood as she settles into her pregnancy. With her hormones and body changing, she'll also need lots of rest. She can't be fighting or throwing herself into the fray, and we need to keep you alive and healthy for her. Therefore, as much as you want to fight, Sam, you cannot risk yourself either."

"I'm a soldier, Doc. I'm not disagreeing with you, but I might not have a choice." Particularly if our enemies decided to bring the fight to us, much like Roman had when he invaded the naval base in search of Abbey. Not only that, if my grandfather's message to my father held any truth, then I was instrumental in the coming war.

"I know. But we need to be cautious, and with her grandmother in the picture, it's even more important to keep both of you under the radar. Especially Layla."

I wasn't worried about Harriet for myself, but when it came to Layla—for sure. "You did warn me about Harriet," I mumbled. My head was still reeling about the old lady and her intentions—in particular, allowing her granddaughter, Rianne, to be a model lab rat for her sick plan. "There's something I can't quite figure out. The Aberdeens have killed vampires for centuries. Now Harriet wants to build an army of supernatural soldiers to take out people like me. If something like cobalt oxide can burn us from the inside out, why not just load us up with the shit instead of using humans to experiment on? That seems like a no-brainer to me."

"I can't speak to Harriet's decision, and you make a great point. We know that the cobalt burns us on the outside, and a blade of that same metal will singe our hearts to ash if held in long enough. However, we don't know how much cobalt oxide it would take to burn us from the inside out. I suspect a large amount, as in more than a syringe full. And like any drug, it would depend on body weight and mass." He adjusted the stethoscope around his neck. "It's probably easier to set us on fire than inject us with cobalt oxide. Still, maybe Harriet has an underlying motive other than building her own army. Maybe she wants immortality."

The crap was bubbling to the surface like a volcano ready to erupt. "If you can't beat them, join them, so to speak."

Doc straightened out the tubing from the needle to the bag. "Exactly."

I rested my head against the pillow. "By the way, the antidote I took before we left to meet Jack and Ray didn't prevent me from passing out, but it might have helped counteract the gelsemium. According to Carly, the gelsemium should've blocked my powers, and it didn't—though maybe it was because my abilities are too strong."

"I'm not surprised by the ketamine. The antidote we developed was for the endotoxin Edmund had used. Interesting about the gelsemium, though. I'll add that to my research list. Anything else you learned while there?"

I chuckled. "Other than going through whatever the fuck Carly was doing to my brain and Dane's? No."

"I'm quite surprised Intech is testing shifters," he said.

I had been more than shocked to find Dane in the bed next to mine. "You can thank Roman Brown. He was the one who snagged him." I had yet to learn how or why, but Roman would go down with the Intech morons and the Aberdeen family.

"Just to be sure, I've got a call into a friend at the local hospital in the city to see if I can use the MRI machine for a quick scan of your head." He headed for the door. "I'll return shortly to check on the blood draw. Oh, and I thought you would like to know—Ben is fine. His wound healed, thanks to the shifter's blood. Actually, it was a combo of shifter blood and Abbey's."

My eyes widened. "Abbey's? How did you figure that mixture out?"

I was sure my sister was all over learning how her adoptive daughter had magical healing powers. The more we learned about my niece, the more she was becoming the Holy Grail of the supernatural world. Which meant the bounty for her life had just increased.

"Hours and hours of testing." Doc sounded exhausted.

I admired him for his persistence. He put his heart and soul into his research and finding answers that would heal us, keep us alive, and improve our abilities. His resolve was ironclad, and he would work tirelessly for days on end until he found a solution.

I grinned. "I'm happy to hear about Ben. Where is he?" The last time I'd seen Ben was in the infirmary about five days ago, if my math was right.

"Last I knew, he's on a mission with the SEAL team. They headed out this morning for Chicago. Hang tight." Then he waltzed out.

Man, I wanted to be on that team. Webb probably sent them out to find Noah Aberdeen and maybe snatch Carly. On the way home, Webb and my father had been concerned about my uncle Patrick's data—and rightly so. His research on genetically transforming humans into monsters falling into the wrong hands was a recipe for disaster. One of Patrick's first test subjects had been Blake Turner. He'd been a bully at the high school Jo and I attended as humans. Blake had had it out for my sister, and somehow Edmund's sick plan was to change Blake into a monster to kill Jo. Edmund succeeded, but not the way my uncle Patrick had planned. Blake turned into something far worse than any supernatural creature in existence—red eyes, fangs like a saber-toothed tiger, and allergic to the sun.

But Blake hadn't lived long. Jo had been accused of killing him, stood trial for his death, and in the end the genetic experiment fucked with Blake's heart, which was why he died.

Despite that, Blake was just one of hundreds or more humans who'd lost their lives at the hands of Edmund and Patrick. Who knew what Carly would produce if she finally had what she needed to experiment?

We had to stop her at all costs.

16

LAYLA

Darkness flowed in through the window as I sat on the edge of Sam's humongous bed, naked and feeling like I'd been hit by a Mack truck both physically and emotionally. The morning sickness was beginning to take its toll on me, and the impact of the explosion had done more damage than I'd wanted to admit—resulting in soreness, mostly.

Steven and Webb apologized for blowing the door, but when the chip in Sam's hip had reengaged, they knew exactly where we were and acted as quickly as they could. Apparently, the vampire military didn't travel without their arsenal of weapons and explosives.

But none of that was important. Sleep and rest were. The problem I had was, I couldn't keep my mind quiet or my eyes closed. I'd spent last night underneath a weight of blankets, restless and sweating. I tossed and turned every hour, and during those few minutes when I dozed off, I had a recurring dream on repeat where fire rose on both sides of a long stretch of road while I was chasing someone. I'd had the same dream the night before we left to meet my uncles, and recently a similar scene had played out when I'd fallen asleep in the hotel room.

Although my anxiety had grown tenfold, thanks to Rianne and

my grandmother, I made a pact with myself. I wouldn't put any more effort into trying to change Rianne's mind about Sam or even about her idiotic decision to become Carly's number one lab specimen. On top of that, I couldn't shake Rianne's question. Did I want to turn?

When I'd first learned of vampires and started hunting, I'd never been more frightened and fascinated at the same time. How a deadly creature could walk among humans and blend in. Their physical makeup was mind-blowing—fangs, a thirst for blood, they didn't age, and they lived for eternity. I would be lying if I said I'd never thought about becoming a bloodsucker. But the more I hunted and killed and witnessed their destruction of humans, the more my answer was a *hell no*. They had no soul. But Sam did, which was enlightening and surprising. I didn't see him as a monster. Even despite his arrogance and that snarky attitude, he was kind and caring. He protected humans as did his brethren.

I recalled what Jo had said on the plane right before we'd met with my uncles. *Our mission from the day we turned has always been to use our abilities to protect humanity and to find a way for our people to flourish and coexist among humans.*

I had yet to ask Sam specifically why he and the others went out of their way to protect humanity. My theory was that since they'd been human until their teenage years, they valued that part of their life. Sure, they depended on human blood for survival, but other animals existed to support their diet.

Nevertheless, I wasn't any better than Rianne. I was in love with one of the monsters that I'd been programmed to wipe out of existence. I understood her hatred for the bloodsuckers. I wished she would accept my choice or at least not be so hell-bent on her revenge against Sam. In the end, no one would win, not even Sam. His craving to decimate my sister was unwavering, but my intuition told me he wouldn't because of me. Why couldn't we find a way to coexist together like Jo had said? Most vampires had found a way to do just that. It was families like mine who disrupted their habitat.

Yet, despite everything, I wanted to watch my child grow up, no matter what species he or she turned out to be. I wanted to be by

Sam's side for as long as I could. But it was suicide to alter my DNA. Someone like Ben, who was half human and half vamp, had gotten lucky. According to Steven, humans had suffered and died at the hands of his deceased brother, Patrick, and his enemy, Edmund, in their efforts to build a vampire army. In truth, if there was a natural way of making a genetic change, I would definitely consider shedding my humanity. Particularly if it allowed me to spend eternity with Sam and my child or children, if fate bestowed more kids on me in my future.

Twirling wet strands of hair around my fingers, I stared at the picture hanging on the wall. The sun peeked over the horizon, spraying orange and yellow streaks across the sky over the serene ocean. My guess—someone had taken the photo from Jo's house in Maine. I would give anything to be there right about now. I couldn't believe it was just last week that I stood with my toes in the sand, the sun rising and the salt air drifting around me.

I inhaled and exhaled, listening to nothing. Sam's bedroom was soundproof, with a heavy metal door that could withstand a bomb if need be. The clock on the nightstand flashed one thirty in the morning. I'd been waking up at the same ungodly hour of the morning on several occasions, for some odd reason.

I lay back on the bed. When I did, my tits bounced, and I winced. Damn breasts were heavy, rock solid, and hurt like a bitch. Dr. Vieira and I figured out, by normal human pregnancy timelines, that my due date was in November, sometime during the first week. He couldn't say for sure if I would deliver early, given that I might be having a vampire or a witch or maybe both. The other unknown was twins. They ran in Sam's family, of course. My uncle Jack and Aunt Tab had a set of twin boys as well. With everything that had happened, I was numb to the idea of twins, and even to a baby witch or a child like Abbey.

Dr. Vieira also tested my blood to make sure I didn't have any crap in it since I'd swallowed a few drops of Sam's. In doing so, he found that my pregnancy hormone, HCG, was on the rise and indicated I was close to four weeks pregnant.

I would give anything to have my mom with me. I wanted to ask her every detail about having a baby. But considering I couldn't raise her from the dead, I would consider flying Aunt Tab, Jack's wife, out here for the next nine months. Not one person in this building knew what it was like to carry a child. Aunt Tab had six children. Then something wild and crazy came to mind. Since my mom had witches somewhere in her heritage, maybe I could whip up a spell to bring her back to life. I laughed out loud. I was officially nuts.

Tears threatened as my thoughts wandered. I swore I had to find a way to clear my head. Maybe Sam could erase my memories. *Are you looney? You can't forget about the good times with your sisters and parents.* Then Sam could zap only specific ones like what had happened at Intech. That way, I wouldn't see Rianne as a monster, or even my grandmother as one. Nerves fired to life, spreading out through my extremities. I needed a distraction, and I knew just what kind.

I closed my eyes, rolling a nipple between my fingers as I settled my other hand between my legs. A quick orgasm would definitely lessen the tension. I scooted farther up on the bed so my head was on a pillow. I raised my knees, then dove into pleasing myself.

I opened my legs wider, giving in to the tingling sensation, picturing Sam's huge cock driving in and out of me when his woodsy scent of sandalwood drifted in.

"Fuck me." Husky and dark, Sam's voice glided over me like melted butter as desire to continue what I'd started feathered along my skin.

When the locks clicked into place, my heart followed suit, and my mind cleared. Sighing, I licked my lips, hiking my gaze over his gorgeous body. He looked like a god among gods with that defined pussy-clenching V. His six-pack belonged on billboards around the country. His thick muscular thighs symbolized power, and his growing erection triggered an orgasm as I rubbed myself into a frenzy. My mouth parted as I released a sigh, my pulse pounding in my ears.

"Beautiful," he said as he watched me watch him.

I brought my finger to my mouth and sucked. "Your turn."

He gave me a lopsided grin, the silver banishing the green in his eyes as he shucked the towel and flung it to the side. Then he crawled on the bed like a lion, ready to devour his prey. Hunger, raw and pure, swam in the depths of his sparkling silver eyes. "Your pussy is glistening, baby doll. Are you ready for this?" He stroked his cock once, then twice.

I whimpered. "I'm always ready for your dick, you, us. So, what are you waiting for?"

He sat on his heels, admiring my naked body "Fuck. Your tits grew overnight."

I giggled. "They hurt like a mother."

He bit his bottom lip. "I'll be gentle. I promise. But first"—he dropped his gaze to my thighs—"I'm hungry." His fangs descended.

"Feast away." The anticipation of his mouth on me or his fangs in me caused goose bumps to blanket my body.

He licked his way up my leg, groaning. Then he bit, quick and sharp, sinking his fangs into the sensitive flesh of my inner thigh. He sucked with great pulls, and the more he drew my life's essence into him, the more my belly dipped and rolled and fluttered. A hum began deep in my core, and I swore I was ready to orgasm again.

It was crazy how a bite could elicit such a strong response of sexual passion.

He peeked at me through half-lidded eyes, his silver orbs twin beams pulling me home on a foggy night. My breathing increased as I threaded my fingers through his damp black hair. I could feel the love pouring through his veins. I could feel his lust as strongly as I could feel my own. Our magical connection was beyond anything I'd ever known, and I would die before I let anyone take me away from him.

As if the music died, I tensed.

Instantly, he retracted his fangs, and any passionate connection we had vanished. "What is it, baby doll?" He was hovering over me in a flash, his gaze searching mine. Then he traced a finger between my eyebrows. "This crease doesn't look good on you. Talk to me."

This room was our sanctuary. Absolutely nothing belonged in it except the love Sam and I shared. But he would persist until I told him.

"I'm sorry. I'm a mess, Sam. I can't stop thinking about Rianne."

His eyes darkened to a deep burnished silver as he mashed his lips together. "She won't go through with it." He sounded optimistic.

I blinked several times. "She will. I saw the look in her eyes and heard the confidence in her tone. I know my sister. When she makes her mind up, there is no changing it."

He moved hair off my forehead. "Baby doll, the SEAL team will stop Carly and Intech before they try one dose of whatever Carly is brewing."

I didn't share his confidence. I cupped his scruffy jaw. "Believe it or not, one of the things I love about you is your arrogance. But not even you or the SEAL team can promise me that."

He kissed my nose. "How little faith you have in us. This isn't our first rodeo."

"You're sweet for trying to make me feel better," I said with a half smile.

His grin was blinding. "I know something that will, no doubt, take your mind off things."

I giggled. "What's that?" I asked, even though I knew what he was referring to.

He trailed light kisses down my neck and over my breasts and lingered for a second on my nipples, nibbling and licking. Then he continued traveling along my body, eliciting goose bumps and flutters along the way until he reached my belly. He pressed a hand into the mattress on one side of me while he dragged his fingertips over my flat stomach. "I can't wait for your belly to grow—to feel him kick."

I wrinkled my nose and snorted. "You want to see me fat?"

He flashed his dimples in a boyish grin. "I want to see you pregnant. Big as a fucking house because that will mean my son will be strong and powerful."

I laughed until tears surfaced. "You're weird. And what if it's a girl?"

He dipped his tongue into my belly button. "Same."

"That doesn't make any sense."

"You know what does?" His silver gaze held me prisoner. "Women are hornier when they're pregnant, which means sex every night."

I dropped into another fit of giggles. "You already shared that fun fact with me during our last round of sex, you know." He had, the night before we'd taken off to meet Jack.

"Just a friendly reminder," he teased.

I lifted my hips. "Less talk, vampire. Fuck me, hard and fast."

He chuckled. "See, I was right. You're horny."

I rolled my eyes and pushed him off me, or rather, he let me. When he was on his back, I straddled him. "It's my turn to play."

He folded his arms behind his head. "Use me. Fuck me. I'm all yours, baby doll."

I traced a slow sensuous path along his toned chest, over his six-pack, and followed the thin line of hair that ended at my playground. I settled between his legs and wrapped my fingers around his thick shaft before squeezing.

He grunted, bucking slightly.

"What do you want, Sam Mason? Tell me."

His heated silver eyes swirled with lust and love. "Take me deep, baby doll. Then I want to fuck your brains out from behind."

I was ready to orgasm at his dirty talk. On an exhale, I closed my mouth over the head of his cock, flicking my tongue over the tip, licking the precum as I pumped him once, then twice.

He watched in quiet fascination, and when I took him deep, and the head of his dick touched the back of my throat, Sam bucked and growled.

I dove into a rhythm—pumping, licking, and sucking while he fucked my mouth like a man possessed.

"Scrape your teeth over my cock, baby doll."

I did as he commanded, and he went ballistic as he clutched the sides of my head. The sounds coming out of his mouth caused a string of passionate ripples to spread out to every nerve ending in my body. I swore I could orgasm just listening to his grunts and moans.

"Harder." Pain and pleasure dripped in his raspy voice, making me whimper.

Again, I did as he ordered, and this time, he shot up. "On your knees, butt in the air, now!" The silky yet dark timbre of his voice made my nipples hard as stone.

I giggled as I stuck my ass in the air toward him.

He grasped my hips and drove into my pussy from behind.

I squeezed around his cock, and he roared like a lion who'd won the prize.

"Play with yourself, Layla." So much lust-filled pain was laden in his voice.

The headboard knocked against the wall as we fucked like wild animals in the jungle. Skin slapping skin. Lust in the air, and love in my heart.

"I need your tits in my mouth while I fuck you." He pulled out and flipped me on my back.

When he shoved his cock inside me once again, I squealed, clutching the sheets.

He suckled a nipple into his mouth, and I met him thrust for thrust as a spiraling tickle of awareness teetered on the edge.

I could fuck this man all day long. His grunts and growls, his gorgeous body, his undying love, and the way we fit together was too much—and yet, not enough.

He gave my tits equal attention before trailing kisses up to my neck. Before I could take a breath, he bit. As if the sting of his fangs into my flesh was the key to unlocking my orgasm, I moaned out my release, shouting his name as a sheet of white light flashed behind my eyes.

He drank and fucked, and on his last pull of my blood into his mouth, he threw his head back, and a guttural roar filled the room, his cock pulsating inside me.

I coasted my hands over his sweat-slicked chest, basking in the glory of how much I was in love with him.

He righted his head and zeroed in on me, his silver eyes shining like diamonds in black sand. "Marry me, baby doll."

Time stopped, and the room spun. I heard him, or I think I did.

"Come again?" I pushed out a shaky breath, and when I did, Sam grimaced.

I sat up on my elbows. "What's wrong?" Horror writhed through my stomach.

He grabbed his temples, pain etched on his face as though his head was about to explode. Then he gulped in air, and his body went limp.

17

LAYLA

I ran through the building braless, my tits bouncing like basketballs and hurting like a bitch. I'd only had time to throw on my jeans and a sweatshirt of Sam's I'd found on a chair in his room.

My heart was drilling a hole into my chest, and tears were pouring out. I had no idea where the heck I was going or what the fuck had just happened. I couldn't wake Sam. I assumed when he'd come into the room that Dr. Vieira had allowed him to leave. Maybe not. Sam played to his own tune and wasn't the type who listened well.

Breathe, girl. Stop right now and focus.

I slapped a hand on a wall in the stairwell, bent over, and gulped in stale air. I dashed away tears, trying to see my phone's screen stuck in my sweaty palm. One of the few numbers I had was Dr. Vieira's. Once I brought up his name, I tapped on it. The line rang and rang until his voice mail connected.

"Damn it!" I shouted out loud. "Answer the fucking phone." My voice blared and echoed.

Dr. Vieira had spent so much time tending to Sam and me that he was probably dead to the world. After all, it was the middle of the night.

The only people in the building who were awake were in the control room, which I think was on the second floor, or maybe the first. I had no freaking clue. *Note to self: memorize the layout of this maze when I have the chance.*

Steven was in Boston. I would guess Jo and Webb were home tucked in until morning.

I vaulted down another flight of stairs, threw open the door to level two, and ran down the hallway. My breathing was erratic. My vision blurred, and I wanted to scream for help. The thought stopped me in my tracks. If my scream was as loud as the vampires claimed it to be, then someone in the building would hear me. Or… Harley. I could call Webb's assistant. I found her number and banged on her name. *Please, please, please answer.*

"Hello." Her sleepy voice lowered my pulse slightly.

"Harley, this is Layla. I need your help. Where does Dr. Vieira live? Sam passed out. Where does Jo live?" I'd been to Jo's house, but for the life of me, I wouldn't be able to find it at this hour or in my panicked state.

She cleared her throat. "Whoa! Slow down and tell me exactly what happened."

"Sorry, there's no time. I need medical assistance in Sam's apartment. Stat." I almost choked on my own spit. I sounded like an EMT, which was comical because my mind wasn't firing on all cylinders.

"Where are you?" she asked.

"Harley, Sam's apartment. Please. He needs help."

"I'm on it." She hung up.

With somewhat of a plan, I ran back to his place. When I reached his apartment door, I grabbed the handle and pushed. Terror gripped my insides. I tried again, holding in a scream, praying I hadn't locked myself out. But, nope. Somehow I had.

Don't freak. Help is on the way. If they have a key.

I silently scolded myself for my stupidity.

I called Dr. Vieira again.

The line connected. "Layla, Harley just told me something happened to Sam."

He answered her call? I shook off my ire, tears pricking my eyes. "One minute he was fine, and the next he was out cold."

"I'm on my way," he said.

"Doc, I'm locked out. We need a key."

"Jo has one. I'll swing by her house." Then the call ended.

I pressed my hands into the wall, wishing like hell it would swallow me up and transport me to a place where there was nothing but sunshine and happiness. I slid down the smooth surface until my butt hit the floor, then I brought my knees to my chest and cried. I wasn't one to shed many tears. But why did the universe keep throwing me wicked curveballs? I felt as though I was dodging bullets left and right.

The squeak of the stairwell door ricocheted off the walls as the sound bounced toward me. I lifted my head to find Harley running my way.

I hadn't seen the pretty strawberry-blonde vampire in weeks. If my memory served me correctly, the last time I'd seen Harley was shortly after Sam and I had had our first romp in the hay on the night I conceived. Since then, I'd been in Montana, and when I returned with Sam, Harley had been out of town.

She slowed to a walk as she approached. "Layla, are you locked out?"

Sighing, I nodded. "I'm sorry to wake you."

She swept her fingers through the air, her red nails glinting in the lights shining from above. "No need. Doc is on his way. I thought you could use a friend." She wiped her hands on her blue leggings that were tucked into suede boots before she sat beside me. "Sam will be okay." She kicked out her legs and crossed one ankle over the other. "He's a tough dude."

"He has a pulse. At least he did when I sprinted out to find help." But now… I gnawed on a fingernail. He might not be dead, but after what he'd been through with Carly, I wasn't sure he would be the same.

She hooked her arm in mine then grasped my hand.

I shuddered, a queasiness taking hold of my stomach. "I'm pregnant." I didn't know if she knew. I hadn't told her. I couldn't see Webb gossiping to her about my predicament either.

Her blue eyes brightened. "My brother, Sawyer, told me. I had every intention of visiting you in the infirmary a couple of days ago, but Webb has been keeping me busy. Anyway, I'm stoked for you and Sam. You must be blown away. I mean, did you know you have the rare blood type?" Her tone indicated she was happy and curious in equal measure.

I smiled at her. It was nice to have a friend—a true friend. Not a sibling or other family member of mine or Sam's. But someone unbiased and nonjudgmental. "Blew me away. Still does."

She squeezed my hand. "I'm here for you, Layla. Anything you need, I'll help. I can only imagine how hard it is for you to deal with everything you've been going through, let alone a pregnancy by a vampire, no less."

And a marriage proposal. I wasn't ready to divulge that piece of shocking news. I'd never thought of tying the knot. I'd always seen myself as a loner despite my longing to have children.

The stairwell door creaked open.

I jumped to my feet when I saw Dr. Vieira, Jo, and Webb.

Harley stood. "He brought the cavalry."

Oh crap. Sam was naked. Heat pinched my cheeks. Jo had probably seen her brother naked as a kid, but I doubted she had seen him that way as a man. Then there was Harley. But she'd seen him in his birthday suit since she and Sam had been friends with benefits before he'd met me.

I shrugged off the insignificant thought. Sam's life was more important.

The three of them wore expressions conveying varying degrees of worry. Dr. Vieira's was the least intense over Jo and Webb, which married up with his profession. Doctors were supposed to be calm and not show an ounce of fear.

Jo unlocked the apartment door and entered before I could rush past her to cover Sam's lower torso. Webb and Doc trailed behind her.

So much for my efforts. The minute I crossed the threshold into Sam's room, my heart fell to my feet. Sam's mouth was open with spit dribbling out. "He's not dead, is he?" He hadn't been when I'd left. *Please say no.*

Harley kept her arm tethered to mine, and good thing, because my legs were trembling as hard as my hands.

Jo felt for a pulse but really didn't need to with her acute sense of hearing… unless she couldn't hear his heart beating.

Sweat dotted my forehead while Dr. Vieira waved a penlight in Sam's lifeless eyes.

"He has a pulse, but Layla, take me through what happened," Dr. Vieira said.

The breath I'd been holding rushed out of my lungs as flames scorched my cheeks.

Jo covered Sam with a blanket. "Did Sam give you any indication what was wrong before he passed out?"

I quivered, remembering the pain in his eyes. "He grabbed his head and winced, then he was out cold. It happened so fast. One minute he was fine, and the next, he was out."

Dr. Vieira returned his penlight to his lab coat pocket. "Webb, can you carry him to the infirmary? Maybe I missed something in his blood work."

Highly doubtful. Dr. Vieira was thorough and dedicated to his profession, which was what I liked about him.

My heart punched my ribs. "Do you think it was something in my blood?" My recent test results were clear, but I had to ask anyway.

Webb fished around in the dresser and pulled out a pair of gym shorts.

Doc angled his head at me. "I told you. Your results were clear."

"Then maybe it's his brain. We know Carly had messed with his head. He was wearing a metal device when I found him," I added.

"Sam told me about that," Dr. Vieira said. "I suspect Carly was taking snapshots of his brain and Dane's to compare them to a human's."

"Maybe she was doing more than that," Webb chimed in as he managed to put the shorts onto Sam.

"I'll run more tests, and we might need to take him to the local hospital tonight for that MRI," Doc said.

Once Webb had Sam over his shoulder, Jo threw a blanket on Sam. Harley and I scurried into the hall as Jo, Webb, and Dr. Vieira hurried out. I was about to go with them, but my bladder protested.

"I'm right behind you guys." I shrugged out of Harley's hold. "I need to use the bathroom first."

She curled her strawberry-blonde hair behind her ear. "I'll wait in the living room, then I'll take you to the infirmary."

"That's great, because I don't know how to get there from here."

I closed myself in the black-and-white masculine-style bathroom across from Sam's room. I relieved myself as fast as I could. I wanted to be there when Sam woke up. I was praying he would. Once I was done, I quickly washed my hands while glancing in the mirror. *Holy shit!* I looked as if I'd just come from the depths of hell. Dark circles ringed my blue eyes. My hair was a rat's nest, and my skin was chalky. I seriously could be mistaken for a dead person—and I wasn't referring to a vampire. The ones in the building had color and were handsome or pretty. I didn't fit into that category.

Maybe this was my new look for the next nine months. My mom had a pregnant friend who had severe tooth decay. Presumably, hormonal changes were the cause. What scared the crap out of me was that I wasn't having a human baby, so my unborn supernatural child would probably steal every ounce of my young life. Horror careened through me at the thought I might look ten years older after I gave birth. Although part of my current appearance was a result of wild monkey sex.

I splashed cold water on my face, then pinched my cheeks, hoping to infuse color into them. There was no doubt I needed to rest, stay healthy, stay alive, and stay sane. I couldn't do any of that on the navy base. My family knew where I was. Sam's enemies did as well. If Roman Brown could storm the naval base and take out guards, so could anyone.

Once Sam was awake, we would pack our bags and get out of

Dodge. If he didn't come out of whatever was happening to him, I would murder the arrogant vampire with my bare hands. I was not having this baby without him. No fucking way.

I pressed my fingers into my chest and inhaled, trying to relieve the terror stealing the air from my lungs.

Knuckles rapped on the door. "Layla, are you okay?" Harley asked.

I shut the water off. "Yeah. I'll be right out." I snagged the brush off the marble counter and dragged it through my hair several times. "Mm," I said to myself in the mirror. At least my hair looked better. Now for a bra and a top that fit. Maybe then I wouldn't resemble a corpse.

Pivoting on my heel, I spotted the mound of clothes near the wicker basket by the shower. In particular, my bra was poking out from beneath Sam's charred cargo pants. It was the only undergarment I had at Sam's. What little clothing I owned was at Harley's, come to think of it. Jordyn and I had crashed at Harley's while she'd been visiting her mother.

I snagged the black lacy garment, but it caught on the cargo pants. As I untangled the two articles of clothing, a piece of paper fell out of one of the pockets.

Curious and nosy, I unfolded the note. A phone number I could hardly read was scribbled on it. The last two digits were smudged as though the paper had come in contact with water. But I didn't recognize the area code. I wasn't sure if the number was important to Sam, but I stowed it in my pocket, just in case. After I slipped my bra on and redressed in Sam's sweatshirt that practically hung to my knees, I met Harley in the living room.

She was waiting by the door, texting someone.

"Good news about Sam, I hope," I said.

Her rosy cheeks whitened.

"What happened? Did Sam…" I couldn't say the word or even think the worst. All I could do was clutch my heart and pray.

18

LAYLA

I stood at the foot of Sam's bed in the infirmary, my hands trembling and my muscles tense. I'd bitten every nail on my fingers down to nothing. Two fucking weeks had passed, and Sam still hadn't woken up. Dr. Vieira had performed every test he could. He'd even taken Sam to the local city hospital for an MRI after Sam's seizure. The latter was unheard of for vampires.

The MRI scan showed an object the size of a rice grain sitting on Sam's brain stem. We speculated Carly had implanted a microchip, and our fears were confirmed when Sawyer's team found a recent study on innovative technology of a BMI—a brain-to-machine interface—that collected and analyzed data. The article named Camden Industries in partnership with Cobra Technologies as the leader in paving the way for people to complete everyday tasks with just a thought. The deeper Sawyer's team dug into the technology, the more they'd found. In an interview, Adam Emery had said that the BMI could be the next generation of weapons in a war against our enemies.

Bingo! Emery was testing the technology out on supernaturals, using them as guinea pigs in his attempt for money and definitely power. Case in point: that was precisely how Adam, my grandmother, and the other investors would lead an army of what I believed would be mismatched predators if they succeeded in altering human DNA.

But I couldn't care less about all the mumbo jumbo about the BMI. We had to focus our efforts on removing the stupid thing from Sam. Since it was sitting on his medulla, Dr. Vieira was hesitant to rush into an operation. According to him, it was too dangerous and paralleled a beheading. More than that, he wanted more information. For all we knew, the chip acted like a bomb—if Sam didn't follow orders, then they could blow up his brain. Maybe that was one way to control him.

I shivered at the thought as the urge to strangle Carly was pulsing in my fingertips. I wanted to see her suffer for what she'd done.

The heart monitor beeped, a sound that steadied my pulse and pumped up my hope. Sleep was nonexistent. I spent most nights at Sam's bedside. I barely showered, and I resembled a zombie out of *The Walking Dead*.

The only routine I had was eating like a horse and drinking blood. *Good stuff.* My belly was growing, my body was changing, and that weird tingling sensation I had in my stomach was more intense but irregular. The feeling always spread upward into my chest. It didn't hurt, and it wasn't heartburn, which were the answers to Dr. Vieira's questions when I mentioned the issue. Given that I was pregnant with a preternatural being, I believed I was developing some magical abilities, and my banshee scream was one of them. Dr. Vieira agreed.

I slid over to Sam's bedside, dropped into the chair, and entwined my fingers in Sam's. "Come on, vampire. Open those soul-stealing green eyes and say something snarky. Your kid needs you. I need you." When I kissed the back of his cold hand, a prickle snaked up from my tummy to settle in my chest, then quickly vanished.

I rested my head on the mattress, our conjoined hands tucked near my chin as I stared at the sexy bloodsucker. His black hair framed his angular, unshaven jaw. A slight smile shaped his lips, and he seemed at peace as his chest rose and fell.

I inhaled and exhaled in rhythm with him, the act hypnotizing me as my drowsiness set in.

Suddenly, I was on a road in the dead of night.

Flames danced along the edges as my bare feet slapped the warm, cracked pavement. "Stop!" I shouted at the figure ahead of me.

"No, Mom. Don't. She's not the person you think she is," a little boy said behind me.

I whirled around. But there was nothing there but an old beat-up truck.

"Layla." A woman's alarmed voice speared through my subconscious. "Layla." A hand grabbed my shoulder.

I jerked upright, searching and blinking.

My sister, Jordyn, stood beside me with unease creasing the skin surrounding her brown eyes.

I flew off the chair and threw my arms around her.

She squeezed me to her. "I've missed you too."

Sighing, I edged back and whistled. "Look at my beautiful sister."

Her brown hair was styled into a messy bun with wispy strands framing her oval-shaped face. Her navy-blue pantsuit was tailored to her curves, and her black boots with two-inch heels made her the same height as me. Jordyn was the shortest, while Rianne was an inch taller than me.

"You look fab, sis," I said. I hadn't seen her in over a week. But she seemed to have blossomed—or maybe I hadn't noticed before now.

Her red lips spread into a weak smile. "We should make an appointment to have our hair done."

I snorted. "Is that your way of saying I look like crap? Because your hair doesn't need any help."

She tucked strands of my somewhat-oily hair behind my ear. "It's time you do something for yourself before the baby arrives. Besides, Sam is in excellent hands." She stuck me with a stern scowl.

I hated to leave Sam's bedside, but I could use a few hours of pampering.

She grasped both of my arms. "If I have to kick your ass to whip you into Layla Aberdeen, I will."

I rolled my eyes. "You know I'm the better fighter."

She gave me a challenging but teasing glare. "I would bet my paycheck you wouldn't win, not considering the way you look. Sis, I know your hormones are probably off the charts and affecting your emotional well-being, but I'm here to change that. You need new clothes. Your belly is growing, and quite fast, I might add."

Feeling my stomach, I said, "I know. I've been eating like crazy. But the morning sickness isn't as bad."

She swept her hand up and down my body. "Those jeans are tight. The sweater doesn't fit you anymore." She checked the ends of my hair. "And you have split ends."

If any of what she'd said came from someone else, I would've told them to fuck off. But Jordyn always tried to keep Rianne and me in check, and I loved Jordyn for that. Just the same, I snarled more at myself. I was one hot mess, and when Sam finally came back to the living, he would probably freak if he saw me looking this way.

She plucked her phone from the pocket of the handbag draped over her shoulder, then typed out a text. "Harley is waiting for us downstairs. We've set up a spa day for us—masseuse, hairdresser, and manicurist." She raised a finger. "Before you give me lip, you're leaving this room. Afterward, I hired a chef to cook us dinner at Harley's place. If anything changes with Sam, Dr. Vieira will let you know."

I laughed through happy tears, hugging her tightly. "I love you." I didn't know what I would do without her. She and Harley were my rocks. "Any new info on Carly or our family?"

One of Jordyn's assignments was helping Sawyer. She'd been surfing the black web for any scuttle on Intech or humans disappearing. Everyone on the SEAL team was working around the clock to find Carly, Adam Emery, Rianne, my grandmother, Noah, and even Jack. He'd dropped off the face of the earth.

Conrad, the vampire scout who worked for Steven, had flown to Montana to check on Jack and Ray's families. Both Jack's ranch and

Ray's house were empty. No sign of Aunt Tab, Ray's wife, or my cousins. I suspected my grandmother had all of them at a secure location. She'd probably blown a gasket when she'd found out Ray was dead.

Webb and Steven were surprised, though, that Jack hadn't shown up at the main gate to claim his brother's body, which was on ice somewhere on the naval base. I didn't care to know where. What I wanted to know was how he died. Did my scream kill him? Or did he have a heart attack? Dr. Vieira was planning an autopsy, but it wasn't high on his priority list.

As far as the SEAL team went, they'd joined forces with Dane's brother, Ross Gray, since the Gray Pack hadn't heard from Dane since he'd been taken by Roman. But no luck finding the shifter—at least not that I knew of.

Jordyn snapped her fingers. "Did you hear me?"

I blinked rapidly. "Sorry, I spaced. You're right. I need a distraction." I went over to Sam and kissed him on the cheek, then whispered in his ear. "If you can hear me, handsome, I love you. Come back to me." I said those two lines to him each time I left. Then I held out my arms to Jordyn. "I'm all yours."

She clapped, giddy with too much excitement that I wished I shared. I was stoked to see her happy. It was also good that Jordyn had a purpose other than hunting vampires or doing my grandmother's bidding. I envied Jordyn. Maybe that was what I was missing—a job. But my skills were lacking for anything other than hunting. Then an idea sprouted—one that didn't pay, but one that I'd planned to do but never had time. I wanted to research my mom's family. That vampire, Kendra, came to mind. She could be a wealth of information. Plus, I was ready to question her, prepared to ask if she'd killed my father. Though my gut said she didn't. For the brief time I'd met her during our showdown with Jack and Ray, I got the vibe that she'd adored my father, and I believed she would seek me out when she wasn't in any danger from my family.

As we left Sam's room, Jordyn hooked her arm in mine. "I can see your wheels turning."

I kissed her on the cheek. "Thank you."

Jordyn had a way of cracking through my doom and gloom. I could always count on her to help take my mind off things, even if it was only for a few hours.

"You know I'm always here for you," she said. "And you need to stay positive."

Although she was right, it was a monumental task to be happy and free and feel like I had a wonderful life ahead when Sam was in a coma. I couldn't be a single mom. I couldn't raise a supernatural kid on my own. I did have an extended family with the Masons. I had a wonderful friend in Harley, and we'd grown close over the last two weeks. She'd been right there for me, if only to listen, which I appreciated greatly. I had the best doctor to handle any issues that would arise from having this baby. However, Dr. Vieira had asked if he could invite one of his longtime friends and colleague, an ob-gyn, to assist with my pregnancy. I didn't mind, and if Dr. Vieira trusted him, I did as well. Still, none of them could mend my broken heart.

It was hard not to feel like the world was crashing down around me. It was hard to fathom a future of sunshine and bliss. I was in love with a freaking vampire who was on the most wanted list of every sick and twisted asshole out for money and power. I had no regrets about falling head over heels for Sam. But, for fuck's sake, I needed him alive, awake, and for him to see his kid born. I needed him to be my other half, my rock, my partner in crime, and the father he was excited to be.

I had to believe he would come out of his coma, and if he did, I would shout to the world that I would marry him.

19

LAYLA

Flames danced along the darkened road as my bare feet slapped the warm, cracked pavement. *"Stop!"* I shouted at the figure ahead of me.

"No, Mom. Don't. She's not the person you think she is," the soft voice of a young boy warned.

I looked in all directions, but I didn't see anything except an old beat-up truck.

The fire died suddenly, and I was enveloped in a sea of darkness. Blinking rapidly to adjust my vision, my breathing increased. As if someone had flipped a switch, the double white lines on the road beamed a vivid orange. Bright stars glistened in the inky-black sky, twinkling like tiny diamonds. A red ring circled the radiant moon that seemed ten times larger than I'd ever seen.

"Over here," the young boy called.

I oriented my vision ahead of me.

A five-year-old boy surrounded by an iridescent glow held out his hand. "We need to go." Fear coated his small voice.

I was frozen to the heat of the pavement.

"Please," he begged. "She needs your help."

My limbs unlocked, and I jogged toward the little boy with black hair and eyes so familiar I lost my breath.

"Who needs my help?" I asked as I reached the boy.

139

"My sister," he said with a slight lisp. *"You're the only one who can help her."*

"I don't understand. Why me?"

His green eyes were high beams in the dark of night. "Because you have the power." He tugged on my fingers. "We don't have much time."

"Who are you?"

"I'm your son," he said, as if I was supposed to know that.

A gasp tore from my lungs as I shot up from the pillow, disoriented. I pushed out a heavy sigh, running my hands through my sweat-dampened hair. *Holy crap!* Was I having twins? I'd been having the same recurring dream in a way—fire, flames, dark road, a little boy, a girl needing help. But until tonight, the boy hadn't revealed who he was.

I pulled my T-shirt away from my heated skin and climbed out of bed. Maybe twins were the reason my stomach was bigger than normal for eight weeks. Dr. Vieira claimed it was bloating, hormones, and my uterus preparing for the baby's growth, which made sense. Still, twins would not surprise me. After all, they ran on both sides of the family.

The clock on the nightstand flashed 1:30 a.m. A chill skittered through me. I'd been waking up at the same time for over a month, and I would bet my life that one thirty in the morning was relevant for some reason.

I needed to clear my head, cool my skin, and feel the crisp air filling my lungs. Another two weeks had passed, and Sam was still in a coma. In total, a month had gone by since Sam had asked me to marry him. A month of long days and sleepless nights.

I had planned to do some research on my mother's ancestors, but I'd never gotten around to it. My days had been filled with working out in the base gym, mainly to expend nervous energy in the hopes it would help me sleep better. In part, the yoga and practicing my fighting skills had enabled me to fall asleep, but my problem was staying asleep. In addition, I sat with Sam for hours, reading about pregnancies, deliveries, and anything related to giving birth. When I wasn't at the gym or with Sam, I cooked for Harley and Jordyn when she wasn't in Boston. Or I baked yummy cakes and cookies, which I devoured.

My stomach growled at the thought of the chocolate cake in the kitchen. But the sugar would only keep me awake. Maybe a spin on the bike in the gym would help burn off my adrenaline. Or maybe Dr. Vieira was in the infirmary, and I could talk to him about my dream and twins.

I decided going to the gym first would be best since Dr. Vieira was probably tucked into his own bed, even though he'd been known to work through the night.

That familiar tingling wormed its way from my belly into my chest as I threw on a pair of yoga pants. I was regularly experiencing more and more of the fluttering sensations as each day passed. But I had yet to encounter any sort of magical abilities.

I rubbed my stomach and laughed. If I was having twins, that meant my belly would be fucking huge. I giggled again, but this time it was because of nerves. I'd put on weight and would continue to do so. How would Sam react? I was confident he would pounce like a sex-starved man when he laid eyes on my humongous tits. But by the time I delivered, I would be bigger than a two-story house. I puffed my cheeks. No sense in worrying about my weight. I just had to stay in shape and healthy.

I shrugged into a clean T-shirt, stepped into my suede boots, and grabbed a jacket off the chair in my military-style bedroom—twin bed, a dresser, a chair, a small closet, and a table for a nightstand, much like the rooms in the women's barracks. Harley's house was initially designed for navy recruits who had graduated from boot camp and were temporarily stationed on the base. I wasn't complaining. I had a bed and a roof over my head. I could've stayed in Sam's apartment, but I preferred the company, spending time with Harley when she wasn't working or with Jordyn, who was staying with us. She was helping Sawyer and had a temporary cubicle alongside his.

Both Harley and Jordyn had kept me abreast of the SEAL activity as much as they were allowed. The SEALs had been scouring Chicago and Montana nonstop for Carly Aberdeen and her team of fuckups, including my family, but they'd struck out. Apparently, no one was surprised that they'd seemingly disappeared. Five years ago, when the SEALs had been at war with Edmund Rain, he constantly moved his location to throw them off track. In addition, there was no sign of Dane Gray. His family and pack had been hunting from New England to Chicago, searching for him.

On top of that, Webb and Jo had set out to find the scientist who had developed the chip. Peter Landon worked for Cobra Technologies, who'd partnered with Camden Industries. After digging deeper into both companies, the tech team learned Peter was no longer with Cobra. Jordyn had found out in one of her chat rooms that there was a contract out on Peter's head. I wished upon a star that Webb and Jo found the man. I believed he might be the only one who could help Sam.

Aside from the tension hanging over us, the living situation in the three-bedroom house reminded me of when Rianne, Jordyn, and I would hang in front of the TV, drinking, laughing, and talking. But Harley wasn't Rianne, and *I* wasn't consuming alcohol. Still, the three of us chatted about everything and anything, including baby names.

Harley suggested Liam, if I had a boy—a name that meant a strong-willed warrior and fit Sam's personality perfectly. Jordyn liked Liam, but she preferred Marcus. I added both names to my list, but I wouldn't be able to decide until I saw his or her face. Plus, Sam needed to weigh in with his choices.

I tiptoed down the hall by the other two bedrooms, careful not to wake Jordyn or Harley. The floor plan was much like Jo and Webb's home—spacious kitchen, living room, and arched doorways, but with one exception. Jo's house had been remodeled and decorated to give the home a lived-in feel rather than the sterile environment of Harley's abode.

When I slipped out the front door as quietly as I could, my bodyguard, Lane, jerked to attention. His charcoal-colored uniform blended in with the blackness surrounding us. If it weren't for his dirty-blond hair or the steam from his breathing, I wouldn't have known he was standing guard.

He climbed the four stone steps, snatched my coat from my hands, and helped me into it. "Put this on. It's below zero out here." The cold didn't affect him in the least. Vampires seemed immune to the frigid winter weather.

The official day of spring had come and gone, and the snow on the ground, which wasn't unusual for the end of March in Massachusetts, was keeping the flowers from blooming.

"Are you just out for fresh air?" he asked, searching the wooded area across the road.

I pushed out a shoulder, zipping my coat to my chin. "Something like that. I would like to see Sam and work out for a bit in the gym."

He started for his camouflaged Jeep parked alongside Harley's Mini Cooper in the gravel driveway.

I inhaled the brisk air, pine and cedar wafting on the soft breeze. "Can we walk?"

"Sure. I have to call it in first." He adjusted his earpiece, then pressed a tiny receiver device on his belt.

I tuned out Lane's voice, ambling down the stone path to the gravel road. The moon's rays peeked through the dense mixture of conifers and deciduous trees. The latter showed signs of new leaf growth, which would sprout quickly once the weather turned warmer. I couldn't wait for the heat of the sun on my skin or the humid air to blanket me. The snow, cold, and ice invoked too many terrible memories as of late.

We'd fought Roman in a blizzard, we'd flown to meet my uncles in an oncoming winter storm, and it had been snowing on and off since Sam fell into a coma. Besides that, I wanted to hear the birds chirp, see the flowers bloom, smell their fragrant buds, and maybe walk along the beach in Maine. I couldn't stop thinking about a hideaway for Sam and me. The only place I had in mind was Jo and Webb's home in Maine. I loved it there—sun, beach, ocean, the salt air, the soothing sounds of crashing waves, and digging my toes into the sand as Sam and I walked along the ocean's edge.

As awesome as that sounded, if Sam came out of his coma, I doubted I could keep him contained. He was a soldier, fighter, and protector, and to keep him confined would be like waiting for a bomb to explode. Still, a few days alone on the beach wouldn't hurt. With no one chasing, hunting, or kidnapping us, and that our enemies had fallen off the face of the earth, it would be a perfect time to take a vacation.

But rest and relaxation were a pipe dream, and I couldn't entertain happy thoughts, not until Sam was on his feet, staring at my tits, or saying something snarky in that husky and sexy voice of his.

"Copy that," Lane said into his earpiece as his long legs ate up the space from his Jeep to the end of the driveway. "I know a shortcut through the woods." He led the way to the edge of Harley's yard and onto a dirt path alongside her house.

Harley didn't live far from the central hub of activity. The one building where everything took place—control room, war room, infirmary, a floor with barracks, cafeteria, gym, weapons room, and the list went on. I imagined that, from an aerial view, the structure spanned at least a football field in size.

"You're not the wolf leading Red Riding Hood into danger, are you?" I teased.

Lane was one of the more talkative SEALs on the team. He loved history and had rattled off facts about old historic structures in the city of Fall River. The one that gave me a chill was the Lizzie Borden house. Living in Montana, I'd never heard of Lizzie Borden.

But the day Lane had driven Jordyn, Harley, and me to the spa, he'd pointed out the house on the way into downtown and explained how Andrew and Abby Borden had been hacked to death with a hatchet in 1892. Andrew's daughter, Lizzie, had been accused of their murder but had been acquitted. I couldn't help seeing the parallel between Lizzie and me. A hatchet hadn't been used in Ray's death, but Jack had accused me of killing Ray when I'd screamed. But no one knew if I was to blame. Still, I had no doubt my grandmother, Ray's wife, and his kids would consider me guilty.

Leaves crunched under our feet as we trampled along a narrow path. Memories of that night we battled Roman Brown and his team of merry vampires surfaced. Olivia Brock, the only female vampire SEAL on staff, and I had fought off our attackers as they'd darted out of the thick brush.

But tonight was quiet. The silence was soothing until a howl stopped Lane and me in our tracks. He angled his head toward the ground, opening his acute senses, listening, and sniffing. Then he pressed a finger to his mouth.

I held my breath.

Another howl cut through the brisk air, sounding as though the animal was calling for backup.

Lane whipped out his gun. "Let's keep walking."

I was ready to run. But when we rounded a curve to our right, my heart jumped out of my chest. A white wolf sat on his haunches, blocking our path, his red eyes glowing.

Lane trained his gun on Dane. I was sure it was him.

I inched up to the snarling wolf, who was about to attack Lane. "He won't hurt you," I said to Dane. "Where did you come from?" Like the damn shifter could talk.

He angled his head one way, then another.

I held out my trembling hand. "It's Layla," I said, even though if the wolf was Dane, he knew it was me.

Nevertheless, Dane sniffed as I drew closer.

"Layla," Lane warned.

"He won't hurt me. It's Dane Gray." I petted his damp, dirty fur. "We've been looking all over for you."

The enormous, beautiful, and scary creature was almost level with my shoulders, and he was sitting down.

He leaned into my hand, seemingly enjoying the contact. Then he sniffed my neck, my hair, and my coat, and lingered on my stomach. As if he knew I was pregnant, his eyes glowed a brighter red, like he was trying to tell me he knew. Then he ran his snout along my arm and pushed his nose at my wrist.

I pushed up my coat's sleeve and exposed Sam's leather strap. I hadn't taken it off since I wrapped the hair tie around my wrist in the bathroom on the plane after Sam had been kidnapped.

Lane's arm held steady as he continued to aim the gun at Dane. "Is he trying to tell you something?"

"I think so," I said. "Do you want this?" I hooked my finger through the leather tie.

A horn blared.

Dane's large head jerked, and within a second, he had darted off and out of sight.

"That alarm indicates we have a breach," Lane said.

"The alarm probably went off because of Dane," I said, trying to convince myself I wasn't about to see my grandmother or Emery's men invading the naval base.

My heart sputtered at the thought that Intech, Roman, or maybe my grandmother had tracked Dane to the base. I would bet they were waiting for Sam and Dane to be in one place, then they would attack. Or worse, they had dropped Dane off here, and they were controlling him now.

20

———

LAYLA

As Lane and I jogged along the dirt path, my stomach fisted into a knot.

Lane pressed on his earpiece. "Repeat that, please." A second later, he responded to the other person in his ear, "Copy that."

The blaring alarm died.

Lane slowed to a walk. "Ross Gray breached the gate."

I pushed out a sigh. "He tracked Dane here then."

"It looks that way," Lane said.

When we reached the clearing where the wooded lot ended and an open, grassy area began, a blue truck skidded to a stop in front of the main entrance. Tripp marched out of the building like a warrior ready to fight. Crossbow at his side, daggers strapped to his legs, his sandy-blond hair tied in a ponytail at his nape, and his bronze eyes lasering on the vehicle.

Déjà vu soared back like a flash flood after a hard rain. Not that long ago, I'd stood in the same area watching Roman slice off my uncle Ray's finger.

A bald guy emerged from the passenger side, his head glistening beneath the spotlights shining from the corners of the building.

147

"Is that Ross?" I asked Lane. I'd heard of the man but had never seen or met him.

Lane held his gun at the ready, just in case. "I believe so."

Another howl ripped through the night, sounding like a cry for help.

Baldy stiffened, seemingly familiar with that howl.

Crossing the grassy area, I scanned in all directions, as did Lane.

Ross whipped his head my way, his striking blue eyes boring a hole in me. "I thought I smelled a human."

Tripp growled as if to say, touch her and die. "Ross, explain why you practically ran my guard down at the gate?"

Ross swung his attention to the furious vampire, who was ready to use the crossbow on him. "Dane finally managed to shift long enough to call us and tell us he was headed here. Your guard was stalling. Dane sounded like he was in dire straits, and I'm worried he might be rabid."

Approaching Ross and Tripp with Lane on my tail, I said, "Dane is on the premises. He doesn't look rabid." At least not that I could tell.

Ross's nostrils flared. "You must be the hunter who started this fucked-up mess."

"Ross, easy. You're on my turf." Acid burned in Tripp's voice.

Ross wasn't wrong. I had started the shit show, but arguing about it wouldn't help anyone. Still, that guilt in the pit of my stomach broke free.

Ross dropped his bulky arms when a dark-coated wolf with gold specks trotted into view from around the corner of the building.

Lane trained his gun on the massive wolf. Tripp didn't seem bothered by the animal. Then again, Tripp had wolf blood running through his family tree.

"Easy," Ross said. "That's Vera, one of my pack members."

"Lane, lower your weapon," Tripp commanded.

Vera trotted over to Ross, her luminous amber eyes riveted on me. I imagined she still wanted Jordyn, Rianne, and me to suffer for killing her sister. We'd been the ones to shoot drug-filled darts at the vamps in the nightclub in our attempts to capture Sam. We had no idea the concoction we'd used had a cocktail of powerful drugs harmful to shifters.

Blowing out a breath, I tucked my hands into my coat pockets, not taking my eyes off Vera. She was a beautiful specimen but freaking scary as hell—more so than Dane. I wouldn't want to be caught alone with her in wolf or human form. Those claws of hers and her canines gave me a chill. I would never forget that night at my rental house on the outskirts of the city when Vera had been ready to sink her talons into Jordyn.

Suddenly, bones cracked, snapping me out of my reverie. Within seconds, Vera morphed from animal to human. She stood beside Ross, matching him in height at about six feet—naked and dirty. "Dane needs medical attention." She stabbed her finger behind her. "He's around the building."

Ross glanced at the driver. "Cooper, get Vera her coat."

Cooper flew out, tossed Vera the ankle-length leather coat, then bolted to Dane's rescue as the wind grabbed his ball cap off his dark head of hair.

Ross and Vera joined him.

"Lane, call Dr. Vieira," Tripp ordered.

Lane holstered his weapon, walked toward the opposite end of the building, and pulled out his phone.

Tripp tilted his head at me, his bronze eyes shimmering. "What are you doing out at this time of night?"

Worrying about Sam. "I couldn't sleep. I thought working out might help." My gaze darted to the oncoming shifters as Cooper and Ross rushed toward us, carrying a limp wolf.

"He's barely breathing." Panic was stamped on Ross's unshaven face.

Tripp opened the entrance door. "Layla, have Lane escort you and Vera to the infirmary. The elevator is not big enough for all of us."

I followed the men inside and stopped at the circular reception desk while the three of them hurried over to the elevator. The moment Tripp stabbed the button, the doors opened.

"My brother, Cooper here, has been talking to Sawyer. Cooper might have a way to disengage the chip," Ross said as he entered the elevator. "We think that fucking thing is why Dane hasn't been able to shift completely."

My ears perked up and excitement fluttered to life when I heard that, and then Vera glided up with a duffel bag in her hand.

She flipped her dark hair off her face. "You know this is all your fault."

It was clear the Gray Pack wanted my head on a silver platter. I choked out a nervous laugh. "So I've been told. Are you still after revenge?" I'd apologized to Vera shortly after Roman had been carted off to jail. But no matter how many times I said I was sorry, it wouldn't bring her sister back.

Her claws emerged from her fingertips. "I'm still angry, but more so at Roman at the moment."

I lifted my chin despite the hurricane of nerves whipping around in my stomach. "I admit fault here. Again, I am extremely regretful and sorry about your sister. I didn't know what was in those darts or the ramifications of it with shifters. All I'd been told was that the drug worked on vampires." It wouldn't have mattered if I'd known what her sister was. That night at the club had been a madhouse of chaos. Wrangling in vampires was a tall order, and my sisters and I started shooting as quickly as we could. Hell, we hadn't been confident that we could pull off the job. In the end, we'd failed.

She stepped into my personal space. "The next time you decide to shoot at a room full of people, think twice. The consequences of your actions, especially in a world you have no clue about, will get you killed." She traced a line from my chin to my carotid artery with her sharp claw. "Because the next time you fuck with anyone in my pack, I will tear you to pieces." An evil grin split her lips wide.

I stuck out my chest. "Save your threats, Vera. I don't plan on screwing with you or your pack. On the other hand, I can't speak for my family, and they are a problem."

She slid back, giving me room to breathe and to settle my jitters. "Same goes for your kin."

I wouldn't argue with her. "Stay away from Jordyn. She's on our side." I would've liked to add Rianne to that statement, but I couldn't find it in me to care about her.

Vera released a low growl. Jordyn had been the one to shoot her sister, but I wasn't sure or couldn't remember if Vera knew that or not. It didn't matter. Vera wanted revenge against Rianne, Jordyn, and me.

It was time to cut through the tension because we could argue for hours and still hate each other. At this point, it wasn't about liking each other. We were on the precipice of war. A war that involved everyone on the planet—humans, vampires, shifters, and all supernaturals.

I opened my coat and revealed my stomach. "You wouldn't want to hurt me anyway. Sam would murder you before you had a chance to touch me."

Her brown eyes widened. "I sensed that there was something different about you."

"I'm eight weeks along," I said.

"You look further along than that."

"Possibly twins," I returned.

Her claws retracted. "I guess you're right. I can't rip you to pieces." Her tone was eerily serious.

An awkward silence stretched between us until Lane strutted in.

"Ladies, I need to run. So step on it, please." He breezed past us and pushed the button to the elevator.

Vera slung her duffel bag over her shoulder. "Do you know for sure if you're having twins?"

I skirted the reception desk. "Not unless my dreams come true."

"Always pay attention to your dreams," Vera said. "They hold the key to the future. At least that's what my ancestors believed."

"Do you?" I asked her.

She nodded. "If I can remember mine, I write them down."

I made a mental note to do just that.

21

LAYLA

It was four thirty in the morning, and the last three hours had been nail-biting.

I paced between the two black marble benches that traveled the length of the state-of-the-art medical facility, or as Dr. Vieira liked to refer to the place—his home away from home.

My heart rammed against my ribs. My nails were down to the nubs. Sweat coated my body, and my stomach was in a ball of knots. Essentially, waiting for Sawyer and Cooper to figure out how to do something with the chip in Sam's head was a mixture of hope and hell that felt as if a school of piranhas was eating at my insides.

I prayed they knew what they were doing. Then again, they couldn't touch Sam without Dr. Vieira's approval. With the chip on the brain stem, anything was risky. Still, we had to try. We couldn't keep Sam in a coma for the rest of his life.

Our best bet was to find the scientist Peter Landon. But again, we couldn't wait forever. Hell, Peter could be dead, considering he had a contract out on his head.

Nevertheless, Cooper Gray, a mastermind in his own right on coding, had an idea to download the chip's program and recode it. In turn, the process would shut the damn thing down. Still, they couldn't say for sure if that was the key to bringing Sam out of his coma. Anything sounded good in theory, but in practice, maybe not.

The double doors squeaked open before Steven marched in dressed in casual attire—jeans, a navy SEAL T-shirt, and flak boots. The Sam look-alike had a disarming nature to him when he grinned at me.

I swayed to a stop. I'd made myself dizzy, trampling back and forth like a crazy woman. "Did Webb and Jo find Peter?" *Please say yes.*

Steven ponied up to the bench opposite Cooper and Sawyer. "Not yet." He tipped his chin at Sawyer. "Lieutenant Tripp filled me in on your plan. How risky is it?"

I stood next to Steven, worrying my bottom lip.

Cooper extended his hand to Steven. "I'm Cooper Gray." The man was bulky, like Ross, with a muscled chest and thick thighs, but where Ross was bald, Cooper had a crop of brown hair. Both had blue eyes.

After a quick handshake, Steven crossed his arms over his chest. "Take me through your thought process—pros and cons."

Cooper plucked a thin, palm-sized gadget out of his computer bag. "According to the data Sawyer downloaded on this technology, the chip has Bluetooth capabilities. If I can connect this hard drive to the chip, I can reprogram it so the fucker will either shut down or reboot. If it does reboot, the small jolt might be enough to move it off his brain stem, if that is the reason Sam can't wake up. That's the good news." Cooper took a breath. "The bad news… it could malfunction and overheat, potentially frying his brain stem. I don't know how fast your kind heals, but it could be catastrophic." He scratched a spot behind his ear. "Look, I'm reaching here. But… I can't stand around. The longer my brother can't shift, the more chance he has of his wolf overtaking him. And I can't try my theory on Dane, since I don't know where the chip is in him."

I swished saliva around in my mouth to coat the dryness. None of what Cooper explained sounded good. Even if he successfully reprogrammed the stupid thing or fried Sam's medulla and Sam healed, the chip would still be in him. In my mind, the risks were the same if we did surgery. A surgeon with steady hands could perform the procedure without killing my hunky man. Besides, I was confident Dr. Vieira would find a way to make sure Sam healed quickly if the surgeon screwed up.

"Keep working on your plan," Steven said. "If we fail to bring in Peter Landon, then we'll decide the next step." Pulling out his phone from his jeans pocket, he stalked in the direction of Dr. Vieira's office, then closed himself in.

Sawyer, the vampire with kaleidoscope eyes, stretched his neck from one side to the other. "I'm confident Jo and Webb will come through."

"Whether they do or not, I'm murdering Roman Brown when we find him," Cooper said through clenched teeth.

On our trek from the elevator, Vera had explained how Roman had lured Ross and Dane to a diner under false pretenses. Ross had gone to the restroom, and when he'd returned, Roman and a human were shoving Dane in the back of an SUV. Bad blood existed between Roman and the Gray Pack. Frankly, their feud with the head of the blood cartel was none of my business. I had my own shit to deal with. I was curious where my uncle Jack fit into Intech's scheme and if he knew his mother was in the States.

Jordyn and I had tried calling Aunt Tab and Jack, but there was no answer. Before my grandmother waltzed into the picture like General Patton, I had hoped Jack would come around to our side since he didn't believe in genetic engineering.

"We have several people to axe," I added as I skirted by the bench and ducked into Sam's room. Maybe I would take a page out of Lizzie Borden's playbook. An axe would definitely chop off heads in one swoop.

I sat in a chair next to his bed and sighed. I'd only gotten two hours of sleep. My mind was wired, but my body was slowly shutting down. I didn't know how much longer I could operate on so little sleep. Just about every night was the same—dream, wake up, bite my nails, snack, work out, watch TV, and take catnaps. I couldn't keep going on like this. My sleep problem wasn't exactly related to Sam's comatose state. My hormones were to blame, as well as my nightmares.

I entwined my fingers with Sam's and kissed the back of his hand. When I did, a spark tinged my lips as though he was giving me a sign that he could feel me. "I'm crazy about you, vampire." I kissed him again, and his arm twitched.

I jumped up and leaned over him, still holding his hand. "Sam, if you can hear me, squeeze my fingers."

A minute passed and nothing. Maybe my exhaustion was making me hallucinate.

I whispered in his ear, "I love you. Give me a sign you're in there."

His hand jerked in mine.

Tears pooled in my eyes as I smiled for the first time in a while. "We're trying everything we can to bring you back. Your babies need you." If I was having twins, that was. I was far enough along where an ultrasound could detect the number of fetuses.

I couldn't wait for my ultrasound now. I was scheduled to see Dr. Vieira's colleague, Dr. Martin, next week. One of the reasons Doc had suggested bringing in Dr. Martin to help wasn't only because of his expertise, but Dr. Martin also had the tools. The infirmary wasn't equipped with a transvaginal ultrasound machine.

"We found the scientist," Steven announced in an excited voice.

Hallelujah!

I dropped into the chair and cried. We weren't out of the woods yet, but finding Peter Landon was a step in the right direction.

22

LAYLA

At four forty-five that morning, Steven had announced that Webb and Jo had found the scientist. By six that night, a wiry Peter Landon, who looked to be in his late forties, set his hard-shell silver suitcase on one of the lab benches.

His salt-and-pepper hair was disheveled. His cheeks were splotchy, as though he had blood-pressure issues, his brown eyes were tired and hollow, and one side of his wrinkled button-down shirt hung out of his black trousers.

Looking at him, my heart broke. The man appeared fragile and scared. I imagined that, with a price on his head, he was. Or the cause could be the fact that he'd been taken by vampires. But I was grateful he was standing before us because I was hoping he could bring Sam out of his coma.

Questions started flying at him like a tennis ball in a doubles match. His head even mimicked a spectator in the stands—volleying back and forth from Steven to Jo to Sawyer to Ross to Cooper. Dr. Vieira and I were the only two who weren't jumping down the poor scientist's throat. I had questions, lots of them. But first, Peter needed to figure out how to get Sam out of his coma. Frankly, Peter should be the one asking us the questions.

I held up my hands, almost knocking Jo in the shoulder next to me. "Please, can I say something?"

Ross narrowed his blue eyes at me and sneered from his spot at the end of the lab bench. "No."

I flipped him off. "I didn't ask you." I was tempted to grab one of the daggers strapped to Jo's leg and fling it at Ross.

"This fucking mess is your fault, Layla," Ross spat.

I clamped my mouth shut, glaring at his bald head. Arguing with him wouldn't help Sam or Dane. However, when the time came, I would give Ross a piece of my mind. I didn't care that he was second-in-command of the Gray Pack. I'd apologized to Vera for her sister's death, but the wolves needed to stop blaming me. I hadn't forced Vera's sister to go to the club that night—or to date Roman Brown, for that matter.

Across from me, Dr. Vieira moved a microscope to his left, pursing his lips. "Okay, everyone. We're all on edge. Let's give Peter some space to catch his breath. Ross and Cooper, why don't you check on Dane. He should be stirring soon."

Jo went over to the fridge in the corner of the infirmary and returned with a bottle of water. "Here, Peter. I'm sorry we haven't given you a chance to collect your thoughts."

Peter accepted the water from Jo. "Thank you."

Cooper slapped his brother on the back. "Come on. We should be with Dane to ensure he stays calm or if he tries to shift. Vera will need our help." Vera hadn't left Dane's side.

Reluctantly, Ross trailed behind Cooper but not before Ross gave me another disparaging glare.

I returned the gesture, holding my tongue and closing my hands into fists. If I were in Peter's shoes, I would be pissing my pants. It had to be daunting to be surrounded by creatures who could easily eat him alive.

The second Ross was out of the picture, the tension between us died a quick death. Even Peter's face began to show some color rather than his ghostly appearance of a second ago.

After Peter downed some water, he set the bottle on the counter and pushed his black-rimmed glasses higher on his bulbous nose.

"Like I told Jo on the way here, I don't know that I can do anything. Before I went into hiding, there were multiple scientists on Cobra and Camden's payrolls. I'm sure they've tweaked the technology."

I pressed my hands into the edge of the marble bench. "But you're the one who designed the microchip. Surely you have some insight on how to help."

Sawyer's phone rang and vibrated on the countertop next to me. The name of the control room flashed on the screen. "I have to take this." He grabbed his cell and left.

Steven slid into Sawyer's spot. "Continue, Peter. Tell us more about the chip."

Peter adjusted his glasses again, a nervous tic for sure. "I don't have much to say. You found me, so you must know that Adam Emery is using my technology to build a weapon for the Department of Defense." He took a swig of water. "But if you must know, I originally created a prototype for the handicapped community. For those who'd lost their motor functions." He loosened his tie. "Not for a human—or in your case, a supernatural—weapon who can be controlled. If Adam succeeds, his victims will become assassins who will kill on command." He shivered.

"Like robots," I mumbled, picturing a supernatural army led by my freaking grandmother.

"Will they know what they're doing?" Dr. Vieira asked. "Will they still have their humanity, that is?"

Peter pulled out a handkerchief from his blue slacks and wiped sweat from his brow. "Their ability to make a decision can be overshadowed by the chip."

My eyes widened. "You mean Sam will know he's being controlled but he won't have a way to stop it?" *Holy moly fuck!*

"Yes and no," Peter said. "We found in our experiments that some completely lose who they are, essentially their humanity, and others know their actions are not their own and fight against it."

Horror careened through me. Either scenario was a ticking time bomb. If Sam did something horrible and knew it, he might not recover from that. On the other hand, if he lost his humanity, what would that look like? Would he even know our child or me? At that point, I would rather have an army of genetically altered creatures to fight against than a fucking brain-to-machine computer that could control anyone.

Doc dragged a hand through his brown hair. "Why do you think Sam passed out or Dane can't shift? I'm assuming it was because the chip moved."

Peter's Adam's apple bobbed. "The movement wouldn't cause a blackout or coma. I suspect the chip malfunctioned in Sam. In the wolf's case, my theory is they programmed him to not return to human form."

I held a fingernail between my teeth. "But he did shift back to human, and he was in his right mind to call his family."

"Probably not for long," Peter said. "We tested the chip on a couple of shifters, and the results were all over the place. One couldn't stay in wolf form for long, while the other couldn't return to human." He sighed, frustration washing over him. "Keep in mind, this technology is nowhere near ready. Adam might think it is, but when we're dealing with the brain, there will be a multitude of challenges, problems, and failures. What works in one might not work in another. Plus... where magic is involved, it's a crapshoot as to what can happen. Each species has different abilities, and that alone can determine the outcome."

Steven grabbed the back of his neck. "This is so fucked-up, it isn't even funny."

Peter's jaw hardened, annoyance pouring off him and onto me. "Tell me about it. I left for that reason. Now I have a price on my head because I violated the terms in my contract with Cobra Technologies. They think I'll talk, so they want me dead." He blanched.

"Are you sure it isn't Adam Emery who is trying to kill you?" Jo asked.

He lifted a shoulder, the area around his eyes wrinkling. "Does it matter?" he asked in a quiet tone. "Look, I want to help, but I need your assurance you'll protect me and my family."

Jo placed her hand over his shaky one. "I told you on the way here that we will protect you and your wife and daughter. They're in the cafeteria. My daughter and yours are hitting it off. As soon as we're finished, I'll take you to them."

"We'll discuss a path forward later," Steven said. "But you have our protection."

Peter slumped his shoulders. "There's one more thing you should know." His tone trembled.

I couldn't fault Peter for his nervousness. I hadn't trusted Steven or Sam when I'd first met them, especially Steven. He'd scared the crap out of me. But I would've done anything to save Jordyn and Rianne despite disbelieving anything the vampires offered or said to me.

Regardless, we were putting Sam in the hands of a stranger—one who had worked for the enemy. Could we trust Peter? My answer was a resounding yes, and only because I was more than certain Jo had read his mind. Otherwise, she wouldn't allow Peter near her brother.

"I can't take the chip out," Peter said. "That would have to be done surgically. But I can look at the chip through my software program. I don't want to get your hopes up. As I've already said, each victim reacts differently." Peter plucked out metal headgear from his suitcase.

My mouth parted at the sight of the contraption in Peter's hand. "That's what Sam had on at Intech."

Peter swept his gaze around. "This device codes the chip through a software program. I'll do some troubleshooting. I want to warn you. It could take me five minutes or five weeks to figure out the problem."

"Other than surgically removing the chip, is there a fail-safe option to, say, somehow dissolve it into the bloodstream whereby the device would be removed naturally?" Dr. Vieira asked.

"I hadn't gotten that far in my research and testing, so if my colleagues found a way, I'm not aware of it," Peter replied. "But I will do my best to figure out what happened."

A muscle jumped along Steven's jaw. "You mentioned test subjects. Who? Vampires, shifters, humans?"

Sadness washed over Peter. "All the above, and… when I was part of the team, all our victims died."

Fuck me! I felt like he'd just punched me in the gut. "Are you saying Sam could die?" He *was* saying that, but I had to ask just the same.

Steven wrapped an arm around me. "Let's not think like that."

I leaned into him, enjoying the warmth of his arm and his emotional strength. "Kind of hard not to." I didn't want to be the downer or poor-me person, but the knowledge that all the victims had died wasn't exactly reassuring me that Sam would come out of his coma. My baby wouldn't have a father. I wouldn't have a chance to build a life with Sam. We'd barely scratched the surface of our relationship.

"What about genetic engineering?" Dr. Vieira asked. "Do you know anything about Adam's efforts?"

Peter shrugged. "I wasn't privy to that project, but I know that Carly Aberdeen had a lot of data on DNA mapping sequences and had been testing the research on humans. Whether or not she was successful, I don't know."

At the mention of her name, I snarled, fisting my hands, hungry to expel the air from her lungs until she took her last breath.

Steven squeezed me to him. "She'll pay for what she's done."

Damn right she would, if I had any say in how she suffered.

Steven released me. "If Adam is successful, we're looking at world war, not only for supernaturals, but for humans too. So thank you for helping, Peter."

Peter gathered his equipment. "Don't thank me just yet. Shall I get started?" He seemed more relaxed now than when he came in, which was good news because if he couldn't keep his hands from trembling, then he might have a hard time helping Sam.

"I'll escort you," Steven said.

Jo's cell trilled, and Dr. Vieira went to check on Dane.

"I'll be right there, Steven. I need to use the ladies' room." My bladder was nagging at me, and I had time. After all, Peter had warned us it could take five minutes or five weeks.

Once inside the restroom, I released an enormous anger-frustration-and-anxiety-filled sigh. I leaned against the door and closed my eyes.

"Sam will come out of this. Sam will not die. Sam is strong," I whispered. "Whoever is listening above, please, please bring Sam back to me." I placed a hand on my stomach. "Hey, little one or two. Your daddy will be alive to see you come into this world." At least I had to believe that. Otherwise, I might lose my mind and my will to live.

Inhaling, I pushed off the door and quickly relieved myself. After I washed my hands, I stared at myself in the mirror. My blue eyes were dull. My face had lost its color. Then again, my skin was on the fairer side since I was a redhead. Still, I needed sleep. I swiped a hand over my wispy strands, combing them down and blowing out a breath. Between my peaked appearance and weight gain, I hoped Sam wouldn't run. Then a frightening thought gripped me—one I had earlier and couldn't seem to shake. *What if he doesn't remember me? Or he loses his humanity? Will he be feral?*

I wouldn't think the worst. Nope. Positive thoughts.

I shook off the bad mojo and left. The second I stepped into the infirmary, Steven's deep baritone carried through the room. "Don't move, Peter."

What the hell?

I ran, dodging equipment and benches.

Jo flew out of Dr. Vieira's office, which was adjacent to Sam's room.

Dr. Vieira ordered the shifters to stay put before he rushed up on my tail.

I skidded to a stop in the doorway while Doc plowed into me.

Sam was awake, but he was sucking on Peter's neck.

Steven held Peter by the shoulders. "Stay still."

Jo climbed on the bed and leaned into Sam's ear. "Brother, it's me, your sister, Jo. You can have my blood."

"What happened?" I asked. I found it odd that Sam was feasting on Peter with Steven in the room.

Dr. Vieira urged me to keep my distance while he left. I imagined he was getting a sedative. That would be the only way to pull Sam off Peter, or at least I thought so.

Nevertheless, I slipped into the room, staying close to the supply cabinet in the back.

Steven grabbed Sam's hair. "Son, stop." His voice was even.

"The chip is activated," Peter said. "You'll have to give the order with a little more force than that. He's programmed to receive harsh intonations."

"Soldier, I command you to stop!" Steven's voice boomed.

Flinching, I pressed my fingers to my chest, trying to ease the stabbing pain, trying not to freak out.

Steven's command did nothing.

"Sam," Jo said softly. "I know you're in there. Please, let go of this human."

Peter grew pale as Sam continued to drink from him.

Dr. Vieira rushed back in with a bag of blood. "Out of the way, Jo." He worked quickly to secure the bag to the IV stand. Then he pulled out a syringe from his lab coat.

"No, no sedative." Jo's voice was lethal. "We need him awake." She whipped out a dagger from the sheath on her leg. "I'm sorry, brother." Then she drove the blade into his arm.

Sam released Peter and growled at Jo like a hungry animal who'd been disturbed.

Fuck me. He was feral.

I jumped backward into the cabinet, and the contents inside rattled—or maybe the noise came from my throat because I was trying to suck air into my lungs.

Jo waved him on. "Come on, Sam. I'm ready for a fight."

Better her than me, and only because I didn't have a weapon on me, although I might be able to get through to him.

"Can you shut the chip down?" Steven asked Peter.

Blood dribbled out of Peter's bite marks and seeped into his white shirt as he typed on his keyboard but not quickly enough.

Sam dove at Jo.

Dr. Vieira jumped out of the way as Jo slammed into a silver metal rolling tray before falling to the floor.

My heart was in my throat until Sam sniffed the air. Then my fucking heart leaped out of my chest as he rushed toward me like a linebacker in a football game.

I swallowed thickly, my breathing nonexistent. Memories of hunting in the woods on a stormy night soared back. A hungry vampire with his fangs bared and dripping with blood had his sights set on me.

"Don't move," my dad had said in a hushed voice behind me. "Stay completely still. Show no fear."

Not an easy task when a predator was stronger, powerful, and bloodthirsty.

Sam stood toe to toe with me and angled his head one way, then another, his silver eyes glowing with bloodthirst and something else I couldn't quite discern.

I touched his long, ugly beard. "It's Layla, vampire. Do you know who I am?" My tone was surprisingly calm, but inside, I was shaking to beat the band.

"Hurry, Peter," Steven urged in the background.

"I'm trying to download the data before the chip shuts down," Peter responded, breathing heavily. "We need to analyze it."

I swallowed thickly, my gaze never wavering from Sam's.

"Don't move, Layla," Jo said as she crept up behind Sam like a cat about to catch a mouse.

Tension and fear charged the air.

Dr. Vieira came toward us with the needle, ready to strike.

Sam whipped his head around and growled at Doc and Jo as though Sam was protecting me.

I guided Sam's face toward mine. "It's okay. He won't hurt me." I was ninety-nine percent sure he wouldn't, only because I could feel his confusion. Drinking Sam's blood gave me his empath ability, albeit weak at best. Still, his mind seemed to work overtime to understand what was happening.

Sam returned his attention to me, his silver eyes swimming with sadness.

Smiling at him, I dragged a hand along his jaw. "I love you."

He leaned into my hand, holding my gaze captive.

I beamed through my nerves. "We're having a baby."

He squatted, clutching my hips as he pressed his ear to my belly.

I held my breath, attempting to thread my fingers through Sam's hair, but that metal device was in the way.

"Don't touch the headgear," Peter rushed out, typing like he'd taken magic mushrooms—wired and shaky.

I dropped my arms to my sides while Sam kept his ear glued to my stomach. Whether he could hear a heartbeat, I wasn't sure. But my soul hurt for him, and beneath the emotional pain, I felt the need to gouge Carly Aberdeen's eyes out.

"How did the chip activate?" Jo asked while watching her brother.

"The second I connected the program, the chip must've rebooted," Peter said.

"And I had no time to reach Sam before he pounced," Steven added.

Peter typed furiously. "I'm almost there."

A growl filtered into the room, and Sam jumped up, baring his fangs at the white wolf in the doorway.

Great! The two would eat each other alive, especially now that Dane had positioned himself in front of me as though he was my protector.

I patted Dane on the head. "It's okay. He won't hurt me." I swapped places with Dane. The last thing we needed was a fight of epic proportions while Peter was trying to nix Sam's chip.

Sam yanked me to him, and our chests collided.

I squealed as pain spread through my breasts. *Fucking vampire.* My reflexes kicked into gear before my brain registered my actions, and I kneed Sam in the balls.

He expelled air as he bent over, clutching his boys while giving me a heartbreaking look through the pain on his face.

Suddenly, I felt horrible. "I'm sorry."

Peter banged on a key. "Sam's chip should shut down in five seconds."

Sam winced before he collapsed on the floor with a thud.

A collective sigh raced around the room.

Ross, Cooper, and Vera hurried in while Steven helped Sam into the bed. Doc hooked the blood bag to Sam's arm, and Jo came over to guide me into the chair.

"Why didn't my command to him work?" Steven asked.

Peter shrugged. "He might be programmed to only follow orders from one voice."

"My grandmother's," I muttered as I eased into the cushioned seat.

"Or Adam's or Carly's," Jo added.

The shifters stood by their alpha, watching and listening intently.

"Will he remember anything when he comes to?" Dr. Vieira asked Peter.

Peter banged on keys. "Not sure." He sighed. "But the chip is off."

Jo returned her dagger to its sheath. "Any way to turn it on again?"

"Whoever has access to the program can, but I'm not sure if they'll need the headgear or not."

"But the data we found on the chip says it has Bluetooth capabilities," Cooper chimed in. "So why would you need a contraption to engage it?"

"We were close to adding that technology, but then I left the company," Peter said. "So you might be right. I downloaded as much data as I could before I shut it down. I'll need time to analyze it in more detail." Peter rubbed the area on his neck where Sam had bitten him.

I might just cut the son of a bitch out. Sam was not about to become a robot for my grandmother's army.

23

SAM

Voices seeped into my psyche as my head pounded like someone had beaten my skull in with a baseball bat. I opened my eyes and was met with blurriness until I blinked several times. Silver eyes, green eyes, and brown eyes came into focus.

"Welcome back, brother." Jo's voice sounded hollow.

"Welcome back, son," my father parroted.

"You gave us quite the scare," Doc said.

I squeezed my eyelids shut, inhaled, and Layla's cherry scent seeped into my nostrils. My eyes flew open, searching, hunting, salivating to see her.

But a strong, disgusting smell singed my nose hairs, overpowering her fragrance. The fucking aroma evoked a memory I thought I had long forgotten. The Old Spice aftershave flipped a switch inside me, and I jerked to a sitting position, my gums throbbing, my throat burning, and the need to snap necks pulsing in my veins. My head swiveled one way, then the other as I looked for the fucker who'd tried to rape my sister.

"Where's that asshole Cliff?" My narrowed gaze landed on a scrawny man with salt-and-pepper hair standing at the foot of my bed, fear soaking his bloodstained shirt.

167

Jo pushed on my chest as if she could hold me back. "Cliff? Why would you think Peter was our old foster dad?"

But Jo and Peter, or whoever the fuck the man was, vanished in an instant when Layla rose from a chair in the corner and stood next to the scrawny human.

Her beauty erased that dark memory, even though her body was rigid and her cheeks were pale. Something terrible had happened, and my veins filled with the need to murder whoever had my beautiful auburn-haired huntress basking in fear.

She studied me—no smile, no light in those ball-squeezing, electric-blue eyes.

My gaze skimmed her gorgeous body. Her yellow V-neck sweater accentuated her mouthwatering gargantuan tits. Her hair was piled on top of her head, bringing out her long, smooth neck. Then my mind short-circuited. Her belly was big. Since when?

I scanned the room. What the fuck was I doing in the infirmary? My mind frantically searched for a reason why I was in a hospital bed with people staring at me as though I was the main attraction at a museum.

My memory latched onto Layla and me in my bedroom with her underneath me and my cock inside her.

I sucked her nipples into my mouth before kissing my way up to her neck. Then I sank my fangs into her perfect flesh. She shouted my name as her orgasm crashed into me, heightening my senses and tightening my balls as I fucked her like a man on steroids. A minute later, I roared my release, my cock throbbing in her tight pussy. A wave of deep emotion infiltrated my heart as I looked into her eyes. "Marry me, baby doll."

I blinked several times before our gazes collided.

Trepidation drenched her and wrapped around me, about to suffocate me. What had her spooked?

"Do you know your name?" Doc's concerned tone cut through my gray matter as he wormed his way into my sister's spot at the head of the bed. "Look at me." He had his penlight in his hands.

I growled at him, not taking my attention off Layla. "What's going on? What happened?"

My father cleared his throat. "Son, answer Dr. Vieira. What's your name?"

I clutched onto the blanket. "Fuck… It's Sam. Now tell me what's going on." The bed began to shake, my elemental powers on the brink of destruction if no one started talking. "Why does everyone look like they're about to crap their pants?"

Layla gripped the footboard, her knuckles white as snow. "Do you know who I am?"

I reared back, my forehead wrinkling. "For fuck's sake. You're my baby mama. I love you, and I asked you to marry me. Please tell me you said yes." That part I couldn't remember, although if she didn't agree to be my bride, I might crawl back into a hole or wherever the fuck I'd been and die.

Jo gasped. "What?" She jerked her head at Layla, her black ponytail swinging behind her. "You didn't mention a proposal."

"Focus," Doc said in a tone that permitted no argument. "Is that the last thing you remember?"

"Yeah. Now can I talk to Layla alone?" I scowled.

Doc waved his penlight in my eyes, unfazed by my irritation. "Not yet."

I swatted the air, hoping Doc would calm the fuck down. "I can see just fine. Someone start talking and tell me what is going on."

Layla smiled for the first time, her shoulders lowering, the tension slowly waning. "You remember asking me to marry you?" She sounded surprised.

One side of my mouth quirked upward. "How could I forget something as big as that? Did you say yes?"

Layla's face flushed a deep red. "We should talk about this later."

My pulse screeched to a halt for a split second until Jo's voice entered my head. *Brother, Layla's been through hell, and so have you. I think you need a better setting than this where you two can be alone.*

She had a point, and come to think of it, I wanted to remember her answer.

"Son, do you know that you attacked Peter?" Dad asked, changing the subject, no doubt feeling Layla's edginess.

"I've never seen this man before in my life," I returned.

Peter touched the vein in his neck. "You bit me."

Layla interlocked her fingers in front of her and rubbed one thumb over the other. "You've been asleep for over a month, Sam. Carly Aberdeen put a microchip in your head to control you, but the stupid thing malfunctioned, which is why you've been in a coma. Then Jo and Webb found Peter. He's the scientist who originally designed the technology, although he invented it to help the handicapped. When he came in to analyze the program, the chip rebooted and you…" She shivered. "Then Jo stabbed you to distract you off Peter, and you attacked her."

"We thought you were going to hurt Layla," my father added. "You don't recall any of that?"

I would never hurt Layla. *Ever.* My eyebrows creased as anger bubbled free. Not at them but at the situation. "Not at all." I was also enraged that I'd lost a fucking month of my life. The bed shook again, as did the supply cabinet. My ferocity wasn't meant for them but for Carly Aberdeen and the rest of her fuckwads.

That fear Layla harbored minutes before hurtled back as she lost the color in her cheeks.

"Is forgetting a normal reaction to the chip?" Doc asked, eyeing Peter.

"As I told you, when we're dealing with the brain, anything can happen," Peter said. "Sam, any headaches?"

"My head throbbed when I woke up, but the pain isn't as sharp as it was." I gritted my teeth. "I knew the bitch had fucked with my head. Did you take it out?"

Doc frowned. "You'll need surgery to remove it."

"Just rip the fucker out," I said through a growl.

Peter yanked on his tie. "It's not that simple. The microchip is slightly bigger than a grain of rice, and it will take a keen eye and steady hands along with the right equipment to remove it."

Doc tucked his penlight into the pocket of his lab coat. "Which I don't have here. And we need to tread with caution because it's on your brain stem. If we sever that, vampire or not, you'll die. Think of it as a beheading."

Fuck me sideways. I would be all for taking the chance if Layla wasn't in my life or I didn't have a kid on the way.

"The chip shouldn't activate unless you're near someone who has access to the program, like Carly Aberdeen," Peter said in a bleak tone.

"Then you better figure out a way to remove it. Because I can promise you, I will be near the bitch to murder her."

"What about recoding it?" Layla asked. Her honeyed voice sounded like a siren's calling me home. "So that Carly can't access it at all."

Look at my huntress going all techie. "What she said."

Peter swung his sorrow-filled brown eyes at Layla. "I'm hoping that after I analyze the coding, I can do something like that. But… it will take time, and I might need to access the chip in Sam again."

An eerie silence dropped over us.

"Let's hope you don't have to," my dad said. Then he squeezed my shoulder. "It's been a long and tiring month. I'm glad you're back, son. I need to make some phone calls."

Jo kissed me on the cheek. "I'm off to find Webb and tell him the good news. You need to shave and shower, brother." Then she bounced out, happy and giddy.

Nothing was better than seeing my sister happy. *Oh, wait. I take that back.* I would be stoked if Layla would come closer or give me a vibe that she was itching to be alone with me. Considering I'd attacked Peter, maybe she didn't want anything to do with me. My heart fell out of my chest.

Doc pinned a stern look on me. "I want you to stay put until that bag of blood is empty."

My bloodthirst was fine, but I imagined he was taking precautions just in case the chip had done some damage.

Doc waved at Peter. "We need to work on the wolf."

"Dane?" My voice hitched. "Is he here?" I'd forgotten about him.

"He's in the next room," Doc said. "But he's having problems shifting, and we think it's because of the chip."

"I'm not sure if the wolf will be as easy as Sam." Peter collected his computer and followed Doc out of the room.

I had several questions pinging in my head.

"We'll fill you in on what you missed later," my dad said, reading my mind. "For now, rest. Layla, will you be okay alone with Sam?"

My heart came to an abrupt halt at the notion that I could hurt the woman I was deeply in love with. No one had confirmed if I had done something to her. I would die a thousand deaths if I'd laid an angered finger on her.

"Did I hurt you, baby doll?" *Please say no.*

She shook her head.

My dad cocked an eyebrow. "You didn't. But you weren't yourself earlier, and I'm not sure I trust that fucking chip."

I was wary too. But… "Pops, you heard Peter. I have to be near someone who has access to it. I doubt Carly is lurking nearby." Although that would be awesome. Then I could torture her until she was screaming for me to end her misery.

Layla blew out a breath. "I can handle Sam."

Maybe so, but her anxiety was saying otherwise.

My old man crossed the room to leave. "Layla, are you sure you'll be okay?"

"Sam would never hurt me," she said, this time with more confidence. "Besides, he knows I would rip his balls off."

As painful as that sounded, I chuckled. "That's my feisty huntress."

My dad grinned at Layla. "You did react quite quickly when he pulled you to him."

I cocked my head. "Care to share?" I asked.

She smiled. "Later."

"Scream if he gets out of hand," Dad said on his way to the door.

"You mean, if he screams." Layla's bright smile warmed my black heart.

My dad shook his head before he left.

Once we were alone, I blinked and stared into her gorgeous blue eyes, inhaling her essence that had a way of driving me mad. My throat burned to taste her, to feel her sweet nectar fill my veins. More than that, I had to show her she was safe with me. I tore the IV out of my arm. "Come here, baby doll." I swung my legs over the bed.

She eased between my legs, beaming.

I raked my fingers through her hair. "Did I hurt you?" I asked again since she hadn't exactly given me her answer out loud.

"Not at all. But you scared us, Sam. You were such a different person with that chip activated. More animal. At first, I thought you would attack me, but you seemed confused and sad when you looked at me. Then I told you I loved you, and we were having a baby. You squatted down and pressed your ear to my belly. I knew you understood me. Even when Dane came in to protect me from you, you were the one who wanted to protect me from him." She lifted a shoulder. "But mark my words, Sam Mason. If you ever do hurt me, chip or not, I will slice and dice your balls, pulverize them, and serve them to the crows." She yanked on my beard.

I barked out a laugh. "You love me, don't you?"

She snorted. "Fuck no. I'm in love with you."

"Explain what my father said about you reacting quickly."

She took a breath. "When you pulled me away from Dane, my tender breasts hit your chest, and my reflexes from the pain made me knee you in the balls."

I couldn't help but chuckle. "Good to know you haven't lost your feistiness, and I'm so sorry."

"No need to apologize. You weren't yourself."

"So you're not afraid to be alone with me?" I needed a solid confirmation because beneath that tough exterior of hers, I could still sense her nervousness about something.

She pursed her lips. "Well, maybe I was at first. But I'm furious at Carly and my family, dizzy, tired, confused, and… I was kind of afraid of what you would think of me."

My forehead wrinkled. "What do you mean?"

She snagged her bottom lip between her teeth. "Do you don't think I'm fat?" She glared, daring me to say yes.

I rubbed her belly. "Fuck no. You're stunning. I can't believe how much you've grown in such a short time. As far as Carly goes, that bitch will be lying in a pool of her own blood when I'm done with her, and so will anyone else who fucks with you and me."

She searched my face. "You mean you, me, and our *babies*." She emphasized the last word.

I cocked my head. "Come again?"

"I keep having this recurring dream of a boy who says he's my son, and he asks for my help with his sister, who seems to be in danger. I don't know, but I think that's why I'm big for eight weeks."

Holy fucking hell. I was stuck on eight weeks. If we had twins, no biggie to me. I was one, so that made sense. But I'd lost time that I would never get back because of the sick fucks who wanted to control me.

Suddenly, I was tripping down memory lane to the time when I'd been kidnapped by Edmund Rain and my uncle Patrick. They'd captured me when I was human, and I woke up a fucking vampire. My father had surfaced after about fourteen years, and Jo was also a vampire. After my uncle had drained my human body of blood, the only way to save me was to turn me without my consent. But the key to my survival had been my sister. Jo had given up her humanity to save me. A scientific process unheard of in my world. A process Dr. Vieira hadn't been confident would work. But I was living proof it had.

Layla snapped her fingers. "Sam, where are you?"

I blinked, homing in on her pretty face. "I'm sorry. I am so fucking pissed at people using me. Did we find Carly or Emery?"

She frowned. "No, and we've been looking everywhere. I called Jack, but no answer. I'm afraid my grandmother has done some-thing to him. I can't even reach my aunt Tab."

I growled. "I'm ready to hunt."

She knitted her eyebrows. "I thought we were going into hiding. Maybe we should spend some time in Maine at Jo's house."

I recalled Doc being worried about Layla and me fighting in battle, how I needed to stay alive and healthy for her and the baby, and that she needed rest. On top of that, he'd recommended we find a quiet hideaway. But Layla and I would never be safe anywhere except on the naval base. Sure, our enemies could penetrate our gates, but we had a better chance surrounded by soldiers than anywhere else.

I pushed out a disgruntled sigh. The need to end the madness grew by leaps and bounds and pulsed in my veins. Then something my father had said hit me.

She rubbed my face. "You're spacing out again. What is it?"

"When my dad was on his deathbed after the explosion, he saw his father. Anytime my grandfather graces his dreams or Jo's, he always has a profound message, and one that we need to take seriously. Anyway, in a nutshell, my grandfather told my dad that a war was coming that could wipe out our existence, and… my dad couldn't die because he had to help me."

A crease dented her smooth forehead. "Help you how?"

"He woke up, so he doesn't exactly know. My dad and I believe he and I are the keys to stopping the war that's coming."

She captured a nail of her index finger between her teeth. "So, do you think the little boy in my dream is a warning or true?"

I pulled her hand from her mouth and kissed her palm. "Jo sees the future through her dreams. I wouldn't brush off the little boy. But what I'm trying to say is, I might not have a choice but to fight."

"Sadly, I think all of us will have to fight, especially if the little boy is right, and I need to help our daughter or save her." Despair laced her tone.

I had to take her mind off her nightmares. Hell, I had to stop recalling my fucked-up past. "We should go to my apartment." I buried my nose in the crook of her neck and inhaled. My eyes rolled back in my head. Beneath the cherries was a hint of citrus, which was new and intoxicating. It didn't matter if we were having twins, the world was on fire, or the building was blowing up. There was no place else I would rather be.

She scraped her nails along my scalp. "You heard Dr. Vieira. You can't until that bag of blood is empty."

I licked her carotid artery. "I pulled it out. And since when do I listen?"

"True," she said. "Um… Sam." She yanked on my hair, causing my head to fall back.

I waggled my eyebrows. "I like it when you're rough."

She narrowed her eyes. "Sam, about the marriage proposal?"

I touched her lips with my finger. "Shh. I want to ask you again, but not here, and not while I stink and look like a bear. So hold your answer." Although by the way her heart was galloping, I knew she would say yes. But I wanted a ring in my hand first.

She clamped her teeth around my finger. "You mean you want to romance me?"

"I want to ravish you."

She giggled, releasing my finger and my hair from her grasp. "You can do both. I won't complain."

"First." My fangs clicked into place.

As if she was programmed to do so, she angled her neck. "Drink."

"I want your inner thigh." My dick jerked at the thought of sinking my fangs into her soft flesh with her pussy glistening before me and the aroma of sex in the air.

Lust billowed around her as I moved a wispy strand of hair around her ear.

She swallowed audibly, her eyes lowering to my cock through my gym shorts, and mewled.

I tipped up her chin with the pad of my finger. "You can suck me off when we take a shower."

She beamed, her lust making me hard as granite.

I brushed a hand over her stomach. "Pregnancy becomes you. But I won't lie. Your tits are making me want to fuck you into next year."

"You have such a way with words, tit man. What else do you want?"

I swirled my tongue below her earlobe, the blood pumping furiously through her. Fear tasted sweet, but excitement was even sweeter, especially from Layla. She had a way of igniting an erotic and orgasmic high I was addicted to.

"Aside from you splayed out naked on my bed, I want to cherish you, Layla. I want to give you everything you ever wanted." I peppered kisses down to her carotid artery. "I'm so in love with you that my heart would stop without you."

She became putty in my hands, and I pounced, sinking my fangs into her neck. The first drop of blood exploded on my tongue, sending heat straight to my balls.

She whimpered.

Man, I would give anything to have her teeth scraping my cock right now like she'd done before I'd blacked out.

I sucked with great pulls, my nerve endings on fire, my body coming more alive than ever. She tasted like candy apples with caramel drizzled on top.

After one last sip, I retracted my fangs and lashed my tongue over the puncture wounds, lapping up every last drop I could. Then I crashed my mouth to hers, savage in my delivery, yet tender in my execution as I took what was mine. Layla Aberdeen would become Mrs. Layla Mason before our baby or babies came, and I would slaughter anyone who got in my way.

24

SAM

Later that night, I strutted into the command center. I would like to say I'd fucked for the last several hours, but no cigar. Layla had hardly slept in the last month. She'd complained that keeping her eyes closed for longer than two or three hours had been difficult.

After I'd showered, I'd found her curled up in my bed, softly snoring. I didn't want to wake her, and I wanted to catch up with my team on what I'd missed in their efforts to find any of our enemies. It didn't surprise me they hadn't located Carly, Emery, or Harriet. Or maybe they had. Our missions weren't for everyone's ears, so they probably wouldn't tell Layla.

The atmosphere in the command center was quiet at midnight. Other than Tripp and Ben standing in front of one of the seven monitors that spanned one wall, Petty Officer Ryan Hawk manned the radio and phones.

The new recruit nodded at me. "Sir," Hawk said.

The blond, green-eyed vampire had passed our SEAL training with flying colors. His first assignment was to learn the ins and outs of the control room, much like I had when I'd been a newbie, which was one requirement my old man had instituted many years ago when he'd been in charge of the SEAL team.

I returned the gesture as I scanned the map of Chicago featured on the largest of the displays.

When we'd been at war with Edmund Rain and my uncle Patrick, we had every state from New England to Alaska on the screens. We'd scoured the terrain from east coast to west. But Edmund had gone dark while they lured humans in and experimented on them. If Carly had what she needed for testing, then she, too, had found a place off the grid.

I strutted past occupied and empty cubicles.

"Ben. Holy fuck," I said, approaching my best bud.

Ben turned around with a cheeky grin, looking like he'd been reborn. Bright reddish-brown eyes. Military-style haircut. Black uniform crisp and loaded with weapons. The shifter bite had kept him confined to a hospital bed until Dr. Vieira whipped up a magic potion of shifter blood mixed with Abbey's.

A jealous streak coursed through me. I was in jeans and a button-down shirt, and aside from daggers in my flak boots, I wasn't dressed for battle, but I was chomping at the bit to join my team-mates and help out where I could since I couldn't dart off without risking the lives of my Layla and the baby or babies.

We exchanged a hug, patting each other on the back.

My half-human and half-vampire friend sized me up. "As always, you're a hard vampire to keep down." He chuckled.

"A month was too fucking long, though. I've missed a ton."

Tripp clutched my shoulder. "We'll debrief you. But I'm glad as fuck that you're back."

I pointed to the map of the Catskills. "What's going on?"

Tripp smoothed a hand over his sandy-blond hair. Like Ben, he was garbed in black—SEAL T-shirt, cargo pants, boots, and weapons. "We've scoured the country, tracked every hot and cold lead, but nothing until a week ago."

Excitement stirred in my gut. Crossing my arms over my chest, I tucked my hands underneath them, resting my ass against the edge of an empty desk in front of Ben and Tripp.

Ben twirled the laser pointer around in his hand. "We've been monitoring several mountain areas of the country for an increase in activity—from truckers to power sources. If you remember, Edmund had moved his operation to Alaska."

"Oh, I remember it well. Mammoth piles of human bodies stacked to the ceiling in the caverns of that Alaska facility." I could almost smell the stench as if I were there at that very moment. "It would make sense for Intech to find a less populated area." That would be something I would do. I stabbed a finger at the screen. "The Catskills?"

Ben circled an area on the monitor with the laser pointer. "The power grid here has lit up like a heavily populated city."

"Have we got eyes and boots on the ground there?" I asked.

Tripp switched maps using an iPad, then zoomed in on the city of Cleveland. "Not in the Catskills, but outside Cleveland. Viking II is on the ground here. Roman's men have overtaken Cobra Technologies' manufacturing plant. That's the company making the microchip."

I ground my teeth together at the mention of Roman's name. "What about Jack Aberdeen and his crazy mother? Layla told me she hadn't been able to reach Jack or his wife, Tabitha."

"A mystery," Tripp said. "But we have them on our radar. Our priority is Roman and digging up more in the Catskills."

I begged to differ. Harriet Aberdeen was part of Intech's genetic-engineering plan. Therefore, she needed to be stopped as well. But I wasn't in charge, and I wanted Carly Aberdeen more than Roman or Harriet at the moment. Carly was the brainpower and the queen of the colony. Take her out, and we might be able to destroy Intech's operation—at least long enough to buy us time to demolish it completely. Sure, someone else could fill Carly's shoes, but not quickly.

Man, desperation rode me hard to jump into the fray and murder my enemies. Sitting idle wasn't my strong suit. My dad had traipsed off to war and had left my mother with Jo and me. But these circumstances were quite different from my old man's. Jo and I were already born. We didn't need his blood to survive.

A radio crackled, echoing in the control room. "Hawk, locate Sam Mason for me, please." Petty Officer Olivia Brock's voice blared in the room. "Let him know he has a guest. Also, inform Lieutenant Tripp that the perimeter is secure. No suspected activity."

"Who wants to see me at midnight?" I mumbled, scanning the screens as my adrenaline ticked up a notch. Maybe Carly decided to grow some female balls and show up. After all, I believed she was more interested in the science behind the Masons' powers than in controlling me. The latter was Adam Emery's objective. But when I found the monitor with a direct view of the main gate, a feverish dose of excitement surged through me. "Are you kidding me?"

Ben and Tripp followed my line of sight.

"That looks like Jack Aberdeen," Tripp said.

"That's Jack Jr.," I returned. He wasn't Carly, but he was married to the woman, and that had me itching to interrogate him.

At the gate, Olivia frisked Junior Aberdeen. He had his arms out to the side as she tore the ball cap off his head and inspected it. Then she continued to pat him down. Once Olivia was done, Junior snagged his hat off the hood of his car.

"He's clear," Olivia said through the radio.

"Copy that." Hawk stood and peered over the sea of cubicles in the distance. "Lieutenant and Sam, did you hear that?"

I nodded once. "Got it, man."

"Ben, fill in for Olivia," Tripp ordered. "Petty Officer Hawk, radio Petty Officer Brock and let her know to escort our guest to the conference room in the lobby once her replacement arrives."

"Copy that, Lieutenant," Petty Officer Hawk said.

Tripp clapped me on the shoulder, grinning. "Maybe we just got a breakthrough. I'll meet you up there. I need to check in with the guards at the back gate. If Junior Aberdeen is here, I want to make darn sure he doesn't have an army with him."

Junior didn't strike me as stupid enough to raid a naval base of vampires. If he did, I hoped Emery, Harriet Aberdeen, and Rianne were part of that army. If I couldn't fight in the field, then bring the fucking battle to me. I was ravenous to hang Emery by his toes off a high-rise building, skewer Rianne over an open fire much like she'd done to me, and Harriet… Well, I didn't have anything in mind just yet. In the meantime, we had prison cells with their names on them. For all I cared, they could rot until I was ready to inflict my revenge. Regardless, I shouldn't be cocky. The Aberdeens were hunters with brazen balls and thick skulls, and with Harriet in charge, who knew what we were up against.

"I can walk the perimeter," I said to Tripp. I would love to find Rianne waiting in the shadows.

"Nah, we have the base well protected and guards on the rooftops," Tripp said.

Ben collected a bulletproof vest from the chair next to me. "I'll do a sweep of the east wall on my way to the gate."

With a plan in place, Ben and Tripp went one way, and I stalked in the other direction.

When I passed Petty Officer Hawk's desk, he stood to attention. "Sir, I'm glad you're okay."

We exchanged a handshake. "Thanks. Are you ready to take a spin in the field?"

He crossed bulky arms over his barrel chest. "Commander London said soon."

Webb London had handpicked Ryan Hawk to join our band of brothers. He had perfect grades in class and in physical training, but Petty Officer Hawk had a knack for strategic planning. He would give Olivia a run for her money since she was our best strategist on the team.

"I'll see if I can put in a good word to speed things up." We could always use extra eyes and ears on the ground.

But first, I had an Aberdeen to shake down.

SAM

Junior's grassy human odor drifted out of the conference room and into the lobby as I exited the elevator maybe twenty or thirty minutes later. I'd taken a detour to my apartment. I'd forgotten to leave Layla a note and didn't want her to freak if she woke up and didn't find me.

Olivia and Tripp stood by the circular reception desk in the lobby, talking in hushed tones.

"Stop by the transient house and check on Dane, please," Tripp said to Olivia. "I'm not sure if Vera left with Ross and Cooper. We have a guard stationed outside the house, but I don't trust the shifters."

She swept her long brown braid behind her shoulder. "Will do, sir." Then she punched me in the arm, which from her was more of a love tap. Olivia was like a big sister to me. "Dude, don't scare me like that again."

I gave her a hug. "I don't plan on it." Man, I was hugging everyone except the one woman who I should be upstairs snuggling with, especially at one in the morning. But my adrenaline was off the charts, and if I stayed in bed with Layla, I wouldn't be able to keep my hands off her, and she needed rest.

After Olivia left, I asked Tripp, "Why did Ross and Cooper leave without Dane?" Before Layla and I had left the infirmary, Peter had managed to shut down Dane's chip. I gathered it had been a difficult task with him as a wolf. Doc had ordered Dane to stay on base for a few days in case he required more medical attention. Apparently, he'd been severely dehydrated, and Doc wanted to perform some tests. Plus, Peter needed Dane close by in the event he needed Dane, since he was analyzing both our chips.

Nevertheless, the alpha and I weren't friends, but I was relieved he wasn't in the hands of Carly. The verdict was still out as to why Dane was having problems shifting. Peter didn't think Dane's chip had malfunctioned, which was another reason he was studying the data. But actions and reactions to a device that controls the brain differed in each victim, according to Peter. For example, I couldn't recall that I'd attacked Peter or my sister with the chip engaged, whereas Dane's mind remained intact. He just couldn't shift to human form. Peter theorized Intech had programmed Dane to stay as a wolf. If he did, then Dane's wolf would take over, and he would lose himself and his humanity—become the predator he was born to be.

"The Gray compound is in upstate New York," Tripp said.

Immediately, I connected the dots. "Close to the Catskills?"

He hardened his jaw, his bronze eyes loaded with questions. "Yeah."

"Do you think they're working with Intech?" That was a crazy question, considering the fact that Dane was a victim like me.

"I don't think so," Tripp said. "But Ross keeps blaming Layla for their involvement in this."

"He does?" Man, I had missed shit.

Tripp scratched his neck. "I shouldn't be telling you this, only because you'll hunt Ross down, but he seems to have it out for Layla. Frankly, even aside from his hatred for her, I don't trust him. He's helped in the search for Emery, Roman, and others, but only because we were looking for Dane too."

"If Ross even thinks of laying a hand on her, I will behead the fucking mutt." At some point, my patience would self-combust, and my enemies wouldn't see me coming. "Aside from Ross, I can't grasp the shifters siding with Intech. Dane was in that glass room with me. Roman set him up. Unless Ross was a lone wolf." I could get behind that.

"I sent Crysta and Kraft to do some reconnaissance to help out Ross if need be, and they can watch things for us as well."

"Good move, dude." I hadn't seen Tripp's cousin in a while. Aside from her relation to Tripp, Crysta was a shifter and one hell of a tracker. If anyone could find a needle in the haystack, it was her. Her business as a private investigator in the supernatural world was flourishing, and she was in high demand.

She'd been hired to track one of our own at the request of Petty Officer Crowe's parents several years ago. Crowe and his partner, Quade, had gone missing on one of our missions. The Crowe family felt that my government had done nothing to find their son. Not only had Crysta found Crowe but also Webb, Olivia, Kraft, Sloan, and Kodiak. Their plane had gone down over the Alaskan mountains in their quest to follow a lead on Crowe and Quade. Sadly, Crowe and Quade had been found dead alongside Sloan, who'd suffered at the hands of my uncle Patrick's brutal experiments.

Tripp tipped his head toward the room. "Are you ready? The perimeter is clear. If Junior has anyone with him, they're not in the vicinity. But Sawyer is monitoring the street cams around the city and checking hotels."

"We can always have Jo or my dad read Junior's mind." We didn't have to sweat things too much with that weapon in our arsenal.

"Which *will* happen before he leaves here," Tripp said as we entered the room.

Besides the long table and several chairs, the walls were decorated with photos of fighter jets and our mission statement.

Junior sat in a chair with his back to one wall, facing us and texting.

Tripp stabbed a thumb at the phone. "Give that to me."

"Why?" Junior bit out in a derogatory tone. "What I have on my phone is none of your business."

Tripp slapped a hand on the table. The sound boomed in the small room.

Whoa! Tripp never flew off the handle unless he had a good reason. Yet, with the pressure we were under, my coma, and the microchips, the tension was high. I'd felt it when I walked into the command center. Not only that, but we'd been on this road show once before, and the outcome had been death and destruction for both humans and vampires.

Still, a power-hungry enemy wasn't one to treat carelessly, particularly one who would go to great lengths to get what he wanted. Therefore, if we couldn't contain what was to come, humanity might cease to exist.

Regardless, I wasn't about to tell my superior officer to stay calm, because if he didn't take Junior's phone, I would.

Junior levered backward, almost toppling over in his chair. "The fuck." He narrowed his blue eyes and slid his phone to Tripp. "Have a blast, man."

I flipped a chair around and straddled the seat across from Junior. "What would you do if you were in our shoes?" I preferred to play the bad cop, but Tripp was doing a bang-up job.

Junior whipped off his ball cap, shoved his fingers through his dark-red hair, and watched Tripp with a stark intent.

I didn't detect any nerves or that Junior was hiding anything. I was the stronger empath over Tripp. Just the same, I opened up a telepathic connection. *Do you sense he has anything up his sleeve?*

No. But I'm on edge as it is, and this asswipe is lucky we let him in, Tripp replied as he read through Junior's texts.

"These are mostly to Carly, with one to your father, Jack." Tripp pocketed Junior's phone. "I'll return this when you leave."

Junior straightened. "You can't keep my phone."

Tripp eased into a seat at the head of the table. "You're on my turf. I can do whatever the fuck I want."

Junior looked at me for help.

I raised my hands. "He's being nice. If his boss was here, I doubt you would ever see your phone again. So, where's Carly?

Your grandmother? Rianne? Why are you here?" *Might as well cut to the chase.*

A heavy coat of silence hung over the three of us.

"Speak," Tripp barked. "It's late, and I have shit to do."

Junior clammed up, studying Tripp and me as if we fascinated him. I would bet my dick he wasn't enamored with us.

"You're right. It's late," Junior finally said. "I would've been here sooner, but my plane had issues. I'm also tired, hungry, and dying for something cold to drink. And I want Jordyn and Layla to hear what I have to say. My dad also has a message for Layla."

"You've been texting Carly," I said. "Does that mean you're conspiring with her? Is she in town with you?" I glared at him, hoping he would say yes.

His lips spread into a thin line. "No." He tipped his head at Tripp. "He saw my texts. She hasn't answered them. I don't know if she's alive." He slumped in his chair. "After I chased her from the loading dock to the lab, the place was filled with too much smoke. She insisted on getting her notebook. I guess the data she had from taking samples from you and that shifter was on a table in the lab. She complained she hadn't entered the DNA mapping sequences into the computer. Before I could stop her, she ran into the smoke. Then an explosion rocked the lab. I managed to backtrack to the loading dock. But no one was there. That's when my father called me. He was in Chicago looking for Noah, so he picked me up."

I thought maybe the winds were turning in our favor until an icy chill crept along my spine. It didn't matter if Carly was alive or not. We had other assholes who were hungry to get their hands on me, or worse, Jo or Abbey.

"Did you find Noah?" I asked.

Junior frowned. "Nope. He's probably with my grandmother and Rianne."

Tripp scrubbed a hand along his jaw. "Why should we believe you?"

"You shouldn't," Junior said. "I wouldn't if the tables were turned. But I'm also here because I want to help. Like my father, I don't want genetically made bloodsuckers and shifters or whatever the fuck else comes out of the experiments to roam the earth." His tone was rife with anguish.

I draped my forearms over the back of the chair. "How would you help us?" This, I had to hear. He was in shape. I would give him that. But he didn't strike me as a soldier. Not that we would accept him into our ranks or trust him. Layla, however, believed we could convince Junior to side with us. Whatever that meant.

"I'm a hunter," Junior said. "The best one in my family. I'm also a good tracker."

Tripp rubbed his chin. "Then why aren't you out there tracking Carly or your cousin and brother?"

"After my father and I gathered our family and got them into a safe hiding place, he and I returned to Chicago." Junior fidgeted in his seat. "We've been watching my house, Intech, and Camden Industries. Intech's lab was gutted. A buddy of mine at Camden told me Adam and his brother, Fred Emery, had 18-wheelers packing up most of Intech after the fire. He didn't know where they were headed. But my dad and I spotted my grandmother, Rianne, and Noah coming out of my house. They'd loaded up a car with a ton of supplies. Then we followed them onto the highway, going east. We lost them outside of Toledo."

"When was this?" Tripp asked.

"About two weeks ago," Junior responded. "We would've kept looking, but my dad had to return to the family. My mom got spooked, but it was a false alarm. So he recommended I come here."

I could see Tripp's wheels turning.

"If they were going east, maybe they're here in the city," I said. Sure, we had other areas we were watching, like Cleveland and the Catskills. But as badly as Harriet wanted Layla in her grasp, I couldn't shake the feeling she was close by.

Junior shook his head. "I think they were meeting Carly, which was why I think they were at my house. When they were packing up the car, I saw Rianne carrying out Carly's clothes on hangars and stuffing them into the trunk along with a computer bag of Carly's."

"So Carly is alive?" I said with too much excitement. I didn't want her dead. Not until I had a chance to play.

"I'm hoping so," Junior added. "I need answers from her."

From the short time I'd seen them together when we'd been running out of Intech, Carly seemed more in love with her work than her husband. But her marriage wasn't my concern or business.

Tripp's phone went off, and he glanced at the screen. "We'll continue this conversation in the morning." He rose. "I'll escort you to the men's barracks. There'll be a guard posted outside your door, but you'll have food and a place to rest for the night."

"Thank you. Will I see Layla?" Junior's tone was grateful and not as cocky as when he'd walked in.

I stood. "If she's up for it" came out of my mouth before I could stop myself. Layla would be there now if I called her.

"I'm not saying another word unless I see her," he said evenly.

"Layla will be there," Tripp assured him before his voice was in my head. *Get out of here and snuggle up to that woman of yours. She's had it rough while you were in a coma.*

I hated that she'd suffered while I was in a coma. It was one reason I was dying to chop off heads and slice off limbs.

I can take him to the men's barracks, I offered telepathically. *If you need to be somewhere.*

Tripp gave me a no-way-in-hell look. *That wouldn't go well. Go. That's an order.*

I didn't always follow orders. But I didn't think twice about his command. Crawling into bed with Layla was far better than jerking Junior's chain, and Layla might be rested enough and up for a wild night of sex. Just the thought had my dick ready to burst out of my jeans.

I saluted my lieutenant and left, wondering what the hell Junior had to tell Layla.

But Junior and the reasons he was on the premises vanished when I walked into my apartment several minutes later and spied a light spilling out of my father's bedroom. *Odd.* My old man had been bunking at Jo and Webb's house when he wasn't at his condo in Boston.

I padded down the hall. Maybe Layla had wandered into his room. She'd talked about wanting to take a hot bath, but the only tub in the three-bedroom penthouse, as Jo called it, was in the en suite tucked into my father's fortress. At one point, his hideaway had always been locked since he'd kept weapons and other precious belongings there that he didn't want anyone going near.

I peeked in on Layla. She was curled up under the covers with one arm under the pillow and the other stretched out in the empty spot where I should be. If she wasn't in my father's room, my old man had to be, although Jo and Webb also had keys to the place.

I left the door to my room ajar and headed toward the light. "Pops, are you here?" No one could breach the building, let alone the apartment on the fourth floor. Besides, the closer I got, the scent of my father's cologne drifting toward me got stronger.

The white walls of my dad's abode were bare, the top of the dresser was empty, and the king-sized mattress was covered in a sheet. When my father had moved to Boston, he'd taken most of his belongings with him.

"Yeah, son." He came out of the walk-in closet with a brown leather book. "I thought you were sleeping. I didn't want to disturb you and Layla, but I had to get this out of my safe." He stared at the scratched cover as though it held secrets to world domination.

"What's in that book that has you frightened?" I was feeling a mixture of fear and confusion from him.

He ran a hand over the cover. "This was my father's journal."

I slipped my hands into my jeans pockets. "Did you have another dream about him?"

He flipped through the pages. "Not necessarily. But remember Jo's dreams always had a black panther in them? Well, I had one tonight with the same animal. And my father had a journal where he detailed his dreams. I'm curious if he saw a black panther too."

"Do you think he's trying to send you another message?"

He lifted his broad shoulders. "Not sure. What are you doing up? Or rather, where've you been?"

I chuckled. "Just catching up on everything, but Junior Aberdeen is here."

He stiffened. "Is Harriet?"

"I wish." I belted out a growl. "But Tripp has the team surveilling the city cameras and local hotels."

A muscle ticked in his jaw. "I hate to think what Harriet would do if she found out about Layla's pregnancy. The simple fact is, she knows Layla has vampires in her mother's family. Harriet is sadistic enough to use that child to her benefit."

"Over my dead body," I mumbled, sitting on the edge of the mattress as a wave of anxiety punched me in the gut. I wasn't cocky enough to believe Harriet wouldn't try to nab Layla or do something as cruel as to use her own kin to her benefit. But if she succeeded in her endeavors—or tried to, anyway—I would become the predator and live up to the creature Harriet believed me to be. "Junior has a message for Layla." I explained the rest of what Junior had said and finished with, "Junior wants to help us."

Placing the book on the dresser just outside the closet, he leaned against the doorjamb. "Is that so?"

I lifted a shoulder. "Thoughts?"

"Depends," Dad said. "If that's truly the case, and I don't find anything in his head—hostility or manipulation or otherwise—then we could use a person on the inside, especially if he has a friend at Camden Industries." He rolled up the sleeves of his white button-down shirt, seemingly preparing to dig in and work hard at something. "Afterward, it's time to gather the troops and lay out all our intel and where we stand. Then we can make some clear decisions on our next steps." He pushed off the doorjamb. "I'm going back to Jo's."

"One more thing, Pops." I swallowed, my adrenaline kicking into gear.

He cocked an eyebrow, resting an arm on the tall dresser.

I leaned my elbows on my knees. "I'm not exactly a romantic." My dad didn't have a romantic bone in his body. At least I wasn't aware of one. I'd never seen him with a woman, and I had no clue how he'd treated my mom since she died before I even knew her. But when he talked about her, he had love for her in his voice.

He grinned, keen on hearing more.

"I'm going to propose to Layla again, and I want to do it properly. She knows it's coming, but I want to surprise her somehow. Jo thinks I should have a nice setting. I'm not asking how to do it, but I would like to know how you proposed to Mom."

He beamed. "Your mom adored old historic buildings." He glanced past me with a faraway gleam in his eyes. "In particular, she loved the Mount Washington Hotel in New Hampshire. One of the oldest hotels around. That night was spectacular, and to see her light up…" He blew out a breath, staving off the emotions that were hopping off him and onto me. "I proposed in a horse-drawn carriage on a summer evening under the stars." Tears clouded his eyes.

I swallowed my own feelings. I'd never gotten the chance to know my mom. She'd died of leukemia when Jo and I were still in diapers. But I would give anything for her to be at my father's side, to be here with Jo and me. "I'm not sure I can top that." I half laughed.

He rounded his gaze on me. "It's not about who has the better grand gesture." He tapped his heart. "It's in here, son. Make sure Layla knows how much you love her. And you'll know when you're in the right place to ask her."

"Pops, I want her with me for eternity. But I know that's impossible."

Sadness washed over him. "You can't look at it that way. Live now. Live free, and cherish her every moment you have."

I chuckled. "Free, huh? Given what we're up against, and that our kid might be hunted like me, free isn't the term I would use."

"You know what I mean, Sam. Have you thought about a ring?"

I picked at the seam of my jeans. "Kind of. I do want to have one before I propose." I had money saved.

He raised his finger. "Give me a second." He ducked into the closet, and a minute later, came out with a small blue-velvet bag. "I thought of this when the topic came up in the infirmary. Anyway, your mom wanted you to have this for your bride-to-be." He pulled out a ruby ring.

My eyes widened at the beautiful stone that would fit Layla's fiery personality perfectly. "That looks similar to the necklace she gave Jo."

He held the ring up to the light. "Your mom loved the precious gems. The ruby is a carat and needs to be cleaned and can be resized for Layla."

He handed it to me just as a bloodcurdling scream pierced my eardrums.

26

LAYLA

Beads of sweat rolled down my back. I inhaled and exhaled, blinking and trying to regulate my breathing like I'd been running for my life. Actually, I had, or felt that way in my dream.

Two figures burst into the room, and it took me a beat to zero in on Sam. In a flash, he was grabbing the sides of my arms.

"Baby doll, breathe." He picked hair off my dampened face.

I shuddered, swallowing and then choking. "I'm good."

"The fuck you are. Was someone trying to kill you in your sleep?" he asked.

I homed in on his worried expression. "Rianne."

His grip tightened, and a sharp prick of something in one of his hands dug into my skin.

I glanced at my right arm. "What's in your hand?"

He froze, regarded Steven, who stood at the foot of the bed, then quick as a whip, he put whatever was poking me into the back pocket of his jeans. "It's nothing."

"You're not a good liar." I was too groggy and freaked out to push him to tell me.

"You should be happy about that," he returned. "Do you want to talk about your nightmare?"

"No. I want to shower." The hot water would feel amazing against my taut muscles.

He straightened. "How about that bath you wanted?"

That sounded even better. But Steven was there, which told me he was staying in his room where the jetted tub was located. "I don't want to intrude."

"No intrusion," Steven said. "Sam, can I have a moment alone with Layla? Also, call down to the control room to let them know things are okay here just in case they heard the scream."

Sam switched on the bedside lamp despite the light spraying in from the hallway. "Sure, Pops." He kissed me on the forehead. "I'll run the bath," he said before strutting out.

Once Steven and I were alone, a jittery flutter clawed at my stomach.

He sat on the end of the bed, faced me, and set a book he had in his hand beside him. His stark white shirt brought out his black hair and forest-green eyes. "Since you first arrived on base two months ago, you've been through quite a journey."

Luckily, I'd fallen asleep in one of Sam's T-shirts, and the blanket was covering my lower half. Just the same, I brought the covers up a little higher over my lap. "To say the least."

He rubbed his chin. "You and my son have been drawn together from the moment you met. Call it fate. Call it whatever you will, but your destinies are tied together for a reason. In my world, that is something to heed. I'm not saying your love for one another isn't real. I believe it is." His tone was circumspect, but beneath his words lay worry, fear, or something along those lines.

"Steven, if you're about to tell me I have to obey orders and your rules around here, I don't want to hear it. To be blunt, I make my own decisions, and with Sam in my life, we make them together."

He clasped his hands in his lap, chuckling. "If you will let me finish, please. We're on the brink of war—one that will be far worse than the war we fought against Edmund and my brother. We have several enemies with different motives, and the one I'm most concerned about is your grandmother."

I held in a snarl. "And Rianne."

He tipped his head to the side. "Her too, but I've known your grandmother for some time, and the woman can be lethal. Did you know your father was afraid of her?"

"In a way, yeah. But most Aberdeens won't cross her."

"She locked up your father after she found out he'd been talking to me," he said.

I swayed where I sat, anger consuming me. I hated that my grandmother had the audacity to treat people with disrespect just because we didn't bow down and kiss her feet. But I couldn't change her beliefs any more than she could change mine.

"I didn't know that. But I'm learning my father held back many things from me and my sisters."

He crossed one leg over the other. "Her hatred for my kind is stronger than I've seen from anyone."

"She blames vampires for the death of her husband," I mumbled. "Can you blame her? I'm not taking her side. But considering several Aberdeens have been killed by your kind dating back a hundred years or more, a person can't help but hate." I sighed. "Until I met Sam and began to learn that you guys protect humanity, I would've never believed there was a nice vampire out there." Boy, how my view had changed—and how easily Sam had stolen my heart.

"I understand completely, Layla," Steven said. "But I've tried to show Harriet that we want the same things as humans. That we strive to keep the peace in order to coexist. But she won't listen. I'm all for punishing the vampires who don't conform to our laws, and if the situation warrants it, even kill them if I have to. But that's not the issue or my point here. She'll use my grandchild to her benefit or might even—"

I held up a hand. "Don't say it. I know. But considering that she wants to command an army of supernaturals, your first point is valid."

"I would like to say she can't find out, but that might be a tall feat since your stomach is growing." He took a breath. "We could find a place where no one would find you, but even that is a challenge since you need Dr. Vieira and his colleague. To that end, I've ordered Dr. Vieira to equip the infirmary with the proper equipment for pregnancies, but that will take several weeks. In the meantime, the naval base is the best place for you, and not anywhere else."

"But I have an ultrasound scheduled with Dr. Martin at his office next week because of the lack of proper equipment. I'm going to that appointment, Steven. And I understand and agree with every word you said, but I also can't feel like I'm a prisoner. Plus, the base isn't that fortified. Roman Brown was able to penetrate the compound."

On a long blink, he dipped his chin. "You're right, but we've taken measures to secure the compound even further, and Roman wasn't able to get into this building. So, I'm giving you and Sam this apartment. You're family now, and you'll need the space with the three bedrooms. You can turn any of them into a nursery."

"I do feel safe here." Soldiers patrolled the rooftops, and it would be hard for anyone to scale a four-story building without being noticed, particularly with the guards who stood watch at the prison complex across the courtyard.

On a separate note, the spacious abode was chic and furnished. Plus, beggars couldn't be choosers. In some respects, I was a nomad with nowhere to go. Not that I was complaining about the military base. But I needed to set down roots and feel like I had my own space. Staying with Harley was great, but I wanted my independence and somewhere I could call home.

"Good, then it's settled," he said. "I adore you, Layla. I also trust you. You're a strong woman. You'll survive what we're about to face. You remind me of my daughter in many ways, and you're a perfect match for my son."

I smiled even though I could hear a *but* coming. "I won't hurt him, if that is your next statement."

He grinned. "Actually, it isn't. I want you to know that I will protect you and that baby at all costs, and so will Jo and the rest of us here."

Warmth spread through my chest. He had no reason to trust me unless he felt he had to because of Sam. But Steven didn't strike me as the type to do anything because of anyone. "Since we're on the topic, why do you trust me? I'm an Aberdeen, after all."

He picked up his leather book. "Your actions toward my son speak volumes, and you may not like this, but Jo has been in your head. If there were any thoughts on your part that led me or any of us here to believe you aren't on our side, then we would've had a conversation by now. Also, I'm able to read your mind as well, when I'm touching you."

I didn't like anyone in my head, but I also couldn't exactly block Jo or Steven every time I was around them.

Steven rose. "One more thing. Pay attention to your dreams. They could save your life."

I reared back. "How so?"

He glanced at the book in his hands as if it held the key to everything. "If you know what's coming, you might be able to stop it."

My face scrunched. "You mean, I can stop Rianne from killing me?"

He dipped his chin. "One reason my daughter is alive is that she embraced her dreams, the messages in them, and ended Edmund Rain before he took her life."

I swallowed an elephant. "Are you saying I will have to do the same?" I didn't have the heart to do such a macabre thing to Rianne. Except if she tried to hurt my babies. Then all bets were off the table.

"Not at all. But there are other ways to change the outcome," Steven said. "You'll know how to when the time is right."

Pfft. Nightmares, magic, vampires, witches, my family tree, and what was true or not, what was real or not, had been a tall order to process.

Sam cleared his throat as he stood in the doorway. "How goes it?"

Peachy. Steven was the third person to warn me to pay attention to my dreams. It wasn't like I hadn't. Hell, I would never erase the mental picture of Rianne stabbing me over and over again.

Steven strutted up to me and kissed me on the head, then met Sam at the door. "I'm heading back to Jo's. Can I have a minute, Sam?"

"Baby doll, the bath is ready." Sam gave me one of his lopsided grins before he and his dad stalked out of view.

I climbed out of bed, puffing out my cheeks, trying to muddle through what Steven had said. But I wasn't about to slay my problems at two in the morning, and I had a bubble bath waiting for me.

My bare feet sank into the carpet as I padded through Steven's room and into the stark white bathroom—jetted tub tucked into an alcove, a shower on the other side of it, a closet, and drawers and cabinets beneath the marble counter that housed two sinks.

After closing myself in, I stripped out of my T-shirt and panties before I eased into the mountain of bubbles. The hot water stung my skin for the briefest of seconds. Once completely immersed, I sighed heavily, leaning my head back against the tub.

Sam whistled. "Now, that is a sight to see."

I jerked my head toward the powerful vampire with hunger in his green eyes that screamed he wanted to devour me. "I didn't hear you. And you can't see anything except bubbles."

A smile tugged at the edges of his mouth, his dimples peeking out, deep and dancing with the promise of mischief and pleasure. "No, but my imagination is running wild with images. And it's nice to see you relaxing."

I captured bubbles in my hand. "Is everything okay with your dad?" I suspected he'd told Sam that the apartment was ours. "And what did you put in your pocket, by the way?"

He leaned against the counter, his black hair loose around his stubbled jaw, his thick thighs encased in jeans that hung low on his hips. "My dad told me about the apartment, but I heard most of what he said to you anyway."

Got to love vampire hearing. "Are you going to answer my other question?"

His gaze roamed freely over my face. "In time. Do you mind if I join you?"

"Of course not." I couldn't imagine Sam lounging in a bath. Then again, the vampire constantly surprised me.

He shucked out of his clothes in two seconds flat and stood like a god of gods—naked, hungry, and virile. Power and strength molded his body into a beautiful specimen.

I licked my lips, enjoying the view as he swaggered over to the tub, stroking his massive erection before he climbed in behind me.

Waves of arousal swirled in my stomach, and a gooey feeling wrapped me in a blanket of love and protection.

I leaned my head back against his chest. "This is nice." And also new. Sam and I had never lounged or enjoyed each other's company. For one, we hadn't had time, and two, when we were alone, it was all tangled limbs and naked bodies. Though the latter sounded heavenly too.

He caressed my stomach as he kissed my ear. "I love you, baby doll. My world is better with you in it. You know I'll keep you and our little ones safe."

I covered his hands with mine. "I know you will. But there will come a time when you might not be able to." I shuddered to think of my grandmother. "Your dad is worried about Harriet. I am too. But I want you to know that I will protect these babies at all costs. We're in this together, Sam. Partners, right?"

"Forever." He nibbled on my ear.

Silence ticked for a beat.

"We need to start thinking of a nursery," I said. "And clothes and furniture… oh my. What if we are having twins? Then everything will be doubled." I sucked in air. "Can we keep them safe?" I stiffened.

His hot breath breezed over my neck. "Relax." His tone was husky and soothing. "No one outside of our small circle here will get near them."

I had no doubt they would be well protected, but stranger things had happened. I sank further into Sam, feeling his strong arms around me, giving me a sense of security, at least for now.

"On a different topic, Junior is in the men's barracks," he said.

I gaped. "For real?" That anxiety I was trying to shove into a deep hole dug its claws into me.

"Easy," Sam said. "We're checking the nearby area and also city cameras and hotels for any signs of the other Aberdeens. Anyway, we'll talk to Junior in the morning." He kissed my ear, sliding his hands up to my breasts.

I closed my eyes. "They're sore, so be gentle."

"Always," he said, his fingers slick with soap as he teased my nipples.

My pussy clenched as my muscles loosened, enjoying the sensation, him, the atmosphere, and us. The outside world could wait, including Junior. Sam and I had to steal time, even if it was only for a minute.

I climbed out of the tub and held out my hand. "I have another way to relax."

The dark timbre of his chuckle set my clit on fire as he got out, grinning, his cock standing erect. "I like the way you think." He snagged a towel off the rack.

Once we were both dry, he lifted me into his arms and carried me into the bedroom, where he eased me onto the mattress. "Spread your legs."

Happy as a clam, I did as he commanded before he dragged his tongue from my knee to my inner thigh, his hair falling forward, the strands tickling my sensitive skin.

"Your lust is off the charts," he mumbled as his green eyes bled to silver, his fangs front and center.

I giggled, and when I did, he bit. I arched my back at the beesting bite, which only lasted a second before pleasure raced through my veins. While he sucked, I rubbed frantic circles around my throbbing clit. In seconds, I was panting and moaning.

Sam raised his head, blood smeared on his mouth, his eyes hungrier than I'd ever seen. In a flash, he hovered over me and thrust his cock inside me before his mouth crashed to mine. Then he fucked me hard and fast.

I sucked the blood from his lips before our tongues tangoed, groans and moans peppering the air.

"I want to fuck you forever, baby doll. I can't get enough of you."

I pulled on his hair as he rode me like a wild stallion.

The headboard banged against the windowsill. Our kisses were sloppy and wet, our skin slick, our breaths heavy.

We rocked and rolled, staring at each another, saying nothing yet saying so much.

Then his body tightened, and he growled his release, my name dropping from his lips.

I froze for a mere second. I loved seeing the alpha vampire come undone, but I couldn't help but think he might black out again.

But when his dimples winked, I sighed heavily.

"Afraid I was about to pass out?" he asked, sensing my concern.

I laughed. "Yep." Sure, the chip was off, but who knew if any activity on Sam's part would flip a switch and turn the stupid thing back on.

He rolled onto his side and tugged me to him. "We'll get the fucker out of my head." He growled, then brushed hair off my face. "You're so fucking beautiful. You know that?" He kissed my nose. "I hope we have a daughter, and she looks just like you. Thick red hair." He traced an area over my cheeks. "Freckles and those blue eyes. You know, I'll kill the first boy she meets."

I snorted, sliding my leg between his. "Why am I not surprised?"

He yawned, causing me to do the same. I suddenly felt like I might be able to sleep through the night, especially with my hunk of a man next to me.

"Sleep," he whispered. "I'll be right here if you have a nightmare." He scooted closer to me, enveloping me in his arms.

I tucked my head underneath his chin and breathed in his masculine scent. Heaven came to mind. There was no other place I would rather be than in Sam's arms. As I closed my eyes, I prayed we had more of these quiet and intimate moments together. Whatever we were about to face, Sam Mason had my heart and soul for as long as I was alive.

27

LAYLA

The midmorning sunlight streamed in from the wall of windows, giving the open floor plan a warm and cozy feel despite the chill in the air. I stared out at the courtyard below, rubbing my arms, rifling through last night—Steven's conversation, Junior, my nightmare, a relaxing bubble bath, and making love with Sam before falling asleep in his arms.

While I felt better than I had in a long time, I was anxious to hear what Junior had to say, but I also couldn't shake the notion that my grandmother and Rianne were holed up somewhere in the city. I wouldn't put it past Harriet to force Junior to do her bidding.

The hum of the fridge and the gurgling in my stomach sounded ominous, sending more chills to tiptoe down my spine. Something horrible was on the horizon. I could feel a prickle of darkness building deep in the pit of my gut. I believed every word of Steven's that a war was on the horizon, and no matter if Sam and I hid or not, I believed that he and I would have to fight. Therefore, it was more important than ever that I stayed in shape as much as my pregnancy would allow.

I rubbed my hands together, blowing my hot breath into them, shifting my thoughts to something positive for a moment rather than focusing on the darkness. My mom had always said that your mind could be your worst enemy. Hell, if it wasn't true. For the last month, I'd brooded and cried and felt sorry for myself. I had to believe there was a rainbow at the end of whatever was headed our way.

A knock on the door snapped me back to reality as Jordyn came in all smiles and rosy cheeks.

"What has you so bubbly?" I asked, basking in her spirited attitude.

She padded across the room in her fur-trimmed black boots. "What has you so pissed or worried?"

I hugged myself. "Life. Granny. Junior."

She pulled the sleeves of her yellow V-neck sweater over her hands, her burgundy-stained lips turning downward. "I hear ya. Are you feeling okay, though? You look pale."

"I dreamed I was having twins, and I really think I am." I hadn't had a chance to talk to Jordyn since Sam woke up yesterday.

"As I once said, Sam has magic sperm. So don't be surprised if you have a litter."

I swatted at her. "Bite your tongue."

She giggled, and I couldn't help but laugh with her, and it felt liberating.

She curled brown locks of hair around her ear, her long mascara-coated lashes sweeping over her cheeks as she blinked. "What do you think Junior wants to tell us?"

"Other than Granny wants us? I'm not sure. Maybe Rianne had the nerve to be Carly's test subject." My heart skipped a beat. I prayed Rianne wasn't idiotic enough to think she would turn out just like Sam.

Jordyn shook her head. "I still can't believe how our sister has changed. But I'm trying to keep a positive outlook. Human or not, the SEALs will take no prisoners. Rianne will die if she fucks with them."

A string of nerves squeezed my throat. "And you're surprised?"

She frowned. "I'm sad."

I was about to agree when Sam strutted in with Junior and Steven.

Junior looked like a hobbit compared to Sam and Steven, and Junior wasn't a small man. He was bulky, but clearly Steven and Sam had the height over Junior.

My cousin whistled as he took in his surroundings. "Military treats you right. Maybe I should join." He appeared well rested, recently showered, and had no visible cuts or bruises. Sam wasn't a fan of anyone in my family except Jordyn and, of course, me. Still, I wouldn't put it past Sam and my cousin to duke it out. Both had crass attitudes. But Junior's asshole nature was a five on the dickhead scale compared to ten for his brother, Noah.

Junior lasered his focus on me and faltered. "What the fuck? You *are* pregnant. I thought Sam was kidding when he called you his baby mama."

I opened my arms. "Surprise." I guess Jack hadn't told him, which set me at ease. Maybe I could trust my uncle. Though, if he did reveal my secret to anyone, Aunt Tab would be the lucky person.

Steven closed the door while Sam snorted, seemingly enjoying the shock and awe washing over Junior's freckled face.

Junior's blue eyes were fixed on me. "What are you, four months?"

I regarded Jordyn. "Do I look that fat?" I dared her to say yes.

Sam's long legs ate up the space between us. "You're stunning." He kissed me on the lips. "But you don't have much color in your face. You should sit."

I could use a dose of blood, but I wouldn't attempt to drink from Sam's wrist with Junior in the room. "I'm fine."

Sam helped me over to the couch like he was afraid I would fall or pass out. His overprotective nature was endearing, but if he and Jordyn and anyone else around me had any intentions of coddling me, I would scream bloody murder. I hated to feel like I was suffocating.

After we were all seated around the coffee table with Sam

hovering at my side, he said to Junior, "This is your moment to shine."

Junior was perched on the edge of the chaise lounge when his eyebrows knitted together. "What are you doing with Carly's number?" He reached out and picked up the piece of paper I'd set on the coffee table after Sam left to get Junior.

In a chair across from me, Steven exchanged a surprised look with Sam.

Sam shrugged at his father. "Where did that come from?"

"It fell out of the cargo pants you had on at Intech. Did you know it was Carly's number?" I'd found it again when I'd been digging in my handbag that morning for my ChapStick. "You can't read the last two numbers."

"I don't have to," Junior muttered. "I don't understand why Sam has her number."

Sam scrubbed a hand over his chin. "Join the club, man."

"Maybe she was trying to send Sam a message," Steven offered.

"Why don't we call her?" Sam sounded excited.

"I will," Junior fired back.

Sam hopped up and snagged the paper from Junior. "Tripp has your phone. Besides, you've texted her many times, and she hasn't responded."

"Sam told me she ran back into the lab. Do you think she's alive?" I asked.

"I'm not sure," Junior responded in a harsh tone. "There was a ton of smoke and an explosion."

"Maybe she's immortal," I said without thinking.

Steven nodded. "You might have a point, Layla. My brother, Patrick, experimented on himself. But he'd never been successful."

Sam stood next to Junior, the sunlight shining on him, giving him an ethereal glow. "She was quite fascinated with our kind. But she was human when I was there."

Junior shivered for a brief second. "She had plenty of time to whip up a batch of her vampire juice while you were out cold in that glass room." Junior's eyes widened at his own statement.

"Yet last night you told me she went back to the lab for her notes on DNA mapping sequences. That tells me she doesn't have anything ready to test on anyone. But that doesn't matter. What are the last two digits?" He plucked his cell out of his jeans.

"Eight seven," Junior said.

The air thickened as the four of us watched Sam enter the number.

Junior bounced his knee. I bit a hangnail on my thumb. Jordyn seemed relaxed, and Steven eyed Sam.

After a minute, Sam said, "No answer."

Junior grunted out a frustrated sigh.

"Jordyn, after this, pull Carly's phone records," Steven said.

My sister rolled her shoulders back. "Yes, sir. Sam, can you text me Carly's number?"

Sam handed his phone to my sister, then he sat next to me. "Start talking, Junior." He swung his arm over the back of the couch.

I had a ton of questions about Carly. If she was the leader of the merry fuckups, how had she found out I knew Sam if Junior didn't tell her? Did she know the Aberdeens were vampire hunters before she married Junior? As far as I knew, Junior never told Carly about our business, and I didn't blame him, since Jack had closed the doors on hunting right before Junior married Carly. So he hadn't seen a need to bring up an inconceivable topic.

Junior leaned his elbows on his knees. "Layla, I guess you told Granny about your mother and vampire blood running in her family, which, by the way, was a shock for me. My dad never mentioned that. Anyway, she grilled my father about it. He told her as much as he knew. Now... she has this twisted idea that Layla, Jordyn, and Rianne would make good test subjects for genetic engineering. Jack wanted me to warn you what you're up against. It isn't about locking you away to convince you not to be with a bloodsucker. The game has changed. Now she wants you to succumb to her evil plan to command an army of supernaturals, and she believes you and your sisters will lead the charge."

I couldn't help but laugh. She was so deranged on multiple levels, it wasn't even funny.

Jordyn shook her head. "Unbelievable. She has gone stark mad."

I tucked my cold hands between my thighs. "Do you know anything else Jack told her?" If Junior didn't know I was pregnant, I held out hope that Granny didn't either.

Junior swallowed. "If you're asking me if she knows you're carrying a Mason baby, I don't know. My father didn't tell me. I doubt he told her. But knowing Granny, I'm afraid not only for you but that baby. You might be hunted more than him." He stabbed a finger at Sam. "Also, my father wanted me to mention that my grandmother talked about a little girl named Abbey."

The oxygen in the room diminished rapidly.

I slapped a hand on my chest. Roman Brown salivated to get his hands on Abbey, and now another person wanted the powerful ten-year-old. My insides were shredding piece by piece at the idea that my child or children would be hunted like Abbey.

Sam was on his feet. "Fuuuuck. I swear, I'm murdering your grandmother first."

Steven, on the other hand, was as calm as the ocean on a hot, humid day. "Explain more."

Confusion blazed in Junior's blue eyes. "Something about a prodigy and that Abbey could be the key to their success. Who is she?"

Sam was pounding his booted feet into the floor behind his father as he paced. The walls began to shake. The glasses in the dish rack near the sink clinked together.

Steven rose. "Son, calm down."

"The fuck I will," Sam shouted. "Everywhere we turn, someone wants either Jo, Abbey, or me. I'm sick of it, Pops." Sam swung his apologetic gaze to me, silver banishing his green irises. "Now my kid will probably be hunted."

There was no probably about it. I knew without a doubt our children would be, and the thought of anyone putting their hands on them had me breathing heavy.

Steven clutched Sam's arms. "We've won this type of war before. We can do it again."

Sam grabbed the back of his head with both hands. "How many wars are we going to fight before we can live in peace!" He was bordering on shattering the windows.

I rushed over to Sam and flattened my hand on his face. "Hey, Abbey is safe. I am too." I didn't sound convincing as my stomach churned like a violent storm at sea. But all of us had to stay vigilant and optimistic. "As long as you and I are together, they can't touch us. In the end, we'll do whatever it takes to protect us and our family." I couldn't promise we wouldn't endure pain and suffering, but I could promise I would give my life to save my loved ones.

"Does that mean kill anyone in your family who fucks with us?" Venom threaded through Sam's words.

"If they try to even take our kid, then yes." I had never been more serious. My dad taught me to defend myself and those I love. *But you love Rianne?* Despite how I felt about my sister, if it came down to her or me, I would choose me. "I will pulverize anyone if they so much as fuck with our child, Sam. Sister or not. Grandmother or not."

Junior gasped. "You would? You wanted to help them after your scream caused us to collapse in that room at Intech."

Even though he was right, I ignored him and kept my focus on Sam. "We're partners, right, Sam? We agreed we have each other's backs. We have a child or children to think about now. Therefore, nothing or no one will fuck with our growing family."

He pulled me to him and kissed me on the head. "I love you."

I inhaled the clean scent embedded in his black shirt, the aroma coating my frayed nerves. "Ditto, vampire."

Trembling, he hugged me tighter.

Beneath the love pouring out of him, I could feel his fury, lethal and primed. I pitied whoever got in the way of his wrath.

Junior asked about Abbey again.

"She's Steven's granddaughter and Sam's niece," Jordyn said.

"What else do you have to tell us?" Steven asked Junior.

I eased away from Sam, rose up on my toes, and ghosted my lips over his. "Better?"

He leaned close to my ear. "I'm the luckiest vampire alive."

I flushed as my heart sang with glee. I grabbed his hand and tugged him over to the couch.

Junior eyed Sam. "I'm not sure I should say any more. The building might crumble." His tone was serious, his expression fearful.

"Just talk," Sam bit out, keeping me close to him as we sat down.

Junior shrugged. "Okay. My dad also mentioned that Harriet seemed quite excited to meet Abbey."

Silence dropped like a bomb.

"Meet her?" Horror darkened Sam's handsome features. "Abbey will never go near that monster."

I rubbed Sam's muscled thigh. "Easy. Junior is only the messenger."

It was Steven's turn to wear a hole in the floor. "Harriet will regret ever returning to the States."

Jordyn scooted to the edge of the cushion. "You could've told us all this over the phone. Why the visit?"

Junior stood and tucked his hands into his jean pockets. "As I told Sam and Tripp last night, I want to help. Not just to find Carly, but to knock some sense into Noah. My mother is beside herself. And my dad and I want to stop the genetic alteration if we can."

"Good luck with Noah," I mumbled. "His head is thicker than Rianne's."

Steven gripped the back of the chair he'd been sitting in. "You didn't know your wife was mixed up in genetic engineering or that she knew about our kind?"

"I didn't. I never told her about the Aberdeen business. It wasn't necessary, given my dad had shut down hunting. But… there are events and things that don't add up now. Maybe she met me on purpose to further her research?" His tone cracked. "I don't know. I can't help but think that. I've also been racking my brain over how she found out that Layla knew Sam. The only thing I can think of is that she overheard me talking to my dad not long after he'd gotten home from this place with Layla, Rianne, and Jordyn. I was in the kitchen and didn't hear her come home. She'd asked me what I meant by bloodsuckers, and I brushed it off. But I also knew if I didn't give her something, she would continue to ask. So I gave her a story about how Layla got mixed up with a guy named Sam Mason, and my father had to help her."

"Did she interview me to see what I knew about vampires, or was she trying to lure me to her side?" Irritation cut through Jordyn's words.

Junior hunched his shoulders. "Not sure. But does it really matter?"

He had a point. "I'm just glad you didn't take the job," I said to my sister.

"Where is your father?" Steven asked Junior.

"If you want to know, you can call him," Junior said. "The less anyone knows about where he and the family are hiding, the better. Oh, and he wants his brother's body. Is Ray here?"

"He's on ice until our resident doctor can complete an autopsy," Steven said.

"Does Granny know about Ray?" I asked, holding my breath.

Junior nodded. "My father had to tell her. Otherwise, she would've sent out the cavalry. But he told her he died of a heart attack."

"I doubt she believes that," I mumbled.

"Of course she doesn't," Junior said. "She thinks the vamps here killed him."

"Not surprised," Steven added.

My head was about to explode with the mountainous crap piling up as high as the Himalayas. I couldn't discern what was more frightening—my grandmother's desire for Jordyn and me to become monsters, as Junior so eloquently put it, or her finding out I was pregnant. If she was anxious to meet Abbey, I could only imagine what she would do if—or rather, when—she found out I was carrying a Mason baby. Because eventually, she would learn I'd gotten knocked up by Sam.

Hunger pangs pricked my stomach along with pesky and thorny nerves. I pressed my hand into Sam's leg and pushed to a standing position. The second I was upright, a trickle of warmth coated my panties as if it was that time of the month.

My blood gelled. My heart stopped, and hysteria had me running to the bathroom.

Heavy footsteps clamored behind me. "Layla?" Worry etched Sam's tone.

Once inside, I swung the door shut, but Sam plowed in.

"Give me a minute, please," I said, holding in the urge to scream at the top of my lungs.

Sam leaned against the closed door, clearly petrified as he gnawed on his lip. I'd never seen fear on the snarky vampire before.

I pulled down my leggings. I'd been wearing stretchy fabrics more and more. Then I checked my white panties.

"You're bleeding." The color drained from Sam.

And I had to be ghostly white too.

28

LAYLA

From the naval base to the local human emergency room, I was numb from head to toe. Even as I waited in a private room for Dr. Martin while he delivered a baby, my heart wouldn't stop jackhammering in my chest, and not only because of the blood on my panties, but also because I was on edge after Junior had told me about my grandmother. I wasn't that surprised she wanted to build me into a creature of the night, but the minute we drove off the base, my heart was on a collision course with an oncoming train.

I didn't want to think my grandmother was waiting idly in the shadows, but I couldn't help but sense that she was. I wasn't saying Junior lured her there, because Rianne knew exactly where I was. Nevertheless, I couldn't live in fear and lock myself away forever. Besides, I felt protected with Olivia and Ben monitoring the outside perimeter of the hospital. My sister and her bodyguard were in the waiting room, and Lane, my bodyguard, was outside my door, and I had the strongest of them all by my side. Sam would annihilate anyone who he felt was a threat to me.

Though my gorgeous vampire was now glacier solid against a wall just inside the door, if it weren't for Lane driving us, Sam

213

would've probably crashed the Jeep. He'd said nothing since we'd left the base except when he yelled at Dr. Vieira to do something.

But Dr. Vieira's hands were tied. Without a transvaginal ultrasound machine, he couldn't do much except assure us that spotting during the first trimester was normal. But to be safe, he'd called his longtime friend, Dr. Martin, who I had yet to meet.

Sam's hands were glued to the ivory wall as though the structure was his only lifeline. His green eyes glowed in his chiseled face, filled with questions, sadness, and worry as if the world was crashing down around him. Maybe it was. Maybe Sam and I weren't meant to be happy, build a family, or even be together. But I refused to believe we were doomed, destined to live as the enemies we'd been born to hate.

Sitting on the exam table naked from the waist down with a thin paper sheet covering my lower body, I swung a leg out and back, a nervous tic to keep me from having my own meltdown. We had been impatiently waiting for Dr. Martin since the nurse had collected a tube of blood from me.

"Dr. Martin is in surgery but wanted us to run some tests while he was preoccupied," a brunette nurse by the name of Louise had said when she'd taken my vitals.

"We might be here into the night," I mumbled, staring at the collection of gloves, swabs, and tissues neatly placed on the speckled counter next to the sink.

Sam grunted, a muscle flexing in his jaw.

I should call Jordyn to let her know we hadn't been seen yet. She'd tagged along for moral support but was out in the ER waiting room, probably biting her nails and bouncing her knee, impatiently eager to hear if I was okay.

"Dr. Vieira said it's probably nothing. Spotting happens during the first trimester," I said to reassure us both that nothing was wrong.

He finally blinked. "That amount of blood didn't look like spotting."

Shuddering, I couldn't argue with him.

"Where the fuck is the doctor?" His tone was stilted, his words clipped.

I tangled my fingers on my lap. "Sam, I really need you to be the calm one. Otherwise, I might have a panic attack." I was bordering on one anyway.

He pushed off the wall, softening his hard veneer. "I'm sorry." He wedged his way between my legs, combed a hand over my hair, and his forehead kissed mine. "I'm trying to keep my shit together."

His demeanor reminded me of his anxiety over flying. "Then why don't you tell me something about yourself that I don't know." We'd played the same game on the plane, which helped him, so it might help me too. We still had many things to learn about each other. "You don't like to fly. You were in foster care. What else?"

He brushed his lips over my nose. "I was in jail a few times when I was fourteen." He inhaled, rubbing his cheek against mine as though he wanted his scent on me or mine on him.

I leaned into him, purring. "Why am I not surprised?"

His nimble fingers danced in my hair. "Your turn. Tell me a favorite place of yours."

I held onto his waist. "I love the ocean. You spoiled me when you brought me to Jo's house in Maine."

"I want to spoil you rotten," he said. "I will give you the world, baby doll. The house on the beach and anything you desire. I will protect you, our kid or kids, and cherish you until my last dying breath." All of a sudden, his head jerked toward the door.

Normally, I wouldn't flinch since he had vamp hearing, but with Junior in town, my nerves were heightened.

A slender man in a green cap and matching scrubs stalked in.

Sam moved to the side of me. "It's about time." His glare was glued to the doctor.

"You must be Layla and Sam. I'm sorry to have you wait so long. I'm Dr. Martin," he said in an even tone, not fazed by Sam's harshness. "Damon Vieira has filled me in on your situation. I was looking forward to meeting you next week, but I see there's a problem." He set his iPad on the counter, pulled on a pair of nitrile gloves, came over to me, and smiled. "Before we get started, tell me what type of activity, if any, were you doing recently. Sex?" He set his soft hazel eyes on Sam, then me.

My cheeks burned, and they shouldn't, since he specialized in the delivering of babies. "Last night," I replied while Sam glued his hand on the middle of my back, the heat of his palm searing into me.

Louise returned, wheeling in the ultrasound machine. "Here you go, Dr. Martin. Would you like me to stay?" She batted her brown eyes at Dr. Martin, then Sam. The little flirt.

"No, Louise. I'll handle things from here. Thank you."

The pretty brunette's gaze lingered too long on Sam before she sashayed out of the room.

While Dr. Martin readied the machine, he said, "Your labs look great. Your HCG levels are high. I doubt your pregnancy has been compromised. But before I do the ultrasound, I would like to examine you. Can you lie back for me, Layla?"

Relief coursed through me, and Sam seemed to lose that fidgety edge he'd been sporting.

When I was on my back and my feet in stirrups, Sam held my hand, watching Dr. Martin with a keen eye and hard features. I had no idea what was going through Sam's mind, but for me, lying there with an ob-gyn about to examine me, pregnant by a vampire mate who I never imagined would be at my side no matter what, was surreal. I would give anything to have my mom with me, or at least alive, so I could ask her questions. After all, she'd given birth to three of us.

I puffed out my cheeks, releasing the air in my lungs as Dr. Martin examined me like any ob-gyn doctor would. It had been over a year since my last annual visit to see my gynecologist. But I wasn't a newbie to the procedure.

With his head between my legs, Dr. Martin said, "Your cervix looks fine. I see a little dried blood, but nothing to be concerned about." He rolled his stool back. "Keep in mind, as your body changes, so does the cervix, which becomes more sensitive during pregnancy. It's common in some woman to bleed after sex where the partner thrusts too hard."

Sam and I had a rough romp in the hay last night. "Are you saying we can't have sex anymore?" Judging by the crease in his eyebrows, I was sure Sam had the same question.

Dr. Martin rose and inserted the probe it into me. "Not at all. Just tone down the roughness." He moved the wand around, watching the screen, which I couldn't quite see from my position. "So far, I don't see anything to be concerned about. Your cervix and uterus look great. Mm…"

"What's wrong?" Sam asked, squeezing my hand a little too hard.

For a gripping beat, Dr. Martin kept his concerned focus on what he was doing.

That ramming of my heart started again. "Is everything okay?"

Dr. Martin turned the machine at an angle toward me. Then he fiddled with the wand and stopped. "See these dark spots on the screen? Those are four fetuses."

Pulling his hand from mine, Sam listed to one side. "Come again?"

Dr. Martin laughed. "I would be light-headed too if my wife was having quadruplets."

I lifted up on my elbows. "Are you telling me I'm having a litter?" I full-on laughed. If I didn't, I would be gasping for air like Sam was.

The vampire pounded on his chest and looked faint.

"I think you should sit," Dr. Martin said to Sam, pressing buttons on the ultrasound.

Luckily, I wasn't standing. Otherwise, I might be on the floor.

Sam dug a hand into the exam table. "I'm fine."

Snorting, I circled my fingers around his wrist. "Keep telling yourself that."

"Are you not freaking out that we're having four kids?" His voice hitched. "Dr. Martin, are you sure?"

The doctor chuckled. "Son, I've been doing this a long time. I'm sure." He kept moving the wand around and hitting buttons on the machine.

"I guess that's why my belly is big for eight weeks?" I asked for confirmation.

"Yes," Dr. Martin said. "From everything I see here, your pregnancy is healthy, and you are that far along." He pulled out the wand. "Keep in mind that with multiples, there is a possibility you could deliver early."

Sam dragged a chair from near the counter to the exam table. The rickety piece of furniture creaked when he lowered his bulk into it.

Taking my feet out of the stirrups, I sat up, my attention on the sheen of Sam's face. I was certain the news would hit me when it sunk in.

Sam's Adam's apple moved as he swallowed. "Four? Four? Are you sure, Dr. Martin?" he asked again.

Dr. Martin removed his gloves. "A hundred percent." He seemed patient in answering Sam one more time.

Sam massaged his temples. "Four," he mumbled. "Four."

Dr. Martin washed his hands, then collected his iPad. "Layla, you're healthy. Look to be in great shape. I would continue to exercise for as long as you can. That will help with delivery."

Or killing my enemies.

"Sex is fine, but take it easy," Dr. Martin said. "I'll send my notes over to Damon. You two are free to leave when you're ready. I would give Sam a few minutes to recover." He headed to the door. "Oh, and I won't need to see you next week. I'll set up a time to come to the naval base next month." He removed his cap and revealed a shaved head. "If Damon hasn't mentioned this to you, I am well aware that the babies may or may not be human."

Dr. Vieira hadn't, but I just assumed Dr. Martin knew about vampires given he was friends with Dr. Vieira.

He tipped his head at Sam. "I can send Louise in with some water."

"He's good," I said. I was afraid Sam might frighten her if his fangs came out.

After Dr. Martin took his leave, I cleaned up and dressed quickly. "Sam."

He raked his hands through his hair. "Last night, as I was drifting off to sleep, I heard the faint sounds of two heartbeats, not four." His eyebrows came together. "Maybe the chip screwed with my hearing."

I was about to say something to calm him down when my phone rang. I fumbled to find my cell in one of my coat pockets. By the time I fished it out, the ringing had stopped, but Jordyn's name brightened the screen. I called her immediately, anxious and excited to share the news. Though she probably wouldn't bat an eye since she thought Sam had magic sperm and had said that morning she wouldn't be surprised if I had a litter.

I giggled. Maybe Jordyn had unique foresight into the future. We had vampires and witches in our ancestry.

But as the line connected, two things happened at once.

Sam jumped out of his chair, pressing on his earpiece when Jordyn shouted into the phone, "Layla, run! You've got to get out of there."

Sam barked into his comm, "Motherfucker. Are you sure, Olivia?" He flicked his chin at me. "Put Jordyn on speaker."

I gulped in air, obeying his command.

"Talk to us, Jordyn," Sam said.

"Fred Emery from Intech is chasing me," she said, breathing heavily.

"Where's Hawk, your bodyguard?" Sam asked.

"A vampire snapped his neck," she said. "I've never seen him before. I think he's working for Intech."

"Where are you?" I asked my sister.

"I'm hiding behind a car in the hospital parking garage on the third level. I think I lost that creep."

Sam pressed on his earpiece again and relayed the info to Olivia. "Can you or Ben get to Jordyn? Copy that? Layla and I are leaving now." Once Sam ended his communication with Olivia, he said to Jordyn, "Hang tight. Help is on the way."

Well, fuck!

SAM

I pulled open the hospital room door. Lane straightened from the wall he'd been leaning against. "Lane, get the Jeep and meet us at the ER entrance. Now!" My voice boomed, causing the ladies at the nurses' station to flinch as they jerked their heads toward us.

"Fill me in, please," Layla said as I grabbed her hand. "Aside from Fred Emery, who else is here?"

"Roman's men. Three that we're aware of but probably several more," I said. Roman didn't come to a fight without an army. "I need you to stay close to me."

She squeezed my hand. "That explains the vampire Jordyn mentioned."

The fuckers must have been watching us, but Sawyer hadn't found any suspicious activity around the base or on any cameras throughout the city. Though I wasn't sure if Sawyer had been monitoring the city cams prior to Junior showing up.

My bet was that someone had alerted them. *Fucking Junior.* Layla and I had been in a rush to see Dr. Martin, and my old man had been a bit shaken up at Layla's plight and probably hadn't read Junior's mind.

Two hallways flanked the nurses' station. The one to my right led to a set of double doors that read Do Not Enter. The other was our ticket out, with an elevator on one side and the exit into the ER waiting room dead ahead, which was the same direction Lane had gone.

"Do you have the daggers in your boots?" I tossed out to Layla.

She nodded quickly.

"Ben, Olivia, come in," I said into my comm. A beat passed, and no response. I tried again. Nothing.

We stalked past a gaggle of nurses gushing about a man they would like to ride.

One dropped my name, and I rolled my eyes.

Layla snarled, glaring at Louise.

But we had no time for jealousy or for Layla to punch the nurse like she wanted to.

We hurried out and into a packed room of crying kids, sick patients, and nervous loved ones. Too many emotions assaulted me, but I shook them off when Layla stopped, causing me to jerk to a halt.

I followed her line of sight to our left, and my fucking blood froze.

A large group was gathered around something or someone about halfway down a hall in line with a radiology sign that jutted out from a door on the left.

"Maybe it's Hawk," Layla said before she dashed away like a paramedic to an accident scene.

"He's dead, I think," a young woman said.

"Why does he have fangs?" a man asked. "That's odd. Isn't it?"

Motherfucker. The last thing we needed was Hawk on display or even waking up, which he would, and then the shit would hit the fan.

Stalking behind Layla, I muttered several swear words.

My comm crackled. "Sam, you have at least five bogeys heading into the hospital," Olivia said.

I slowed to a walk. "Where are you?"

"Fighting off more of Roman's men in an alley behind the hospital. Ben spotted Roman. So watch your six."

"Retrieve Jordyn. She's in the parking garage, level three."

"As soon as I finish off this fucker," Olivia said through a grunt.

"Either you or Ben call this in," I returned.

"We already did. Help is on the way."

Thank fuck.

"Any idea where Roman is?" I asked her, walking toward the crowd, searching for Roman's ugly mug.

"Ben had eyes on him dodging cars in the parking lot," Olivia returned. "Just get the fuck out of there." Then my comm quieted.

I inhaled the energy around me, feeding off the human scent, their fear, their excitement, preparing myself to unleash my elemental powers at a moment's notice.

Footsteps clamored behind me, and I spun around, prepared to take on my attacker, only to find Dr. Martin with a panicked expression.

"What's going on?" he asked, taking in the crowd.

Layla was pushing her way into the melee. "Excuse me. He's my brother."

I grinned at her white lie as I marched toward her. "One of my men is down," I said to Dr. Martin. "We need to clear out the hospital."

Dr. Martin took off to break up the group as my mind worked to figure out a plan to save human lives. But Layla and the babies were in more jeopardy than the nosy humans who were snapping pictures of Hawk.

The plural form of baby had my mind ready to explode, but this wasn't the time for a meltdown.

As I approached the crowd, I spied the fire alarm. One way to clear out a building. Without missing a step, I yanked on the handle, then kept walking as the alarm blared with a high shriek. Humans scattered like cockroaches, running past me.

Layla was slapping Hawk on the face. "Hawk?"

"Baby doll, I suggest you back away from him. He might be hungry when he wakes up." And angry as a bear. He would definitely go for someone's throat.

Dr. Martin said, "Nice thinking, but the fire department won't be far behind."

Just as I was about to pick up Hawk and toss him over my shoulder, he woke up snarling.

Dr. Martin jumped away.

Layla didn't bat an eye. "You were supposed to protect my sister," she snapped like a viper with an overload of venom.

Hawk jumped to his feet and trained his green eyes on me. "I'm sorry, sir."

Considering many of the SEALs were on missions, given the list of enemies we were surveilling, we had limited choices of men. So Webb and Tripp had given Hawk a chance to guard Jordyn.

I held up a hand. "Save it for later. We'll have bigger problems if we don't blow this joint now." I grabbed Layla by the arm. "Baby doll, Roman is here."

She searched the hallways. "Where?" She sounded way too excited for my liking. Then she whipped out her daggers. "I'm ready."

I chuckled. "That you are. Please be careful." I was confident in her fighting abilities. What I wasn't so positive about was her condition. I didn't want anything to happen to her or our babies. *Fuuuuck! Babies. Shut up, brain. I'm in the middle of a dangerous situation.*

She pursed her plump lips, her big blue eyes filling with rage. "You think Roman is helping my grandmother?"

I hadn't told her Roman's men were guarding the microchip plant outside Cleveland. "Oh, he's part of Intech's team, so I would imagine he is," I said.

Her daggers were secured in her hands. "Well, I'm tired of this shit. I'm ready to kill all of them."

"Dr. Martin, make sure the ER is cleared out," I said. "Lane, what's your location?" I asked into my comm.

"I'm outside the ER in the Jeep. Move, Sam," Lane returned. "Or else we won't be able to leave. Too many people spilling out of the building."

I informed Lane that Roman was on site and to keep his senses open.

"Hawk, head in front of us. Layla, behind Hawk," I ordered.

Hawk drew his gun from his holster.

"Aim for the heart, man," I said. Cobalt bullets would definitely stop a vampire.

We headed toward the waiting room while Dr. Martin darted into what looked to be a hallway beneath the radiology sign.

The energy within me thrashed around like a caged animal struggling to get free. Pulling both arms back, I turned my palms out—waiting, scanning, listening, sniffing. The surest way to kill Roman was to burn him, and I was primed and ready to bury the fucker once and for all.

Hawk raised his fist, coming to a halt. He scanned the door that led into the hub of the ER.

Layla's pulse was beating rapidly.

I tossed a look over my shoulder, meeting an empty hallway. "Keep moving, Hawk."

Just as Hawk took a step, Ben sailed through the doors from the hub of the ER. My best bud landed in front of Hawk with a resounding thud.

Hawk pumped several bullets into the beast of the guy, who marched out with a semiautomatic in hand. One down.

Ben jumped up. "More are coming. Sam, take Layla. We got this."

"Where's my sister?" Layla asked as I snagged her arm.

Ben didn't have time to answer. Another burly vampire with arms bigger than his head marched out behind his counterpart.

"Layla, this way." I spun on my heel, tugging her with me, searching for an exit, which I didn't see.

"I need to find Jordyn," she said, running alongside me.

"We will, but I need you safe first."

"I can't let my grandmother take her." Layla's voice pitched and rolled.

I didn't want that to happen either. "I know. But we have bigger issues. You're carrying four. You and them are the only ones who are important right now. Are we clear?"

She nodded reluctantly as she puffed out her cheeks.

When we reached the end of the hall, a gift shop sat on the right, and there was nothing to my left.

Motherfucker.

"New plan." I scanned the hall for another escape route.

Ben and Hawk had disappeared.

A war raged in my head. The only way out was back the way we'd come. We were sprinting toward the waiting room when two men bulldozed out from radiology. A blond giant tackled me to the ground. "Get her," he said to his scar-faced comrade.

"Run, Layla!" I shouted as I pushed my attacker off me. Before he could react, I lifted my hands, the electricity sizzling in my palms, and swung one fireball at him.

He squealed like a pig, the scent of burning flesh permeating the air. Then he stumbled, swatting at his face to put out the fire.

"Sam!" Layla shouted in a petrified tone.

I bolted, my palms out, my head down, primed to burn the fuck out of the bald scar-faced moron on Layla's tail. The oil on his scalp was sure to set him ablaze.

Out of nowhere, someone barreled into me like a fucking bowling ball. We crashed into a water fountain and then through the wall behind it.

I threw him off me and dove into the hallway with water spraying everywhere. When I jumped up, the bald dude and Layla were gone.

Hawk climbed out of the gaping hole. "Sorry, some fucker threw me." He darted back in through the radiology door.

I closed my fists, clenched my jaw, and ran for my fucking life because she was my life, my heart, my soul, and she was carrying our kids. I banked around the corner, the emergency room entrance directly ahead. I ran out into the afternoon sun, skidding to a halt at the curb. No Lane. No Jeep. Only a parking lot of patients, nurses, doctors, and bystanders.

I jogged across the driveway and over to Louise. She levered back as though I was the Loch Ness monster. I was more than her worse nightmare.

"Y-You have fangs. Wh-What happened to your eyes?" She stuttered out her words. "They were g-green. N-Now they're silver."

One of her colleagues screamed. "Over here. He's the one."

I rounded my gaze on the tiny human woman trembling violently and pointing at me.

A cop rushed up through the crowd with his gun drawn. "Hands up."

What the fuck? "You're kidding. I'm looking for my wife." Technically she wasn't yet, and I still had to ask her again. But the word spilled out easily.

The squat cop, with fear dripping off him, aimed the gun at my chest. "I said, hands up."

I laughed. "The bullet won't kill me." I didn't want to make a scene, but at this point, I was losing time to find Layla. "I'm looking for an auburn-haired woman, about five-seven, blue eyes, pregnant. Louise knows her."

"No, I don't," Louise said.

I got in her face. "Either you help me, or I'll rip out your tongue."

The cop inched closer. The name on his uniform was Davidson. "What are you? You killed my partner."

I swiped the gun out of his hand before he could take a breath. "Sir." I retracted my fangs. "I didn't kill your partner. I don't want any trouble. I'm looking for someone."

He backed away, shaking his head. "Impossible."

A kid about twelve years old walked up as his mother screamed at him not to. The brave soul of a boy smiled at me. "I saw a woman come out. She ran that way." He pointed to the road between the hospital and the parking garage.

"Did you see a black Jeep?"

"Yes, sir. The Jeep followed the woman, and a bald man was chasing the lady."

I almost hugged the kid but didn't want to scare him or his mother, who was holding her breath behind him. "You're awesome, dude." I mussed his brown hair to show I wasn't a monster like the crowd thought I was. They weren't wrong. "Anyone else who looked suspicious with fangs like me?" There was no sense in hiding who I was anymore, and I didn't give a fuck either. Layla's life hung in the balance. Hell, if I had time, I could wipe memories, but I didn't have the bandwidth or energy to erase what these humans had seen.

The boy shook his head and returned to his mother.

I tossed the gun to the now-frozen cop as the other bystanders watched me in horror as a few snapped pictures. The Council of Elders wouldn't be happy. Not my concern.

I dodged cars and ornamental trees. Jordyn was in the garage, so it made sense Layla would go there to try to save her sister.

My phone rang, and my heart skipped a beat when Layla's name flashed on the screen.

I slowed to a fast walk. "Talk to me, baby doll," I said, answering.

"Sam," she whispered. "I'm—" She screamed, but not banshee level. "Get your hands off me."

"Layla!" Fury sent me flying down the narrow road and into the parking garage. "Layla!"

I checked my screen, and my heart fucking stopped cold and dead.

Kill was the only word in my vocabulary.

30

SAM

An eerie silence crawled through the first level of cars, trucks, and SUVs in the parking garage. That snowy night five years ago slinked back like a cat burglar on an eerie evening. Jo and I were human, running into a hospital parking garage with vampires on our asses. However, at that time, we hadn't known the creatures existed.

I sniffed the air, hoping to catch Layla's cherry scent as I called her. Immediately, the line went straight to voice mail.

Motherfucker.

I stood in the middle, sharpened my hearing, and listened. The slow cadence of a heartbeat filtered in. I headed up a slight incline where the garage banked around to the second floor. The *boom... boom... boom* indicated either the person was out cold or that a vampire was waiting, since our hearts beat slower.

Olivia's voice blared in my comm. "Sam, what's your location?"

I couldn't answer until I knew what I was dealing with. As I reached the second level, I stomped my foot once, pulled back my arms, and drew in the natural energy of the sun's rays beaming in. An electrical charge careened down my arms to pool in my hands as the wind began to howl, rushing in, whistling. A paper cup flew by.

A bottle rolled past me, and a collection of paper and trash swirled in the air.

I sniffed again, and the scent of human blood drifted into my nostrils. I tapered off my elemental powers, my fangs elongating. I sprinted up another incline and banked around the corner. A man lay on his stomach behind a white car. Jordyn's scent lingered close by. Where Layla was all cherries, Jordyn smelled of vanilla.

I pressed on my comm. "Olivia."

"Sam, where the fuck are you?" she returned.

"Parking garage. I can't find Layla. Do you have her or Jordyn?"

"Negative," she said.

Sirens blared in the distance as a gust of wind swept through.

"Roman's men are piling up. We have about ten dead," she said.

"A bald fucker was chasing Layla. Have you seen Lane?"

"Negative on both," she returned. "The SEAL team is two minutes out."

The human was bleeding from an area on his lower back where it appeared as though he'd been stabbed.

I rolled him over. He looked like Adam Emery minus the wicked scar on his face. Jordyn had mentioned Fred Emery. "It seems someone clocked Fred Emery. Can you get someone up here to make sure we bring him in?"

"Copy that," she said before she clicked off.

My phone rang.

"Layla, where the fuck are you?"

"Sam," she whispered in a heavy breath. "I'm in the basement of the hospital. Jordyn is bleeding. But there are SWAT men chasing us as well."

"Where in the basement?" I jogged back the way I'd come. "Are they vampires?" Roman's men could very well be in SWAT gear.

"The sign said boiler room. I managed to scream when one of them tried to grab me, and he collapsed. He's out, but not for long. Jordyn passed out too. They're not vampires." She shuddered.

"I'm coming your way."

"Don't," she bit out harshly. "They have those dart guns."

I clutched the phone, almost crushing it. "How many men?"

"I only saw two," she said in a low tone. "I think they're with Intech."

That much was true since Fred Emery had brought his goons with him. "Have you seen Lane? And where's the bald vamp who was chasing you?"

"They were fighting in the alleyway."

Once out of the garage, I hopped over a median, then took off down a road alongside the hospital. "Keep talking."

"Someone is coming," she whispered.

I ran with the phone to my ear, searching for the door into the boiler area. Again, images from long ago fucked with my head. Jo had been stabbed by Cliff, our alcoholic foster dad, and a trip to the emergency room had set us on a course to hell.

"Come on, Jo. Keep moving." I pulled her as we skirted a dumpster in a dark alley, looking for the boiler room.

But it wasn't nighttime, and I wasn't human anymore.

The long expanse of the building had doors punched in it, but no fucking boiler sign.

"Layla," I said. "Are you still with me?"

Silence.

I looked at my cell. *Fuuuuck!* Either she hung up, or she lost the signal.

The smell of detergent drifted out of an open door up ahead, accompanied by a cloud of steam. I tried Layla again. Her voice mail connected. I was ready to throw my phone when a man wearing a hairnet sauntered out with a cigarette in his hand.

He was about to light the cancer stick when his gaze landed on me. His hackles lifted, and he dropped his cigarette in fear.

I smiled, showing my fangs. "I don't want trouble." *Unless you don't answer my question correctly.*

I quickly glanced into the laundry area where industrial washing machines and dryers droned, and bins of sheets were lined up side by side.

"I'm looking for two women. One with auburn hair and the other with brown. Have you seen them?"

He gulped in air. "You have fangs like the other men I saw."

"Describe them quickly," I ordered.

His pulse pounded within his carotid artery like a drummer in a solo performance. "Two of them had short blond hair, fangs like yours, and black eyes." He shivered. "The other one was bald with a scar on his face."

Lane had blond hair and Roman did too. "You saw all three of them together?"

"No. One of the blonds came through the laundry room about thirty minutes ago, carrying a duffel bag. He asked for the electrical room. The other blond was in a Jeep and chased the bald guy." He stuck his finger to his right. "That way."

Fury had me growling, which made the human shake like a leaf.

All I could think about was Layla's rental house blowing up. Roman had lured me there while he stormed the naval base.

"And the women?" I asked, clenching my teeth so hard my fangs embedded in the skin below my lip.

He swung out his trembling arm to the door behind him. "They ran through here too. Are you people the reason the fire alarm went off?"

Ignoring his question, I asked, "Where's the boiler room?"

"Around the back side of the hospital, or you can go through—"

I took off before he could finish, my mind scrambling to figure out what the fuck Roman was up to. Maybe his agenda didn't match Emery's or Harriet's. Maybe he just wanted to kill Layla and me both. But that didn't add up either. Or... he was creating a diversion.

They had to be watching us, waiting for us to leave the naval base. How else had they known Layla and I would be at the hospital? It wasn't like her emergency was planned. Not only that, but Roman was supposed to be in Cleveland, although Tripp and Ben only talked about Roman's men. They'd never said they had eyes on Roman. But the hows and whys had to wait along with the answers to my questions.

When I turned the corner, I came to an abrupt halt as pain clawed at my chest. Lane's head sat in the middle of the road next to the idling Jeep.

Pure hellfire burned through me as an intense need to kill pulsed in my veins.

I shook my head like a dog shaking off water, but it did nothing except spike my adrenaline to new heights.

I took off running like a wild man, scanning doors, seething, and hoping beyond hope I got to Layla in time. The hospital had too many fucking entrances. I passed a door with no sign on it. The next one—electrical. As tempted as I was to find out what Roman was up to, I had to get to Layla first.

I sprinted to the end of the building and came up empty for the boiler area. I turned the corner, but there weren't any doors along that side.

I backtracked and ripped off the door to the electrical room. The electricity in the air hummed and sizzled, and I absorbed every bit of it. Pipes, control boxes, pumps, and tanks crowded the space. Straight ahead, an open archway spilled into yet another area.

Walking deeper into the room, I held my phone in one hand and fisted my other, prepared to unleash my wrath at a moment's notice, when my phone vibrated.

"Layla," I said into my cell.

"Sam!" she screamed. "There's a—"

My heart dropped to the cement floor. "Layla!" I shouted, running farther into the belly of the beast.

I couldn't hear any heartbeats or breathing. Too many sounds—pump motors trilling, electricity sizzling, the loud rumble of the boiler blasting in the machine-packed room. I listened intently, sniffed, checked around more tanks, pumps, pipes, and corners. But my senses were on overload, and the oil permeating the air was potent.

I backtracked a ways. Maybe I'd missed something. She said she was in the boiler room. The dude with the hairnet said a blond vamp asked for the electrical room. I was standing not far from the boiler.

"Layla," I said into the phone but realized the call had ended.

I searched again, my heart freaking the fuck out. "Where are you, baby doll?" I said to no one. I was about to enter the electrical area when an explosion threw me against the boiler. I bounced off it like a fucking basketball and stumbled to my feet. I growled, inhaling the dirt and debris and all the fucking natural energy I could. Then I was wiping the shit and metal from my face when a second explosion rocked the fucking room right in my ear. The boiler blew, sending me soaring through the air.

Motherfucker in hell.

All I could think of was Layla and our babies. Rage, fear, madness, and murder strangled me. I wasn't the type to pray, but I was praying like a priest—not for me, but for my family. Hellfire was about to rain down on this planet. I wouldn't stop until I had the hearts of every last fucker responsible, human and vampire, in my bloody hands.

To be continued…

ALSO BY S.B. ALEXANDER

Visit https://sbalexander.com/all-books/ to learn more about S.B. Alexander books and future releases. Please note release dates are subject to change based on reader demand and the author's schedule. Subscribing to the author's newsletter or following her on Facebook is the best way to stay updated with planned new releases.

ABOUT THE AUTHOR

Bestselling author **S.B. Alexander** is an independent author with over 25 titles to date. She writes paranormal, new adult, and sweet romances that feature hot heroes stealing hearts.

S.B. or Susan as she likes to be called is a navy veteran, former high school teacher, and former corporate sales executive. She's a lover of sports, especially baseball, although nowadays you can find her glued to the TV during football season.

Her motto: "Life is too short to waste. So live every moment like it's your last."

You can connect with S.B. Alexander in the following ways:
Reader Group: https://sbalexander.com/beastsandbitches
Author Website: https://sbalexander.com
Newsletter: https://sbalexander.com/newsletter
Email: susan@sbalexander.com

NEVER MISS A NEW RELEASE:
Sign up for her Author App
iTunes: https://bit.ly/sbalexanderitunes
Android: https://bit.ly/sbalexanderandroid

facebook.com/sbalexander.authorpage

twitter.com/sbalex_author

instagram.com/sbalexanderauthor

amazon.com/author/sbalexander

bookbub.com/authors/s-b-alexander

tiktok.com/@susanbalexander

GLOSSARY OF TERMS

Natural-born vampire: A human born with the vampire gene that, when activated, will turn them into a vampire.

Activation process: Those who carry the vampire gene can only turn by drinking the blood of their vampire father at the age of sixteen years or older.

Council of Elders – A group of five vampires who set the laws.

Genetic engineering: Turning humans into vampires through a process of restructuring their DNA.

Cobalt – A vampire's kryptonite. The metal will kill a vampire if staked through the heart. It will also burn a vampire's skin if they come in contact with it.

Reproduction: A natural-born vampire is born by a male vampire and a human female with a rare blood type of Vel negative.

Council of Eternal Affairs: The legal department of the vampire government.

Vampire characteristics: Sunlight doesn't burn them. Their hearts beat at <5 bpm. Skin temperature is ten degrees cooler than a human. Eye color changes to black except for a few chosen ones.

Steven Mason: Vampire and father to twins Jo and Sam Mason. He's dubbed the most powerful of all vampires because of his many powers, including his mind-reading abilities. He can only read minds when touching someone except when it comes to his children. His normal eye color is green. His vampire eye color is silver.

Jo Mason: Turned at sixteen. Powers include seeing the future through her dreams, mind-reading without touching a person, telekinesis, and she's an elemental with the ability to manipulate water, air, earth, and fire. Her normal eye color is silver. Her vampire eye color is violet.

Sam Mason: Turned at sixteen. Powers include feeling what others feel (Empath), telekinesis, and he can compel a person using a series of numbers woven into a magical spell. He's also an elemental with the ability to manipulate water, air, earth, and fire. His normal eye color is green. His vampire eye color is silver.

Guardians: Vampires who are equivalent to the human police.